W9-BYL-441

"Just be yourself, Hunter. She likes you."

"I truly have no idea how you talk to a child," he said. "I'm guessing golf scores aren't going to do it. And probably not surfing, either."

His chuckle made her smile. Which sent warning notes through her. She was not going to soften toward this man.

Some man. Someday. Sure. If she was attracted to one she felt she could trust.

But not this man. Not a charmer.

"You talk to her like she's a person," Julie said. "I think back to when I was a kid and pull from that."

His attention, fully on her now, warmed her all up again.

She was there to help him for Joy's sake. She had to get it done.

And get out.

Dear Reader,

Joy is the pinnacle of good feeling for those of us living within the human condition! And for those of us who are parents? Holding your child in your arms, hearing his or her voice, watching him grow... These are some of the most joy-filled moments ever.

They're also the moments that make us the most vulnerable ever. Because the shadowy side of joy—the loss of joy—is excruciating. It can be debilitating. We'll go to any lengths to avoid it, to prevent harm from happening to our children. That's what Joy's mother does: she puts herself in jeopardy to protect Joy. So that the child might know joy.

And in this story, the child brings joy to those who are there to help her.

The source of joy isn't just children—the source is infinite, spreading itself more thoroughly than the worst disease (the shadowy side) ever could. It's here where I am and there where you are, touching us both and millions of others. And it's up to us, each one of us individually, to let it in. A lesson Julie Fairbanks, a haunted soul, has to learn. For Joy's sake.

I love to hear from my readers. Please find me at www.tarataylorquinn.com, Facebook.com/tarataylorquinn and on Twitter, @tarataylorquinn. Or join my open Friendship board on Pinterest, Pinterest.com/tarataylorquinn/friendship!

All the best,

Tara

USA TODAY Bestselling Author

TARA TAYLOR QUINN

—

For Joy's Sake

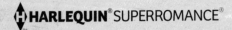
HARLEQUIN® SUPERROMANCE®

If you purchased this book without a cover you should be aware
that this book is stolen property. It was reported as "unsold and
destroyed" to the publisher, and neither the author nor the
publisher has received any payment for this "stripped book."

For Morgan Marie and Baylor Raine—you most
certainly came to this world for joy's sake.

Recycling programs
for this product may
not exist in your area.

ISBN-13: 978-0-373-64037-9

For Joy's Sake

Copyright © 2017 by Tara Taylor Quinn

All rights reserved. Except for use in any review, the reproduction or
utilization of this work in whole or in part in any form by any electronic,
mechanical or other means, now known or hereinafter invented, including
xerography, photocopying and recording, or in any information storage
or retrieval system, is forbidden without the written permission of the
publisher, Harlequin Enterprises Limited, 225 Duncan Mill Road,
Don Mills, Ontario M3B 3K9, Canada.

This is a work of fiction. Names, characters, places and incidents are
either the product of the author's imagination or are used fictitiously,
and any resemblance to actual persons, living or dead, business
establishments, events or locales is entirely coincidental.

This edition published by arrangement with Harlequin Books S.A.

For questions and comments about the quality of this book,
please contact us at CustomerService@Harlequin.com.

® and TM are trademarks of Harlequin Enterprises Limited or its
corporate affiliates. Trademarks indicated with ® are registered in the
United States Patent and Trademark Office, the Canadian Intellectual
Property Office and in other countries.

Printed in U.S.A.

www.Harlequin.com

Having written over eighty novels, **Tara Taylor Quinn** is a *USA TODAY* bestselling author with more than seven million copies sold. She is known for delivering intense, emotional fiction. Tara is a past president of Romance Writers of America. She has won a Readers' Choice Award and is a five-time finalist for an RWA RITA® Award, a finalist for a Reviewers' Choice Award and a Booksellers' Best Award. She has also appeared on TV across the country, including *CBS Sunday Morning*. She supports the National Domestic Violence Hotline. If you or someone you know might be a victim of domestic violence in the United States, please contact 1-800-799-7233.

Books by Tara Taylor Quinn

HARLEQUIN SUPERROMANCE

Where Secrets are Safe

Wife by Design
Once a Family
Husband by Choice
Child by Chance
Mother by Fate
The Good Father
Love by Association
His First Choice
The Promise He Made Her
Her Secret Life
The Fireman's Son
For Joy's Sake

Shelter Valley Stories

Sophie's Secret
Full Contact

HARLEQUIN HEARTWARMING

Family Secrets

For Love or Money
Her Soldier's Baby
The Cowboy's Twins

MIRA BOOKS

The Friendship Pact
In Plain Sight

Visit the Author Profile page at Harlequin.com for more titles.

Cast of Characters

Lila McDaniels—Managing director of The Lemonade Stand (TLS). She has an apartment at the Stand.

Wife by Design (Book 1)

Lynn Duncan—Resident nurse at TLS. She has a three-year-old daughter, Kara.

Grant Bishop—Landscape developer hired by TLS.

Maddie Estes—Permanent TLS resident. Childcare provider.

Darin Bishop—Resident at TLS. Works for his brother, Grant. Has a mental disability.

Once a Family (Book 2)

Sedona (Campbell) Malone—Lawyer who volunteers at TLS.

Tanner Malone—Vintner. Brother to Tatum and Talia Malone.

Tatum Malone—Fifteen-year-old resident at TLS.

Husband by Choice (Book 3)

Meredith (Meri) Bennet—Speech therapist. Mother to two-year-old son, Caleb.

Max Bennet—Pediatrician.

Chantel Harris—Police officer. Friend to Max and his deceased first wife.

Jeremiah (Jem) Bridges—Private contractor with his own business. Divorced. Has custody of four-year-old son, Levi.

The Promise He Made Her (Book 9)
Bloom Larson—Psychiatrist in Santa Raquel. Domestic violence therapist. Divorced.
Samuel Larson—Santa Raquel high-ranking detective. Widower.

Her Secret Life (Book 10)
Kacey Hamilton—Daytime-soap-opera star. Identical twin to Lacey Hamilton. Volunteer at TLS.
Michael Valentine—Cybersecurity expert. TLS volunteer. Shooting victim.

The Fireman's Son (Book 11)
Faye Walker—Paramedic. Divorced. Sole custody of eight-year-old son, Elliott, who is in counseling at TLS.
Reese Bristow—Santa Raquel fire chief.

For Joy's Sake (Book 12)
Julie Fairbanks—Philanthropist and children's author. Sister to Colin Fairbanks.
Hunter Rafferty—Owns elite professional event-planning business specializing in charity fund-raisers. TLS is one of his clients.

CHAPTER ONE

HER BREATH CAUGHT in her throat, Julie Fairbanks
crouched on the floor, hugging her knees, staring
at the television screen. The baby who'd been born
in a man-made bubble town, who'd been raised
and surrounded by people who were only there
to keep up appearances, was a man himself now.
And about to break free...

The creak of a door opening disrupted her con-
centration. Lila McDaniels, managing director of
The Lemonade Stand, stood in the entranceway.
All six women, lounging in various positions on
the couch, chairs and floor, looked at her. Five
were residents at the unique women's shelter. Julie
was a volunteer who hadn't left after she'd finished her art therapy session. Lila's gaze homed
in on Julie. With a sideways quirk of Lila's head,
Julie knew she'd been summoned.

Before the show's hero broke free.

Smiling at the other women, she quietly left
before the happy ending that was coming soon.
And hoped each one of them would find the nec-

essary strength and support to create her own happy ending.

"What's wrong?" Julie asked as soon as the door was closed behind them.

Lila shook her head, but her tight gray bun hadn't moved. "Nothing's wrong. I just wanted to have a chat with you," the unflappable woman said. Her voice was kind—as always. And the words were issued with Lila's usual emotional distance.

The woman both intrigued and frightened Julie. Intrigued because Julie sensed there was so much more to Lila than her ability to maintain calm in an atmosphere of pain and fear. And watching Lila frightened her sometimes, too, because she doubted she'd ever know Lila's sense of peace.

For the most part she'd love to have Lila's life. Unmarried and yet with a huge family of women and kids to tend to every day. Making a strong, positive difference in the lives of others.

They were heading for Lila's private suite—rooms that were her off-duty space at the Stand. Lila stayed there any time she didn't make it home to the condo she owned in town. Julie hadn't been aware of any situation at the Stand that had prompted the director's need to stay over this particular early-October Friday night.

But as a volunteer at the Stand, mostly working with the children, Julie wasn't privy to every circumstance.

Lila offered her tea. Julie accepted. And watched the older woman bring out the exact brand and flavor she preferred. In some ways they were so much alike, she and Lila.

And yet, Julie knew next to nothing about the other woman's circumstances, other than that she'd been the managing director of The Lemonade Stand since day one.

Word was that she'd applied for the job while the resort-like shelter was under construction. She'd undergone a normal interview process and had been hired.

From what Julie had been told, in all the years Lila had been at the shelter she'd never had a personal visitor. Not a family member or friend. And even in town, she wasn't known well.

That was where Julie and Lila differed. Everyone in Santa Raquel knew who Julie Fairbanks was. Many of those people she'd once considered friends. There was still a handful.

A carefully selected, heart-vetted, very small handful.

"How are you doing?" Lila asked, giving Julie a rare, full-on smile as she took one of the two wingback chairs on either side of the claw-foot table in her small but elegantly decorated parlor.

"Good." Julie nodded as she sat in the other

chair, suddenly feeling as if she was onstage under bright lights. As if she could be seen but couldn't see what was out there. "Busy," she added. And then, perhaps to ward off whatever was coming, she continued. "The annual celebrity gala for the Sunshine Children's League is coming up and, of course, I'm fully involved with that..." Her seat on the league's board had won her the opportunity to chair the gala. "And Minoran Child Development is getting ready to open up a thrift shop. The red tape is endless, although Colin's being a sweetheart and helping out tremendously." Lila was well acquainted with Julie's older brother, who not only ran the family's prestigious law firm in town but had recently become a major donor to The Lemonade Stand.

"I hear that Chantel is pregnant."

"Three months!" Julie grinned. Her sister-in-law, who now shared the family mansion with Julie and Colin, had come into their lives as an undercover cop pretending to be a member of their privileged society, and had become her best friend. "I can't wait to have a little one in the house!" These days, that new baby was the first thing she thought of when she woke up in the morning.

She was just the aunt. She'd maintain her proper place. But still, she couldn't wait. "I'm going to watch the baby when Chantel goes back to work.

At least for the first couple of years." If Julie had her way, she'd be the child's nanny until he or she went to school, but it was ultimately up to Chantel and Colin, and they all had time to figure that one out.

Lila's smile looked somehow...worried, suggesting that she saw some kind of sadness in Julie's situation. In her gray skirt and blouse, with her hair in its usual bun, Lila didn't resemble Julie's idea of a psychic, but she felt sure the older woman had otherworldly talents of perception.

Lila's next words confirmed Julie's personal opinion. "I'm concerned about you," she said.

"Me?"

"Yes."

The woman watched her, as though waiting for Julie to confess to something. "Why?"

"There's a wine tasting at your home this evening."

She nodded again. She'd helped arrange the event that was raising money for the Santa Raquel Library fund—a cause that had become dear to her and Colin and Chantel, since the library's fund-raising efforts had been instrumental in creating the bond the three of them shared. Chantel, while posing as a writer from a privileged family in New York, had been dating Colin as part of her cover. She'd agreed to write a script for the library's grand opening party in the renovated mansion that had been willed to the city as a library site. The evening's event had been a mystery caper, and Chantel had written herself right into the hands of a privileged, wealthy, respected man she'd discovered was a serial rapist—Julie's rapist. She'd risked her own life in order to give Julie's life back to her.

"The wine event is there. You're here." Lila stated the obvious, so Julie just shrugged.

"You're cohosting an event, and you aren't there."

Feeling those bright lights again, Julie sipped her tea. Stared at the polish on her toes, the black leather straps of her flip-flops across her pale feet. And then she looked straight at Lila. "I am capable of being there," she said with complete assurance. "Knowing that, I've given myself the option of choosing not to be."

"Why make that choice?"

So maybe she'd recognized from the moment Lila had appeared exactly *why* she'd wanted to see her. The summons. The tea. Julie would've liked to stand up and leave. To defend her right not to be subjected to inquiry. But she didn't really feel defensive. Or upset with Lila.

"You know I'm uncomfortable around that crowd."

True enough, though no one on the night's guest list knew that. The rapist's father was one of the state's most prominent bankers—so the details, including names, had been kept out of the news. Smyth Jr. had accepted a plea agreement. And money really did carry a lot of power. But Lila knew—Julie and Colin had become associated with the Stand through the ordeal. As did others closely associated with Smyth's ten years' worth of victims.

"I also know you've made a point, with Chantel's and Colin's support, of rejoining your social group. I heard that you used to love dressing up for parties, too."

"And I can now attend these things without panic attacks," she told Lila. "It's like I said. I know I can, so I no longer have to."

"We're talking about a function in your own home, Julie. Yet here you are."

She didn't like how Lila's statement made her feel. As though she, Julie, wasn't quite done with moving on. As though she was still broken.

The truth was, she'd never be done with it. Not really. There was no way to erase what had happened, and no way not to be affected by it.

But she was able to live more normally now.

For some reason, she needed Lila—a highly respected professional working with female victims—to see that.

"I wanted Chantel and Colin to be able to welcome guests into their home as a couple. More specifically, I wanted Chantel to feel like the hostess, the woman of the house. Since she came into our lives on a lie, she still sometimes feels like an imposter, like she's not really one of us, especially when there's a gathering that includes people who don't know the details. It can be hard for her. As if making the transition from street cop to detective wasn't difficult enough, she's living in a society that's completely unfamiliar to her. If I was there, people would naturally turn to me as the hostess and..."

It was the reason she'd given her brother and his wife for skipping out on the high-dollar evening they'd been planning for several months. They hadn't been happy with her proposed absence, hadn't thought it necessary, but they'd accepted her choice. Because her reasoning was valid.

"But why are you *here*?" Lila asked.

Julie frowned. It wasn't unusual for her to be at The Lemonade Stand. In a volunteer capacity with the children, but also hanging out with the women. "I don't understand."

"It's Friday night. You're twenty-eight years old. Independently wealthy and lovely. You could be doing any number of things for fun and relaxation. Okay, so you wanted to be away from your home for the night. You could've booked yourself into a resort spa. Gone to the theater. You could have been on a date."

Julie didn't respond to Lila. She couldn't.

Inside her, everything was tense. Poised for escape.

"We need you here, Julie. You know that. And we all *want* you here. You bring a nurturing and understanding and compassion that's special and very, very precious to these women. And to the staff."

Julie raised her eyes to Lila's. And was scared by the concerned crease in the other woman's brow.

"But we aren't being a friend back to you," Lila went on, "we aren't good for you if you're using us as a hideout."

Ironic, considering that the Stand existed so women had a place to hide and be safe while they healed.

"If you need to be here, you are welcome. Always. I don't ever want you to need to come to us and then change your mind. Or your course of action. But if you need to be here, then we need to be doing something to help you."

The band around Julie's chest relaxed a little.

"It helps me just to be here," she assured the other woman.

Lila waited until their eyes met again. "Those women you were with tonight… Do you think any one of them would choose to be here? If they had a place to go, where they'd be safe and could live a healthy life?"

Thinking of the five women she'd had dinner with in the cafeteria and then wandered to the lounge with—women who all had rooms in cabins on the premises—Julie shook her head.

All of them mourned for the lives they'd lost. For the dreams they'd lost. For the sense of security that had been taken from them. They yearned for real homes. Yearned to be in control of their lives again. And they lived in fear, too.

Julie wasn't afraid of being attacked again. She had a lovely home that she cherished, a bed of her own that she'd be returning to that night.

"As a staff member, volunteer or not, you are one of us, Julie. And you will be for as long as you choose to share yourself with us. And also as a friend. You're both things to us."

Okay, good. No problems. She wanted to breathe easier.

But didn't.

"I've come to suspect that you're here for a third purpose, too."

No. No, she wasn't.

"You're aware that most state facilities have time limits on the number of weeks a woman can remain in a shelter like ours, right?"

She knew. The Lemonade Stand, as a private facility, didn't have to adhere to those mandates.

They had their own mandates, loosely based on state laws, but they didn't send away women who were doing everything required of them, who were participating fully in their own recovery, who were making progress but just weren't ready to leave yet.

"Do you know why the state sets those time limits?"

"Because of the money." Obviously. "And we mostly adhere to them because we don't want our residents to start feeling powerless, to lose their sense of self-reliance by relying on us too much."

"And because if they depend on the Stand to fill an emotional void, a void left by abuse, then they lose their ability to fill that void themselves."

"You're telling me not to get too attached to the residents. Not to become personal friends with them because they're going to move on." She was well aware of that. And didn't let herself get too close—even while they were intimately in each other's personal space as they opened up and shared their most vulnerable secrets.

"I'm telling you that I'm worried you're using us to fill a void in *your* life."

The words had come, in spite of Julie's attempts to forestall them.

This was what she'd been afraid to hear.

CHAPTER TWO

JULIE STOOD UP in Lila's parlor, wishing she could escape into any of the antique paintings on the walls depicting faraway places. The way she escaped into her own paintings in her home studio. "I'm sorry. I shouldn't have come here tonight…" As she heard her own words, she heard Lila's earlier ones, too, about not ever wanting Julie to feel that she shouldn't come to The Lemonade Stand.

Lila wasn't telling her to leave. But Julie would rather leave than hear what Lila *was* telling her.

"You can go if you'd like, of course," Lila said, her voice as calm as always. Her teacup sat untouched on the table between them as she watched Julie. "But I hope you'll stay, continue our conversation."

In other words, Lila thought she needed help.

That was what this meeting was about.

Julie was already in regular counseling, with Bloom Larson in town. Chantel had introduced them the previous year when she'd spent time keeping the psychiatrist safe from a threat to her life.

Julie was doing what Bloom called her "personal work"—challenging herself to face the situations that frightened her, dare to live life fully, not to let the bastard who'd stolen her youth have the rest of her life, too. So she had more work to do, and Lila knew full well that these things took time. Maybe even a lifetime.

She met Lila's gaze again. Then focused briefly on the rose-colored silk fabric of her chair. Confusion had her sinking back into the seat she'd so abruptly vacated.

"Have you told Dr. Larson about all the time you spend here when you aren't working or socializing with staff?"

Julie shook her head.

"Needing to be in the company of others who are going through some of the same struggles you face, who've been indelibly hurt by those they trusted, is normal," Lila said.

Julie felt better for a moment.

Was something wrong? Or not?

"But I think that, for the most part, you're beyond that stage," the director continued. "You're more like a mentor to these women than you are one of them."

Right. That was how she'd seen it, too. So... everything was fine?

"Which leads me to suspect, as I mentioned a few minutes ago, that you sometimes come here for another purpose."

Recognizing the defensiveness that suddenly flared within her, Julie slowed her thoughts. "I'm not sure I understand."

"Personal intimacy." Lila said the words softly, almost as though she could diminish their impact. "You're close to your brother and Chantel, as you should be. They're your only family, and the three of you are good together…"

Julie nodded. They had to work at it, she and Colin mostly, but they *were* good together. She with her own wing in the house, he and Chantel with theirs. They all met for breakfast, which Julie prepared every morning. Otherwise they might not see each other for days.

"But besides them, you have…"

A small circle, Julie finished silently when Lila's voice dropped off. She had acquaintances. What seemed like millions of them. And, yes, those few friends.

"There are a couple of women I consider close," she said. Her best friend from high school, for one. Jaime, an artist, lived in New York now, but they were still in touch.

"I hope you consider all of us here your friends," Lila said, finally picking up her cup of tea and sipping. "But I'm not just talking about friends. Look at Sara and Lynn—" full-time counselor and resident nurse at the Stand "—they're both committed to this place and have personal lives, too. They have spouses and children."

"You don't." Even as she let the words loose, Julie knew they came from her defensiveness. Not the right reason at all.

"I'm fifty-three years old," Lila said, appearing completely unflappable. "Past my childbearing years."

"I'm not opposed to having a future," Julie said slowly, trying her best *not* to be defensive. Lila wasn't completely wrong to have concerns. Julie'd had similar conversations with Dr. Larson.

"But you haven't been on a single date since high school."

"That's right." Not that she hadn't been asked—and fairly often, too. Until just over a year ago, she hadn't set foot out of her house for any kind of social function. And not for a business one, either, if it was at night. Except on rare occasions when she'd gone somewhere with Colin—having vetted the guest list to know who would not be present.

"From what I understand, you haven't been out with girlfriends, either. Other than for lunch."

"No. But only because, as you said, they all have lives, families…" Which had come about during the years Julie had been holed up in her suite in the Fairbanks mansion.

Lila nodded. "So what do you say to a girls' night out? You and Sara and Lynn and I? We can go wherever you'd like, do whatever you want, the only caveat being that we don't discuss The Lemonade Stand, our residents or our work for the entire evening."

What? Lila was asking her to do something socially? Not trying to gently tell her she was nuttier than she'd realized? She hadn't seen that coming.

"I've already spoken to them. They're both in."

Julie was confused again. Lila wasn't reprimanding her? "But…why?"

"You're a strong, talented, giving woman, Julie. We all like you and enjoy your sense of humor. We thought it would be fun."

A mental flash of her studio called to her. She needed her easel. Needed a pencil and paper—time to create the simple stories that always helped her see more clearly.

"Why?" she asked again. Was Colin behind this? He'd promised her he'd back off, that he'd let her take charge of her own healing.

"Because we want to show you that you aren't alone."

The threat of tears nearly strangled her. Lila was wrong. In the end, everyone was alone. Alone in your mind. In your secret places. Alone in a pain only you could feel. In a fear only you could fight.

No one else could know what it felt like to live with your own inability to trust.

Lila's hand on Julie's knee brought her gaze back to the older woman. "You're interesting, Julie," Lila said. "You've got such a unique perspective. Don't forget I've read your stories…"

She blinked. Only Colin, Chantel and a few other people knew that she was the author of the newly published and already bestselling children's book series, *Being Amy*. Lila was one of the few. Julie had told the director and Sara about the books when she'd offered to do some storytelling sessions the year before.

"Don't worry, no one else here knows," Lila said, cluing Julie into the fact that she must be showing her horror at the thought of becoming a public figure of any kind. "I gave you my word."

She nodded. At Chantel's urging, because her sister-in-law believed that Julie's books could help children understand the challenges they faced, she'd agreed to have her work looked at. Chantel had an aunt by marriage whose family owned a small nonfiction publishing house—and who had long-term acquaintances with fiction publishing professionals. Within six weeks of sending the original file, Julie had a contract.

"So what do you say? Will you join us for dinner?"

The mere idea of venturing out far enough to go out for no purpose other than to socialize gave her a panic attack…and yet…she'd loved being part of a tribe…

But, in the past, when push had come to shove, when there'd been pressure put on their families by the police commissioner and his best friend, Smyth Sr.—a man who'd owned most of their investments—when they could've been ostracized from their privileged social group, her friends had all chosen to believe that a brutal date rape had been consensual sex.

Not everyone was out for the money, Julie told herself.

Her protective voice spoke up. *But everyone looked out for self. In spite of others' needs.*

Except at The Lemonade Stand, where Lila and Julie and Lynn spent most of their waking hours. She could trust them to be real friends.

I will not let the bastard win…

"When did you have in mind?" Every nerve trembled, but when Lila gave her a date and time, Julie agreed to the outing.

And got out of The Lemonade Stand as quickly as she could.

LATE SATURDAY MORNING, Hunter Rafferty swung. Connected the iron with the ball and sent it sailing. It landed on the green, setting him up for a putt that would make him a shoe-in for the day's grand prize. He didn't even know what it was. Or care.

Hunter didn't really like golf. Never had. Even though he'd been playing since he was twelve. He was good at it.

But then, he was good at pretty much everything he tried.

Looking to the one person in his foursome who'd prompted his attendance at the day's charity event, he asked, "What can you tell me about Julie Fairbanks?"

Brett and his wife, Ella, had stopped in briefly at the wine tasting held at the Fairbanks mansion the night before. Their sixteen-month-old son had a cold, and Ella, a pediatric charge nurse, hadn't wanted to be away from him. But Hunter had seen Brett speaking with Colin Fairbanks, Julie's older brother.

Brett Ackerman, founder of The Lemonade Stand, among other things, turned and looked at him. "About Julie Fairbanks? Depends on what you want to know." He picked up his bag and, with Hunter right beside him, began the two-hundred-yard trek to his ball a little short of the green. If they hadn't been friends for so long, Hunter might have taken offense. As it was, he knew Brett was just being...Brett. He'd actually managed to establish a nationally respected accreditation for charities. They'd invite him to sit on their boards; there, he'd oversee spending and activities to ensure a lack of fraudulent use of funds. All across the United States, charitable foundations were vying for the accreditation, waiting in line for Brett to have time to sit on their boards.

The other two in their foursome at the semi-annual businessmen's tournament were several yards ahead of them.

Depends on what you want to know. Brett would've made a great covert op. Getting information out of him was nearly impossible sometimes.

If he knew what he wanted to know, he wouldn't be asking.

He didn't want to limit what he might learn by narrowing his possibilities.

"I found it odd that she wasn't at the wine tasting last night," he improvised. The event had been in her home. When Brett had issued the invitation to attend as a way to get to know some of Santa Raquel's elite a bit better, Hunter had immediately accepted. Mostly because it would've given him a chance to see Julie outside their business relationship.

Brett had originally introduced him to Julie when he'd heard about the gala fund-raiser for one of the kids' charities she supported. As a result of that introduction, Julie had hired Hunter's company—The Time of Your Life—to run her gala, and they'd been working closely together for months.

He knew nothing more about her now than he had when they'd first met.

Except that she was soft-spoken, often quiet, but when she had something to say he wanted to listen. She wasn't pushy or aggressive, and yet she always managed to make things happen. She dressed more conservatively than any other woman he'd ever wanted to date. She'd never once mentioned that she lived in a mansion or that her trust fund was worth more than he'd ever had in all his investments combined. Her long dark hair was always contained. She had a smile that could melt ice.

And a scent that he dreamed about, waking up on more than one occasion expecting to smell it on the pillow beside him.

Oh, yeah, he had it bad.

But he wasn't about to wallow in it.

He was The Time of Your Life guy.

And it was time for him to have a life.

Or something like that.

CHAPTER THREE

WITH ONE MISSION in mind—getting Brett to give him some information before they left that day—Hunter took a couple of quiet steps in the pristine grass. Trying to come up with a plan.

"She wasn't at the wine tasting because she was busy elsewhere," Brett said a good two minutes after either of them had spoken.

Hunter had spent the evening looking for her when he should've been courting new clients and had left with his hopes dashed.

"You know where she was?"

"Yeah."

"But you aren't saying."

Brett stopped then and turned toward him. "Are you asking?"

He hadn't said exactly what he wanted to know. Or why he was asking about Julie. A key miss on his part.

Brett Ackerman was not a man to hack around with. He had made a mint from one thing most people had but so rarely relied on—integrity. A mint. By being a man the entire country could trust.

Americans Against Prejudice was how Hunter had met him. Hunter's business arranged charity fund-raising events. And Brett had just been starting to earn recognition in the field of charitable organizations. Hunter had withstood intense scrutiny from Brett on the first few occasions they'd met. He'd been completely open. With his books, his intentions, his plans. He'd been eager for Brett's approval, truth be known.

The two had been in contact ever since.

"I've asked her out more times than I can count," he confessed as they reached Brett's golf ball.

Hunter might not be as wealthy as most of the men out on Santa Raquel's most prestigious golf course that Saturday afternoon, but he had money. Good looks. And a knack for showing people a great time.

Brett swung. Hunter watched as his ball landed and rolled five feet closer to the green than his own. Didn't matter, Hunter was there on one. It had taken Brett two.

"I've never been turned down for a date in my life," he said, when Brett remained silent.

"So that's what this is about?" Brett asked, bagging his iron. Slinging the strap of his golf bag over his shoulder, he started to walk again.

"That I'm bugged because she turns me down? I thought so at first."

Glancing his way, Brett asked, "You don't now?"

"Nope."

"I can't tell you much."

He'd figured.

"Don't even think about getting to her through Colin," Brett said, his tone sounding almost as if he was enjoying himself. "She hates it when he sticks his nose in her business."

Hunter had spent some time speaking with Colin the night before. Had liked him. A lot. And he'd obtained a promise from Colin to invite a group of handpicked clients to attend a dinner at Hunter's expense, to allow Hunter to explain what he did and invite them to join his guest list. Wealthy individuals were always looking for charity tax write-offs, and he threw one hell of a party. It was a win-win.

"I left it alone," he said now. He'd been tempted to ask Colin about Julie. Something had held him back.

Like the thought that Colin would warn him off his little sister and he didn't want to piss the guy off by disregarding his advice.

At the edge of the green both men pulled out putters and dropped their bags. Waited while the two guys ahead of them took their putts.

"Julie's not really in your league," Brett said, serious again.

"I'm not after her money." If Hunter hadn't

known Brett so well, he would've been more offended than he was. Still…

"I'm not talking about her money," Brett said. "Julie's…different."

No shit. She wouldn't be keeping him up nights if she weren't. "I know."

"She's not a woman a guy's going to have fun with."

"I'm not out to take advantage of her." Although he could forgive Brett a little more easily on that one. He liked to have a good time. So did many other people, including the women who liked to hang out with him.

"Is she seeing anyone?" He couldn't stop himself from asking, in spite of how stupidly adolescent he felt.

Brett didn't answer, and Hunter took that as a no. If she *was* involved, there'd be no reason he could think of to keep the information private. And in that case, she'd likely bring the guy to her upcoming gala.

"She's careful." Brett was staring at him now. And all of Hunter's senses slowed.

They weren't playing around here.

"She's been hurt." Brett didn't look away as he spoke. "Badly."

He continued to stand there.

"I just want to invite her out to dinner," Hunter said. "To sit at a table with her and have some conversation." Crazy thing was, his words were the complete truth.

He'd take more if it was given. A helluva lot more. He'd take anything she wanted to offer. But he really needed to talk with her, spend enough time with her to figure out why he couldn't get her out of his head.

Brett's expression changed. For a second there, Hunter thought he'd scored the big one. That Brett was going to give him his way in.

And then the other man walked off to sink his putt.

Hunter sank his, too. First try.

The other two in their party congratulated him. Fist-bumped him. Said they'd buy him a beer.

That was when he realized they'd just finished the eighteenth hole. They were done. His win was official.

He didn't want a beer.

He wanted a date.

JULIE WAS AT the storyboard easel in her sitting room on Sunday afternoon when her cell rang. Colin and Chantel were at Chantel's little apartment in town—the place she insisted on keeping so she didn't completely lose herself in Colin's opulence—vegging for the afternoon, and Julie had expected to work uninterrupted.

When she saw who the caller was—Hunter

Rafferty, owner of The Time of Your Life—she debated whether or not to pick up.

She didn't want to deal with Hunter that afternoon. He was likable. Able to put everyone at ease. Make them laugh. He was great at his job. And his charm *was* a job. Which was why his personal attention bothered her.

But…he wouldn't be calling unless there was a problem with the gala. Something that needed immediate attention. He never called to ask her out; he only did that in person. On the walks to a parking lot after a meeting. That kind of thing. Using her private cell number for personal reasons would be inappropriate.

So, there had to be a problem.

The gala meant the world to her. If they earned even half of what Hunter told her they could expect, the Sunshine Children's League would be able to feed real Thanksgiving dinners to homeless and orphaned kids all over the Los Angeles valley.

She answered her phone on the fifth ring.

"Can you free yourself up for a couple of hours?" His hello, by way of that question, put her instantly on alert.

This was what she didn't like about Hunter. For all his ability to put people at ease, he made her uncomfortable.

Julie couldn't consider his attention harassment. Except that, in a way, she did.

Not because he was friendly with her.

But because...part of her liked it. While the rest of her knew not to trust his party face in a personal setting.

"I'm working." She gave him her standard answer. Nice that pretty much all she did was work, of one kind or another, so the words were always true.

"Is it something you can break away from?"

"Why?"

"I'm at a festival in Santa Barbara. There's a great act here. I just caught the tail end of their show, but they're due to be onstage again in an hour. The show's about forty-five minutes long. If you like them, I can get with them right afterward and see if we can book them."

He'd told her about an entertainment cancellation when they'd had a gala meeting on Wednesday. He hadn't mentioned, when she'd seen him then, that he was on the guest list for the wine tasting at her house on Friday. She'd seen his name. She'd already been toying with the idea of leaving Chantel to act as hostess. Hunter's name on the guest list had made up her mind for her.

"We've got nine great acts lined up," he reminded her. "Most of them are fairly short. We need a tenth if we're going to keep the party going long enough to get the money you want…"

The gala was a black-tie affair at a dinner theater in Beverly Hills. Guests paid to be there. That price included dinner and the first three acts. But they could pay more if they were enjoying themselves and wanted the evening to continue. There'd be voting buttons at each seat. If guests wanted another act, they pushed the button. As long as there were button pushes, the gala would continue. And each push of a button served as another pledge.

She wanted ten acts.

If he'd told her about the festival to begin with, skipping the preliminary questions, she could already have been on her way…

Asking for directions, she told him she'd be there in half an hour.

And wasted five of her thirty minutes trying to decide whether she should change from the jeans and the short, waist-hugging black leather jacket she'd worn to brunch with Colin and Chantel in town. By then, considering how long it would take her to get there, she no longer had time to change.

"NICE JACKET." HUNTER'S words had Julie cringing even before she was fully out of her BMW. She should have changed.

"My sister-in-law gave it to me," she said.

Which was why she'd had it on. The only time she'd had it on. Sassy was just not her style.

Not anymore.

Not for many years.

"She's got good taste."

The look in his eye, accompanied by the grin on his face and the tone of his voice—they made her feel warm.

She didn't *want* to like it.

But she did. Sort of.

And that bothered her.

On a day when she'd been all set to enjoy her peace.

As they started to maneuver through the festival crowd at the edge of the beach, he raised an arm and reached toward her, as though he was going to drop that arm casually around her.

She stepped away.

And hated her life for a second.

Hunter always looked good. Great. But in jeans and a blue polo shirt, with that blond hair windblown and just a hint of stubble on his chin, he was drop-dead gorgeous.

The fact that she noticed, that she *always* noticed, made her nervous. Even if she didn't have a lifetime of issues to muck her way through, Hunter Rafferty was not her type. At all. He was a charmer. The kiss of death.

Charmers' smiles were so bright, so compelling, they hid everything beneath them. Everything inside them.

Someday, she might be healthy enough to go out with friends without a panic attack. In a perfect world she might even get healthy enough to date. But she'd never, ever be able to trust a charmer again. One of them had almost killed her.

And he'd condemned her to live in the shambles he'd left behind.

Smyth had taught her something about charmers, though. They smiled even when they were destroying you. She'd never forget his smile as he held her arms above her head...

She turned down Hunter's offers to buy her a cup of shaved Hawaiian ice, a funnel cake and, finally, a chocolate-covered frozen banana. She kept her distance as they made their way to the stage and sat a chair down from him when they settled in to watch the show.

She gave him her approval of the six nine-year-old girls who sounded like Gladys Knight and the Pips, halfway through their show. After that, she excused herself, knowing he had to wait until the end of the act to speak with the girls' manager, or parents, or whoever could arrange to have them in the lineup the night of the gala.

She'd tell him when he called her later that she thought the girls should be their opening act. And to thank him for finding them.

What she *wasn't* going to tell him was that she'd liked the festival and wished she could have dared enjoy herself with him.

But she wouldn't.

Because she knew why she was attracted to him. He was exactly her type—in the most dangerous way. And that meant he *couldn't* be her type. He was upbeat. Energetic. Always with an idea up his sleeve. Adventurous, like she used to be.

She'd fallen head over heels in love with a man like him, a fun-loving charmer, once before.

And had the fun choked out of her.

Literally.

CHAPTER FOUR

HUNTER DIDN'T CALL Julie Sunday night. She'd had to leave the festival, which obviously meant she'd had something else to do. Or so he chose to think.

She wasn't a micromanager. So she didn't need to be told immediately that he'd hired the girls for her gala.

And…he wanted to call her badly enough that he shut himself down. He wasn't desperate. Had never had to be overeager.

And to prove that to himself, he called a woman friend of his, one he'd been dating casually on and off for years, and took her to dinner and then to a club. He enjoyed himself just fine. More importantly, she enjoyed herself.

Mandy was fun. Vivacious. She was easy to please, and pleased to be with him. Best of all, like him, she had no expectations beyond having a good time with someone she could trust. Had no interest in more than that. The only reason he'd ended the evening early—when she'd made it clear that the night could extend until morning—

was that he had an 8:00 a.m. meeting, followed by a packed Monday and a busy week.

But he'd see her again soon.

He'd assured her of that. And had won a glowing smile and intimate kiss for his trouble.

Mandy was the woman he wanted to be thinking of when he woke the next morning, made his way out to the kitchen of his high-end beach condo to put on the coffee, and headed to the shower. Mandy. Not his festival companion.

Julie Fairbanks was only on his mind because he had to remember to let her know he'd signed the girls, and he hadn't put the reminder on his phone.

That need to call her, in the middle of such a jam-packed week, was why she was the first thing on his mind when the phone rang just as he was pulling on a polo shirt. Grabbing the sports coat that matched his pants and gave the shirt the business touch it required, he reached for his phone.

Dad.

"Hey, what's up?" he answered, slipping into expensive loafers and shoving his wallet in his back pocket before picking up his keys from the nightstand. He'd spoken with both of his parents—separately, of course—the morning before. His regular check-in. But he and his dad, who'd moved to Florida after his parents' divorce ten years before, chatted frequently. Mostly about golf scores and such.

"I need a favor, son."

Son. Not *Buddy*, the nickname his father most often used. Or *Hunter*. Which generally meant his father wasn't too pleased with him.

Son. Hunter paid attention.

"Sure. What's up?" His father was a wealthy man. He could afford to buy just about any favor he needed. And that probably meant it involved his mother. Again.

Karen Rafferty only contacted her ex-husband when she had to. Still, she had a way of pissing his father off—almost as if she was doing it on purpose, as his father sometimes thought. Hunter was more inclined to believe that after so many years of living with a man who didn't give her what she needed, Karen's reactions to her ex-husband were automatic. And automatically negative. She was otherwise a kind, decent woman.

As his father was the first to acknowledge.

"You remember Betty's brother, Edward?"

Betty…John Rafferty's wife. Hunter's step-mother of nine years. And Edward…

"Yeah, he was at your wedding," Hunter said. He pictured the man, about his father's age, a primary care doctor like his dad, and boating enthusiast, as he recalled.

A widower. With a pretty companion whose

name he couldn't remember and whose relationship with Edward reminded Hunter of him and Mandy now. Enjoying each other with no strings attached.

"He needs your help, Hunter. Anything you can do… You know so many people."

While John's California contacts were ten years in the past and mainly in San Diego.

"Is he in some kind of trouble?"

"His daughter is—"

Standing in his kitchen, near the door that led to his garage, Hunter shook his head. "I don't remember a daughter. Was she at the wedding?"

Granted, he'd been a bit put out by the speed with which his father had found a new wife in his new town, concerned that the woman was using him. But now that he knew Betty, a nurse in the building where John had his private practice, he approved wholeheartedly.

"No. That's all part of the problem. He hasn't seen her in practically a decade. Her mom died twelve years ago. Edward buried himself in work, and Cara got in with the wrong people. You know how it is on certain parts of the beach—easy to find crowds to lose yourself in."

Hunter, with his love of a good time coupled with the cold-war atmosphere in his home, had come close to losing his whole future on the beach in San Diego. Until his father had set him straight, telling him that his love of a good time was not something to be thrown away, but to be capitalized on. It was his talent, and he needed to use it wisely.

"She met a guy who ran some surfing school shortly after her mother died. Edward was sure the school was a front for drugs, but the more he questioned, the more Cara pulled away, saying that he just didn't want her to be happy. She ended up following the guy to California, where he started a second surfing school. They got married. Had a little girl... He hired someone to check up on her over the years, just to make certain she was okay."

Hunter wasn't seeing the problem. He was seeing valuable time slip away. But when his dad called, he listened. "So the business was legit, and everything worked out."

"Edward hoped the business was legit, that she was healthy and happy. Cara hasn't contacted him in years or responded to any of his efforts to contact her. At one point, before they left Florida, the guy, Shawn Amos, warned Edward to leave Cara alone. Said that Edward did nothing but make her unhappy. Edward was certain, even then, that Shawn was the biggest problem between him and Cara. He says Amos turned Cara against him. He tried to tell Cara, but any time Edward said anything that could be even vaguely construed as a criticism of Shawn, Cara got defensive and quit listening to him."

He was sorry for the guy. But he didn't see what he could do. He was a party thrower, not a trouble solver, and he had to get to work.

They had a dozen events that week, and while he had staff to handle most of the on-site logistics, he always showed up.

"What kind of trouble is she in?"

The phone call to Julie would have to wait. He didn't want it to be rushed. Just in case he could get her to engage in more than a brief business discussion. Still standing in his kitchen, he looked out toward the beach and realized how long it had been since he'd been out there for the sheer sake of enjoying himself, enjoying the surf. He'd known some great guys who taught surfing...

"She's missing, Hunter."

"Hey, wait a minute, Dad. He needs to call the police. Not me. I'm no investigator. I don't even know an investigator." Wait, yes, he'd just met one—Julie's sister-in-law, Chantel.

Just as Hunter was about to suggest Chantel to his father, John said, "The cops know, Hunter. They're looking for her. That's not the favor."

Completely focused now, Hunter stopped thinking about the time he was losing. "What can I do to help?"

"Edward's granddaughter is staying with a

friend, a neighbor, for the moment, but if Child Protective Services gets involved, she might be sent to strangers. She has an aunt, Shawn's sister Mary, who's in the hospital in critical condition. She's in and out of consciousness, but she said that Shawn beat her up and that he hurt Cara, too. She also said Cara told her to take Joy and run. Mary's the last known person to have seen either Cara or Shawn. The family van is still parked at the residence."

The whole thing was way over his head. Completely outside any area of expertise he'd ever even thought about having. His father had to know that. "What can I do?" he asked again.

"Edward is flying to LA this morning. He plans to stay until his daughter's found. But his first concern is his granddaughter. He wants to make certain that until her father's in custody, she's in a safe place and out of the foster care system."

Finally, he understood. "Edward needs a place to stay," he said. "You want him to bunk with me." The condo had four bedrooms: his, the one with a desk and computer in it for when he worked from home, and two that were ready for guests. "I'm an hour and a half north of the city, but of course, he's welcome. Right now. For as long as he needs. Is he renting a car?"

Hunter had vehicle rental connections.

"Or if he needs a place in the city," he added, "let me know."

He had connections there, too. A file folder filled with them.

"I was hoping you'd contact your friend Brett Ackerman, son. You said he shocked everyone a couple of years ago, admitting that he was the founder of a women's shelter…"

"Yeah. The Lemonade Stand." He didn't know all that much about it. Brett kept a hands-off approach. Hunter had thrown some fund-raisers for the Stand, but never on-site. Or even close to the site. And, as always, he didn't ask a lot of questions about what went on beyond his need-to-know part. He'd learned early on that he couldn't do his job, wouldn't have time to help as many charities as he did, if he delved into all the causes for which his clients were fighting.

"As Edward understands it, Mary—Cara's sister-in-law—doesn't have much money. And if she's close to Cara, she probably won't take any from him. But if he could pay Brett, make a donation to the shelter, I…thought maybe they'd have a place for Mary and Joy there, just until the cops find Shawn and we know they're safe…"

"I can talk to Brett, sure, but what about Edward? You said he's flying in today. Where does he plan to stay? I assume he's meeting with whatever police department has his daughter's case. You have a cell number so I can contact him?"

"He's got a room at a place there in Santa Raquel," John said. "Because I suggested he stay close to you." His father's faith in him had been steadfast. "Ventura police have jurisdiction over the case."

About an hour north of LA, forty-five minutes or so south of Santa Raquel, the beach town was a place where teenagers liked to party. Hunter had never set a function there. But a surfing company made sense…

"What hospital is the aunt in? And what's her full name?"

"Mary Amos. Unmarried. Twenty-seven years old. She works at a gift shop down by the Ventura pier. She's at Ventura County Medical Center."

With a Bluetooth earpiece keeping him connected to his father, he took the details on his phone. "And what's Edward's last name again?" Betty was a Rafferty now. Until she'd married John, he'd had no reason to know her as anything but Betty.

"Mantle."

Like Mickey Mantle. He remembered now. Dr. Mantle.

"The little girl, Joy, how old is she?"

"Seven."

He took down Edward's cell number, flight and hotel information next.

"Got it," he said, keys in hand, phone in his pocket, as he headed for the door. "Tell Edward not to worry. And to call me when he gets in," he said before he clicked the earpiece and started another call.

As he waited for Brett Ackerman to answer, his dad's effusive thanks echoed through his mind. Bothering him, oddly enough. This was serious stuff, and he wasn't doing anything but making a phone call.

The doctors in the world healed pain. The cops punished those who created pain. And Hunter…he was the guy who had a lot of contacts and knew how to put on a good party. Who could always be counted on to lighten the mood.

He was the fun guy.

Not the lifesaver.

CHAPTER FIVE

JULIE HAD THOUGHT about Hunter a great deal on Monday. Only because she was bracing herself to hear from him. Hoping she hadn't given him any hint of how much she'd enjoyed being at the festival with him. Afraid he'd turn on the charm even more.

Secondary to that fear was the fact that she'd been at a crowded public festival for more than an hour without a panic attack. She wanted to celebrate her progress, but was too busy worrying that her lack of anxiety had been due to him—that she'd been so taken with him she was distracted from her usual sense of discomfort.

When she got up Tuesday morning to find the late-night email from him, telling her that he'd signed the girls' group, she was relieved that there was no need for a phone call now. She'd see Hunter at Thursday's meeting—a dress rehearsal for the acts they'd be showcasing at the following week's gala—and then one more time, at the gala itself. After that, she'd be done with him.

Yes, she was relieved about all of that.

No matter what Lila McDaniels said, she was not hiding from life. She was living the life she'd chosen for herself. A life of giving.

Of making the world a better place for children who weren't growing up with the kind of privilege she had. For children who didn't always understand the world around them. Just…for children in general, because children brought her joy.

Being a child had brought her joy.

And she spent time with victims of abuse because she felt comfortable with them.

Still, she hesitated when she saw Lila's number pop up on her cell Wednesday morning. She'd been about to leave the house, heading to LA for a lunch meeting with a couple of board members of the Sunshine Children's League. Among other things, the league supported a home for children awaiting adoption, and Julie was on a committee that was planning an October Open House, for later in the month, with food trucks, Halloween fun and tours of the facilities guided by the kids themselves. They were hoping to attract prospective parents for older children.

She made it through three rings before picking up.

"Hello?" In her studio, she looked over the current work in progress, a drawing on her easel—and the words that went with it on the table with her watercolors.

It's okay to have a day that goes wrong in every way.

The drawing showed a glass of spilled milk, a broken toy and a chubby-faced little girl frowning at a big jelly stain on her shirt.

"I need your help." Lila's first words, after a quick hello, made her stomach hurt.

"Of course. What do you need?" She'd step up. No matter what. The alternative, to stay locked away in her fairy-tale world, wasn't right. Or enough.

You didn't die from anxiety. Not her kind of anxiety anyway. And even if you did, she'd rather die than be dead alive.

Lila told her about a little girl, Joy. A new resident at the Stand whose father was abusive and whose mother was missing—presumably taken by the father. The seven-year-old had been with them since Monday night, but so far hadn't said a word to anyone. Or even nodded or shaken her head. She followed instructions.

And she stared vacantly.

Except when it came to Julie's book about a little girl, Amy, who was afraid of her own shadow—*Amy's Shadow.*

"I'm not sure she reads the words, but Sara and the women whose bungalow Joy's staying in, until her aunt's out of the hospital, have read it to her several times. And whenever she's not being told to do something else, she's got the book in her hands. Sometimes turning the pages. Sometimes just holding it."

Tears flooded Julie's eyes. She used to think her sensitivity, her drama and intense emotions, made her special. Then they'd made her fragile.

Which was why she hated when her feelings took over.

There wasn't time for that right now.

"Can I see her?" Julie asked. She might not be a counselor, but she'd studied child development. And she knew Amy, the girl with the shadow, very, very well.

"That's why I'm calling. I was hoping you could make time this morning."

The Sunshine League meeting was important. But it could go on without her. The others could fill her in on any decisions made in her absence.

Within half an hour, she was sitting in the front room of one of the larger bungalows on Lemonade Stand grounds with Joy, a small-boned, dark-haired girl. The child's big brown eyes were filled with a blankness that tore at Julie's heart.

Vanessa, one of the adult residents of the bungalow, sat across from them, thumbing through a magazine. The television was on, a family sitcom playing softly in the background.

Sara Havens Edwin was in the kitchen with the older woman who'd agreed to have Joy stay in her room. Hannah was a grandmother of two. And as soon as she got legally disengaged from her abusive second husband, she was going to be moving across the country to live close to her grandkids. If her own kids had had their way, she'd be there already.

Hannah had insisted that she had to get healthy before she took up life with her kids. Julie had spent an evening with her the week before, baking cookies. And listening. What she'd figured was that Hannah needed time to find herself again before she dared to join the grandchildren she adored.

"Would you like me to read to you about Amy?" Julie asked, hands in her lap. Joy didn't reply. She didn't offer the book. And Julie didn't take it from her.

She just started talking. About Amy. About some of the things behind what was on the page. Things that Julie, as the author, knew. Things that hadn't made it to the page. She explained all of Amy's thoughts and feelings.

Sara had come into the room and was now sitting several feet away. Hannah was there, too. Listening. Vanessa was no longer reading. The TV still droned softly.

Julie tuned it all out.

Smiling at Joy, she talked to her calmly yet confidently. She knew Amy better than anyone.

She shuddered at the thought of anyone, other than Lila and Sara, knowing that she'd written the new bestselling *Being Amy* series of children's books. But considering the confidentiality code at The Lemonade Stand, she hoped that if Vanessa and Hannah had guessed, they'd keep her secret.

The little girl, dressed in jeans and a pink-and-purple short-sleeved shirt, with matching pink-and-purple tennis shoes, opened the book. Turned the pages. Almost as if she was following along with the story. Julie purposely spoke out of page order, to see if Joy got to the right page. Talking about the time Amy was in the bathtub in the morning instead of at night and her shadow was on the wall beside her. Then she moved on to her shadow being in the dentist's office with her. Joy turned back a couple of pages.

Julie wanted to look at Sara, to let her know the little girl was engaged.

But she didn't. She wanted Joy to feel her full attention. As though it was just the two of them there.

Just the two of them—and Amy.

For as long as Joy needed her.

A BUSY WEEK turned into a maelstrom. Hunter got everything done, with his easygoing nature intact. Most of the time he even managed to keep a smile on his face.

Except for the meeting he'd sat in on with Edward and Lila McDaniels, managing director of The Lemonade Stand. He didn't know what he'd expected when he'd called Brett. But it hadn't been an immediate appointment with Brett's top employee at the Stand. He was told to bring Edward in. Hunter had already been vetted for safety purposes when he was hired to run the fund-raisers. And for this one visit, Edward, who had a current medical license, could get in on Hunter's credentials. Just to Lila's office and back outside.

That short trip down one hall had been more than Hunter had bargained for. The entire atmosphere—uplifting, supportive and yet somehow desperate, too—had been unlike anything he'd experienced in his life.

But his visit and Edward's had worked. Sara and Chantel had gone to collect Joy from the neighbors and as of that very first night, Joy had been inside the safe environment, which had round-the-clock security.

Mary would be welcome there, too, if she chose to avail herself of the opportunity once she was well enough to leave the hospital. She'd suffered a severe blow to the head, and it looked like there could be complications, so she might not be out for a while.

Edward had not yet met his granddaughter. He

was voluntarily undergoing a full evaluation, with background checks, to prove to anyone with questions that his daughter's lack of contact with him was not a result of some horrible deed in his past. Or being a horrible man.

What Hunter knew, and others might not, was that if Cara wasn't found alive, Edward was planning to take every step possible to be awarded full custody.

It was all way more drama than Hunter generally had in his life, and he got most of it from Edward, in the evenings, over beer.

He even felt that the strange week had impacted his carriage. His purposeful gait, as he entered the dinner theater he'd booked to host the Sunshine Children's League gala, was different from his usual laid-back style. Hunter always built extra time into his schedule. For things like traffic. Catastrophes. Unexpected phone calls. His world was successful partially because of his ability to leave "urgent" out of his days.

But that Thursday he arrived with barely fifteen minutes to spare before dress rehearsal was due to begin for the following week's gala. Still in the golf shirt he'd put on that morning, he was sweating. At least the dark color of the shirt hid most of the giveaway on that one. Again, not his usual style.

The lack of proper hygiene time irritated him,

which put him even more off his game. And here
he wanted Julie Fairbanks to be impressed enough
to go out with him.

Or rather, accept a single invitation to dinner.

He'd neither seen the woman nor spoken with
her since Sunday. He'd been hellaciously busy, and
still, she was on his mind the second he woke up
that morning. He'd finally reached the day he'd
be seeing her.

That thought had sprung him out of bed and
into the kitchen for coffee with a whistle.

Coffee was the first thing that had gone wrong.
He'd emptied his canister the day before and had
neglected to open a new one. Which meant going
to the storage cupboard out in his garage to re-
trieve the canister waiting there, emptying the in-
dividual white plastic cups into their holder on the
counter, and disposing of the canister.

A small problem. One he'd whistled through.

And then he'd turned on the hot water for his
shower and discovered he had none. The ther-
mostat on his hot water heater had gone out. A
hundred-dollar fix—he knew a guy who'd come
over half an hour later and had it fixed for him
in less than that. Then a quick shower and he'd
been on his way.

His route had been slower due to traffic he usually managed to avoid. Edward had asked to meet
him for lunch, and since the guy was technically

family, knew no one else in town and was really broken up about his missing daughter, Hunter agreed. He'd had a business lunch planned, which he attended, met Edward at two, and had to rush to his midafternoon meeting. From then on, he'd never quite caught up to himself.

No time for the second shower he'd planned before seeing Julie again.

"Hunter. I thought I'd be the first one here."

Either her voice had invaded his brain, along with the images he'd been playing for weeks now, or she was standing behind him.

He turned slowly, his ready smile pasted on his face. "Then you don't know me well enough yet," he told her, immensely relieved to find that in spite of his tardiness, he'd beaten her to the venue. Timeliness mattered to her. He'd figured that out when another board member was late for their first meeting. She'd been gracious. But the way she'd continuously rubbed her hands together while they were waiting had given away her distress.

He was trained to notice stuff like that.

Or rather, the psychology degree he'd earned in college, in an effort to better understand people so that he could better know how to please them, had taught him that he needed a class in body language. Which he'd sought outside of his college training.

"I know you arrive fifteen minutes early for every meeting," she said, coming toward him. Her long dark hair was pulled back, but the white shirt buttoned up nearly to her throat covered any skin she might have left exposed.

Hunter swallowed, pretty sure that she was the most beautiful woman he'd ever seen. Then he shook himself awake. Yeah, Julie Fairbanks had a perfect figure, great features and memorable eyes, but he was a California boy, and he'd had his pick of more beauties than most men met in a lifetime.

"Ah, but this is a dress rehearsal," he said, leading her to the stage at the front of the room. He'd reached for her arm, but he'd somehow missed making contact again, just like at the festival. He wondered if she'd avoided his touch this time because she could tell he was sweating. He stopped just short of sniffing his armpit.

That she would certainly have noticed.

"Tensions tend to run high when acts come face-to-face for the first time," he said. "They're all vying for position in the lineup, while trying to determine which position would be best for them. They're looking at the venue, determining how to fit their act into the space, assessing stage wing options for props or easy entrances and exits. They're also finding out who they know, avoiding people they might've had words—or relationships—with in the past. Plus, they're staking their claim to dressing-room space. And they're doing all this while trying to appear blasé about the whole thing."

In Hunter's world, he and his staff dealt mainly with talent that could make it big, but hadn't done so yet. Galas like Julie's could be a chance at a big break. If the right person noticed them. Was impressed by them. Was in the audience at all…

Usually, with events of this size, there was at least one well-known agent or producer in the audience. He always saw to that. Kept the talent coming. Made the whole evening a win-win. And the level of his talent brought the producers and agents back.

All of it was in a day's work for him.

Not that he expected Julie Fairbanks to know or care about any of that.

"So, what position would be best for them?" She actually met his gaze as she turned her head to look at him.

That was a first. Normally their eyes meeting, no matter how hard he tried to make it happen, turned into yet another near miss.

Blue. Her eyes were blue. He'd known that, of course. His were, too.

Blue and blue make blue. Crazy thought. From a crazy man. He needed to get a grip fast.

She'd asked a question. His mind struggled to re-call it. Position. Right. She'd asked about position.

He had a flash of her on the couch in his study with her shirt unbuttoned…

No. What the hell was wrong with him? Hunter had never looked at a woman he was with and pictured her with her clothes off. Not unless he knew she *wanted* him to see her with her clothes off.

Some men did that. Lots of normal men did. Not him.

Just a rule he'd set for himself after a particularly heated fight between his parents, with his mother accusing his father of mentally undressing some woman at a party. His father had eventually become so riled, he'd admitted to having done that. Hunter, a kid at the time, had been completely sure his mother was wrong, but having heard his father's admission, he'd made the rule for himself.

Julie turned those blue eyes on him a second time.

Position. Oh, yeah.

"I'm not sure there is a best position in a show like this one," he said now, more serious than usual as he considered her question. Serious because he had to focus to stay on topic. "First is good since it guarantees you'll be seen by everyone. But it's so early in the evening that some folks might not have arrived. People are still eating. Chatting. Catching up. Generally just enjoying themselves. And not worried yet that the evening might end too soon."

"Because the first acts are covered in the initial ticket price, no one needs to pay attention or push their buttons to stay. It won't affect their wallets."

"Exactly. It gets more intense, with more people actually watching the show as folks start to really pay attention. They have to decide whether the talent warrants another spend. Some will stay for the duration, just to donate, but a lot won't. They'll stay as long as they're enjoying themselves."

"So maybe, for the performers, it's more about not getting the worst position," Julie said. "Because if the talent that comes ahead of you isn't good, you might not get to go on. And even if you do, there'll be fewer people there watching."

"The evening is wearing down at that point. People are usually quiet and watching the stage. Besides, any talent scouts in attendance are going to stay until the end." At least Hunter's did. Which was why his shows drew the level of talent they did, and why people paid so much money to attend one of his functions...

They'd reached the door that led backstage. Holding it for her to precede him, he told himself not to look at the perfectly shaped backside in the black jeans, or notice the way her wedged heels gave height to legs that had been crashing his thoughts for weeks now.

Still, as she turned toward him, waiting for him to follow, there was something…different about her. Like maybe she'd found the lightness in her step that he'd lost from his. Maybe she'd stolen it from him on Sunday. Yeah, maybe that was it.

Starting to feel a smile coming on, Hunter got to work.

CHAPTER SIX

JULIE HAD THE table set with fruit and fresh flowers, place mats and her favorite breakfast dishes before Colin and Chantel entered the breakfast room Friday morning. The family of three had a housekeeper who also did a lot of the cooking, but Julie had always reserved the right to prepare breakfast. When it had been just her and Colin, she'd needed the promise of time alone with her older brother to get her out of bed in the morning.

Needed to know that *he'd* know if she didn't get up.

And since Chantel had come…it was just as important to start her day with her family together. Maybe more so. Much as she adored Colin, Julie found a greater understanding with the woman he'd married.

Plates of crepes were set down and, when they were empty, snatched back up as efficiently as she could manage without being rude. Ignoring the look between her brother and his wife—one that meant they were sharing silent thoughts about her—she was out the door before they were.

She'd been spending time with Joy for two days and was still the only one who could get any kind of response out of her. Lila and Sara wanted to give her a few hours alone with Joy that morning. She hadn't told Colin or Chantel about the little girl yet. Not that she could say a whole lot anyway. But she hadn't even mentioned that she was working directly, one-on-one, with a single child.

Reading to kids, doing puppet plays with them, having them paint and draw—her most common activities at the Stand—was fulfilling. Worthy expenditures of time.

And there was still that step back from personal intimacy. Allowing her to keep her private self safely tucked away inside.

It was how she wanted it.

And yet, here was Joy, who seemed to need her in a way no one else ever had. And she hadn't been so eager to face a day since the night her beautiful, promising young world had crashed around her feet.

In jeans and a blue, button-down tapered shirt, she grabbed an art satchel out of the back seat of her BMW after she'd parked in the secured lot behind the Stand and headed inside the grounds. No one was sure what Joy might have seen the morning her aunt was beaten and her mother went missing.

No one knew what she'd seen before that, either.

Or experienced herself at the hands of her father. There'd been no outward signs of physical abuse—for which Julie was incredibly thankful.

But that didn't mean the man hadn't hit her. Only that he hadn't done so with enough force to break bones. Or leave scars.

Sara and others were convinced that Joy's silence was indicative of severe emotional trauma. But until the aunt could be questioned—other than the brief inquiry made by police as she was being loaded into an ambulance at the neighbor's—Joy was the only one who could tell them what had happened.

And that was where Julie came in.

EDWARD CALLED, WANTING to meet for lunch again on Friday. And again, Hunter rearranged his schedule. Preparations for the two benefits he had going that night were running smoothly. He was half an hour ahead of schedule, as usual. There'd been some last-minute security issues and road closures with a 10K run he had set to kick off at six the next morning, but those were being handled. And Saturday night's event to raise money for a political campaign was a roast. Other than arranging the venue, ordering food and drink, and taking care of the guest list and seating, his staff of three had little to do for that one.

He'd be attending the roast and had asked Julie

to be his date for the evening. Or rather, had offered to take her so she could taste the desserts. He'd hired the same company to provide an after-dinner sweets table for her gala. She'd politely declined his invitation.

He'd originally thought he'd take Mandy—a first for him, mixing her pleasure relationship with business—but changed his mind. And was thinking of Julie again as he pulled into the posh resort where Edward had a room and saw the older man waiting for him at the valet post. Not an unusual occurrence if they were going out somewhere. They weren't; Edward was just that badly in need of company.

His white shirt neatly pressed, his shined shoes pristine, the doctor held out a hand to Hunter as he stepped up to the curb. Edward had recently come back from the police station.

"If this was a stranger abduction, there'd be more chance that she's already gone," Edward told him, speaking of his beloved daughter as they sat on the patio of the resort's Mexican eatery, the ocean restless in the distance. "But since she's most likely with Shawn, they think there's a good chance of finding her alive. Many abusers tend to become conciliatory, protective, even loving, after an attack. Our hope is Shawn is that type of abuser. If he lashes out when he's drunk, we have a fairly good chance, too. As long as Cara can keep him away from the booze."

Hunter shifted in his seat. He felt completely out of his element. And figured that if Edward's daughter had been able to keep her husband away from whatever caused his heinous acts, she'd have prevented their current situation.

Watching the doctor rub at a nonexistent smudge on his water glass, Hunter felt for the guy. He didn't expect great things of himself in the hero department. But for Edward, a man who'd dedicated himself to saving lives, being unable to save your own daughter had to be akin to burning in hell.

Remembering how frustrated and distraught his father would get when he lost a patient, Hunter looked out to sea.

He had to give his head a shake. The ocean had been a refuge for him back then, too, anytime his dad came home without the patience to deal with the sound of his mother's voice. He'd go out to the beach. To surf. To lose the sound of his parents' anger in the roar of the waves.

And then he'd go home, his usual cheery self, tell a joke, or if things were really bad, ask his dad to watch sports or go to the putting green. Soon all would be well again.

But this, a missing daughter...

"Is everyone positive that she didn't go with

him willingly?" Hunter asked. Maybe it was a horrible question to ask, except that it was a truth Edward had been living with for a decade. His daughter had forsaken family to be with a man who hurt her. So maybe the idea that her disappearance might have been voluntary wasn't as alarming as the thought that his daughter was being held hostage by a maniac.

Nodding, Edward looked older than he had at the beginning of the week. Older than his fifty-two years. The lines around his eyes seemed more pronounced. "Among other things, she didn't take her cell phone with her," he said.

Hunter shifted again, wondering if a cool breeze would be along soon.

"But if they had to leave in a hurry, what with Mary's…situation and all…"

He really wanted to come through for his dad and Betty. For Edward.

The older man's smile was knowing. Sad. Almost as though he was giving up.

"They found her purse," the doctor said. "Three hours north of here. It'd been thrown in a twenty-four-hour box-store trash can and was only found by accident. Her wallet was gone, but inside there was some ID cards, makeup, a handheld electronic reader with children's books loaded and moist wipes. They're going through it now."

"Hopefully they'll learn something…"

"Hopefully." The doctor didn't sound hopeful.

"It's a start," he continued. "More than they had before…"

Struggling to find anything in his repertoire for a situation such as this, Hunter dug deep. And still came up empty.

"I need a favor." It was as though Edward had read his mind.

"Anything," Hunter said, probably too eagerly. Anything he *could* do, he *would* do. They'd ordered but hadn't been served yet. He could flag someone, get their food to go.

Or skip the meal altogether.

"I have a meeting this afternoon. An interview, more or less. I want you to come with me."

"What kind of interview?"

"It's with Joy's counselor at the shelter. And some other staff. Apparently Joy hasn't said a word since Mary got her to the neighbors that day. I want to see her…"

Edward's voice broke. He visibly calmed himself, then said, "The people caring for her aren't convinced it's a good idea, particularly since she doesn't know me. Or probably even know of me. At the same time, I'm family. And being with someone who loves her is vitally important at this point, too."

He'd go. Of course he would. He just wasn't sure what he could contribute…

"I have a tendency to come across as standoff-ish," Edward said, looking him straight in the eye. "But you walk into a room and suddenly everyone feels comfortable."

He wouldn't go that far.

"This meeting is critical to me, Hunter. I can't afford to have it go wrong. They aren't going to risk that little girl's emotional health—and I wouldn't want them to—if everything doesn't go perfectly. I know how much I love her. I know I can care for her. I just need a chance to *get* that chance."

"When's the meeting?"

"Four."

Right in the middle of the time he'd allotted for the shower he'd planned to take before the evening's round of party visits. Well, a washup and change would suffice.

"You want me to pick you up here?" It would take extra time. Meeting Edward at the shelter would work much better for him.

But this wasn't about him.

"If you wouldn't mind."

And he had an idea…one that was growing on him in leaps and bounds. "Then, afterward, assuming they need a while to discuss things and you don't get to see Joy right away, you can come to work with me. I always have two tickets to every event, and one of tonight's functions is to raise money for some technically advanced machine for the new hospital here in Santa Raquel. It's taking place on hospital grounds. You'd fit right in..."

Finally, something truly helpful he could do.

Introduce Edward to his own kind.

That way, he wouldn't feel quite so alone while he waited to learn his daughter's fate.

And his own, too, Hunter supposed, when you considered that he could possibly become guardian to a seven-year-old child he'd never met.

"If I'm not spending the evening with my granddaughter, I'll probably take you up on that offer, son," Edward said.

Sounding just like Hunter's dad.

So much so that Hunter relaxed.

He had this.

CHAPTER SEVEN

AFTER A COUPLE of hours with Joy, followed by a board meeting in LA, Julie pulled back into the Stand's parking lot just after two on Friday. Joy would be out of "school" for the day, and if she wanted to be with Julie, Julie wanted to be with her. According to Sara, they'd had to put Joy's aunt in a medically induced coma—Julie wasn't privy to the details—but it meant that Joy was alone.

A feeling Julie knew only too well. Shortly before the attack that had changed her life, she'd lost her own mother. And her father, too.

Memories of the debilitating fear that had taken over her life crept in even now, eleven years later. And she'd been nearly an adult at the time. Seventeen. Joy was only seven.

She'd coped by losing herself in the memories of her childhood. Expressing them through her drawing. And writing.

Amy, the little girl afraid of her own shadow, had been born during that time in Julie's life. It was no wonder to Julie, and no mistake, in her view, that Joy clung to the fictional character. To the book.

She couldn't stand in for Joy's mother or aunt, but she could be a kind stranger who understood what she was going through during these first difficult days. And if there was a chance that she could help Joy tell someone what had happened the day her mother went missing... If there was any clue to her parents' whereabouts that the child could possibly disclose, then she'd spend every moment she could trying to help Joy come out of her shell enough to communicate with them.

She'd had an idea and was feeling hopeful as she sat with the little girl in the same private room they'd been in that morning, a room in the school wing of the Stand's main building. She'd set up two identical easels with a table in between. The table held pencils. Sitting at one easel, with Joy at the other, she started to draw freestyle. She invited Joy to do the same.

"This is how Amy came to be," she told the little girl, her gaze on the page in front of her. She was drawing Amy. At The Lemonade Stand. Joy might not have figured that out yet. But Julie had faith that she would. "My mom was gone, too, and I was scared, and then Amy came into my head, like an imaginary friend, to play with me. Do you ever have imaginary friends?" she asked.

Kids had them. It was normal. Her minor in child development had taught her that much.

"Mine was a lot like me. I named her Amy. But I wanted her to be out here in the world, you know, so I could see her…"

Amy had been the way she remembered her younger self.

"So I drew her, just fooling around, and I started to feel better. So I drew her some more."

The fictional face that was so familiar to her was taking perfect shape on the page. Usually Amy's expressions were more serious; she was a little girl who had fears and learned that the only real thing she had to fear was being afraid. But today, Julie drew her differently. Today Amy's eyes glowed with hope. There was going to be a grin on her face, too. Not the happy, secure, quiet smile she usually wore at the end of the books. But an ebullient, childish grin. Something she hoped Joy could remember feeling.

As she worked, she chatted. About Amy. Keeping her comments age-appropriate and one step removed. The grin was there on Amy's face. But something wasn't quite right. The chin maybe.

"Sometimes Amy thinks she's the only one who knows stuff," she said. "And sometimes she knows secrets that she's afraid to tell because people who are bigger than her might get mad."

After she'd been brutally raped, Julie had come

home to Colin. He'd taken her to the hospital. They'd gone to the police. Her rapist was known to them. But he was the son of a powerful man, and in the end, she and Colin had agreed, understanding the consequences if they didn't, to let the matter drop.

Amy had taken it all on.

No, the problem wasn't the chin. She looked at the mouth again.

There was movement beside her. Joy had picked up a pencil.

Heart pounding, Julie left Amy's face incomplete, moved down to the neck and shoulders, which she could draw without paying much attention. Dressing Amy in a T-shirt with butterflies, she watched Joy—also in a T-shirt with butterflies—out of the corner of her eye.

Afraid to do anything that might distract Joy, she continued to talk about Amy. About the reasons she liked butterflies—because of their soft wings and pretty colors, which was why Julie had always liked them.

Sara had said that she thought Joy was relating to Julie, or maybe to her childhood self, through Amy. She'd told Julie just to be herself.

Joy's hand, gripping the black pencil, hovered over the page. Black was a color associated with anger. And fear.

But it was also good for outlining.

Julie steadied her own hand. Drew another long stroke. Analyzing Joy's reactions wasn't her job.

"Amy used to love chocolate ice cream best," she said, fixated on that dark pencil in the girl's hand, in spite of her admonitions to the contrary. "Now she kind of likes vanilla better sometimes."

She was babbling. But kids liked ice cream. And she didn't want to scare Joy off.

A circle was forming slowly on the page in front of the girl.

Julie fiddled with the collar of the T-shirt on her own page. Waiting to see what came next in Joy's drawing.

Two dots, where eyes would go.

And then little broken lines straight down from them.

Julie didn't need to be a psychiatrist to get that one. Just as Joy didn't need to be an artist to draw an understandable depiction. Or use words to speak.

The precious little girl, whose father had most likely just abducted her mother, was crying inside.

LILA MCDANIELS, IN brown pants and jacket, with a top that was a darker shade, met Hunter and Edward in the small public lobby of The Lemonade Stand. Other than the nondescript, tiled room, the rest of the premises were accessible only by pass code or key.

"Edward." The Stand's managing director took the doctor's hand briefly, released it and stepped back immediately. Hunter didn't know if Edward noticed or not, but he didn't think the reception boded well. "Hunter." Lila turned her attention to him with a smile that, while not effusive, still held what seemed like genuine welcome.

What the hell?

"I'm so grateful to you for entertaining my plea," Edward said, his tone about as far from standoffish as Hunter had heard. He crossed his hands one over the other in front of him and gave the older woman a smile.

She quickly turned to lead them toward a private door…

Shrugging off his impressions, putting them down to his own discomfort, he followed the other two back down the hall. The same hall they'd walked through when they'd come here a few days ago.

Edward's granddaughter was now a resident at the Stand. Which made him more of a client than the total stranger he'd been the last time they'd visited. The man's daughter was missing. His grandchild was traumatized. What did Hunter know about the nuances of any of that?

Figuring they were heading toward Lila's office again, he was surprised when they stopped short before they reached it. They stood in front of an open door that looked like it led to some kind of small but nicely appointed conference room.

Not a lot of space for mingling, he noticed first. But the upholstered chairs at the long table were an attractive touch. Comfortable.

The beige color on the back wall offset the flowered prints. Not his personal taste, but for an event…

He'd set a dinner there if the room had been offered for his use. It would suit a small charity board consisting of members who all knew each other well—and didn't intend to stay long.

Lila, with Edward standing at her side in the doorway, was introducing him and turned, stepping more completely into the room, so that Hunter could come forward, as well.

And actually see the two women sitting at the table.

He supposed the managing director continued to speak. He heard a voice. But he was no longer paying attention.

Julie Fairbanks was one of the women at that table.

Which confused the hell out of him.

HUNTER HAD AN hour to spare for Edward's meeting. He wished he had all night. While he didn't like feeling superfluous, particularly when he had so much to do, he walked into the conference room, took the seat next to Edward and stared at Julie Fairbanks.

Why was she there?

He tried the silent approach, trying to get her to look at him and read his mind. It failed.

"Dr. Mantle, I appreciate the urgency of your situation, but before we could even consider arranging a meeting between you and your granddaughter, we need to talk with you."

The speaker, Sara Havens Edwin, as she'd been introduced, was a full-time counselor at the Stand. The introduction of Julie had included no title.

Edward nodded. "Of course." His hands were folded on the table now, his attention fully on the blonde counselor. Lila, at the head of the table, had handed the meeting over to Sara.

For the most part, Hunter watched Julie. Was she a counselor, too? No one had ever said so. Surely Brett would've told him if she worked for him, when he'd asked about her on the golf course.

What had Brett said?

That she'd been hurt.

He'd assumed that meant she'd gone through a painful breakup.

She didn't look in his direction. She watched Sara, with a glance or two at Edward as he answered basic questions about himself, including the fact that he'd taken a leave of absence from his practice.

"You can always go through the courts to get an order for visitation with your granddaughter."

Hunter's glance swung from Julie to Sara when he heard the counselor's words.

"I'm aware of that," Edward said. "Ms. McDaniels and I have spoken about it." Edward's smile at the director held gratitude. She nodded, and then he focused on Sara.

"In the first place, that would take time," Edward continued with the air of one in charge, "although I understand there's the possibility of an emergency temporary order. At this point, I'm not interested in my rights. I'm interested in the best care for my granddaughter..." His voice faded as he cleared his throat.

Hunter felt he should jump in. Say something to lighten the moment. It was the whole reason Edward had asked him to be there.

But Edward didn't know Hunter well. When it came to emotional drama, he went surfing.

"I understand that further disruption in Joy's life wouldn't be good. I also know for a fact that family love is a strong healer," Edward continued, then looked Hunter's way.

He figured his uncle by marriage was doing just fine. So, fingers steepled at his lips as though he was completely familiar with such things, he nodded.

"Can you plan to stay around awhile if necessary?" Sara asked, giving Edward a piercing glance.

"Yes."

"He's got a room at my place anytime he wants it and for as long as he needs it." Hunter addressed the counselor.

"I…didn't realize Hunter was going to be here…"

He turned to Julie the second he heard her voice.

"I had no idea you were related to Joy's grandfather," she said.

"By marriage," he felt compelled to say, to be completely truthful on that score. "His sister's married to my father."

Julie looked between Sara and Lila. "I've known Hunter awhile. He wouldn't be here if he thought there was any reason to worry where Edward's concerned."

"Hunter is the reason Joy's here," Lila McDaniels said. "Brett Ackerman referred him to us."

The glance Julie sent Hunter, as though she was seeing him in a new light, sent a jolt through him.

Giving him a "go surfing" impulse again. And yet, keeping him in his chair. What was it about this woman?

Why couldn't he just move on?

"Julie's being at this meeting was kind of last-minute." Lila was speaking again. "She's been…

spending time with Joy. So far, she's the only one who's been able to get any reaction out of her at all."

Hunter wasn't surprised. He should be. But he wasn't.

"You're a counselor, too?" he asked Julie, somewhat disturbed that he hadn't been privvy to that information. He'd assumed she was one of the social elite who sat on a lot of charity boards.

"No," she said. "I…draw." She looked away. Shutting him out again.

And that left him wanting "in" more than ever.

"Julie is doing art therapy with Joy." Sara took over, leaving Hunter with the impression that there was more *not* being said at that table than was actually spoken.

Definitely not his forte.

"And you've had some success?" Leaning forward, Edward seemed about ready to take Julie's hand across the table.

Julie nodded.

"Can you share it with me?"

With a glance at Sara and Lila, who both nodded, Julie said, "She drew a crying stick figure."

The doctor's lips pursed. His chin tightened. And Hunter saw a tear in the corner of his eye.

He cared about Edward and Joy. He wanted to help.

And, not for the first time, came up blank.

CHAPTER EIGHT

No one had told her Hunter Rafferty was going to be in the meeting with Joy's grandfather from Florida.

No one would've had cause to know that she'd met the man. Sara and Lila weren't part of her life outside the Stand.

Still, seeing him there was a shock.

In just a few days, Joy had become an integral part of her waking moments. And she was related to Hunter Rafferty?

By marriage.

"Here's what I'd like to propose," Sara said, drawing Julie's full attention. "Joy is currently in the cafeteria with her house mother, helping make chocolate chip cookies for tonight's movie. We can walk through there, all of us, like any other group of adults on a tour." The counselor turned to Julie. "Are you okay with that?"

"Of course." She'd been planning to spend the evening at the Stand, in spite of the fact that doing so might further stoke Lila's fears on her behalf. Colin and Chantel were going to the theater in LA.

And she wanted to be on hand in case Joy needed her. For the same reason she'd postponed her all-girl outing with Lila, Sara and Lynn.

Sara glanced at Lila. "Let's just walk by, say hello. Give Edward a chance to see the child."

Lila's nod was immediate.

Sara turned to Edward. "This is only going to work if you're emotionally up to seeing her without reacting. If you'd rather wait, we can."

"I want to see her."

"He's a doctor. He knows how to keep his own emotions in check when he's dealing with emotional situations," Hunter said.

His ready defense of his step-uncle, although maybe unnecessary, impressed Julie.

It was the charming smile that she couldn't get past. Didn't trust.

"And then we can talk about an actual meeting. However, I should warn you that we might not tell her right away who you are."

"I, um, think we should," Julie said. She wasn't the professional. Or the boss. "I mean, you know best," she told Sara. "And I don't want you to take risks based on my opinion."

"We asked you to be here because you seem to have an understanding of Joy that the rest of us don't," Lila said. "We want your opinion, Julie."

"It was right after I was talking about secrets that she drew the picture," she said. "I feel we should tell her the truth. She's only seven. It's not like she's going to understand the biological significance. But I just think… Well, she's lost her mom, her aunt *and* her father…"

She paused, looked around the table. "I'm not insinuating that having her father around was a good thing, but it must've been good some of the time or Cara wouldn't have stayed, right? Not when she had a father to run home to."

"She was pretty angry with me," Edward said. "After her mother died… I wasn't home as much as I should've been."

Julie didn't really need to know about that. "Whether Joy was afraid of her dad or loved him, his disappearance must still give her a sense of abandonment—especially with her mom and aunt gone." She focused on Sara.

The counselor nodded.

"So… I think it might help her to know she's not all alone. And it might be good for her to find out that she has a family member who isn't related to her father. And isn't afraid of him."

Sara was studying her. Julie withstood the examination. There was something about her that was calling out to the little girl. Something about Julie's own suffering that was somehow reaching Joy.

"Poor baby. No telling what she's not saying…"

Edward, a tall, commanding man in his fifties, suddenly looked sunken.

"She's responding to Julie," Lila announced to the table. "I have every hope that she'll open up soon..."

"Absolutely," Sara added. "Be assured, Dr. Mantle, that we're all watching her very closely and are doing everything we can for her."

"I don't doubt that," Edward said, standing. "I'm thankful that she's here. Could we take our walk now?"

He'd lost so much. His wife. His only child for all these years—and possibly forever. Yet there he was, ready to take responsibility for a little girl he'd never even met. To slay her dragons. With apparently no thought of himself, or what the ensuing weeks and months could take out of him. He was putting his entire life on hold. His practice.

The man was a rock.

And watching him brought tears to Julie's eyes. They increased when Hunter stood up next to Edward, patted him on the shoulder and stayed close to his side as they walked to the door.

"You coming?" Sara's voice jolted Julie into motion.

In some ways Joy was a very lucky little girl.

In some ways, Julie was lucky, as well.

She'd do better to remember that more often.

"IT'S STRANGE, THE two of us meeting like this."

Purposely staying behind the group walking toward the kitchen, Julie wasn't all that surprised when Hunter lagged back to talk to her.

"I had no idea you were connected to Joy." Even though she was repeating herself, she said the first thing that came to mind other than, "go away." Or "it's good to see you." Because it wasn't good.

"Only by marriage," Hunter said, making her wonder why it was so important to him to bring up something he'd already mentioned.

"You don't like Edward?"

"On the contrary. I highly respect him. He reminds me a lot of my dad."

"Your father?" In the months she'd known him—the months he'd been trying to get her to go out with him—he'd never, ever said anything personal about himself. His business, yes. Himself—never. It was as though, outside of The Time of Your Life, Hunter Rafferty didn't exist. But then that was how charmers were. The facade helped them hide their true selves from the world.

"Yep" was all he had to say about his dad.

"Do they get along?" She was just making conversation. Trying not to get caught up in the emotional drama that was unfolding. Trying not to worry about Joy's reaction to the strangers who were going to be invading her space.

Trying not to worry about the man who was about to see his granddaughter for the first time.

"They work together," Hunter told her. "That's how Dad met Betty, Edward's sister."

Edward was a family physician. "Your father works in a doctor's office?"

"My father is the principal owner of the clinic in which they both work. He's a primary care physician, too."

Hunter never seemed all that serious. Different from Smyth, who was charmingly serious. The son of a financier. Because he didn't seem to take life seriously, she'd somehow assumed Hunter came from a...less responsible background.

"And he married Edward's sister?" Betty. "Yep."

Looking ahead to the older couple walking in front of them, Julie felt herself getting emotionally drawn in to the scene about to unfold.

They were still several yards from the door that led to another hall that ended at the kitchen. There was time for her to escape to the safety of her car before things got too intense, before she found herself entwined in an emotional moment that included the man at her side. Like that would somehow bind them. They weren't going to be introducing Edward to Joy. This was just a walk by. Joy didn't need her for that.

She could get home to her studio.

No one would be there. Or know that she'd spent the evening holed up alone. Even if they'd known, she had the right...

"How long have they been married?" She could hardly get the question out. It was innocuous, unimportant. But it kept her there.

"Ten years."

About as long as Edward had been estranged from his daughter.

"So you've never met Cara?" Joy's mother was a mystery to Julie. And yet, her heart was calling out to the woman. Praying that she had the strength to stay alive until she could be found. Praying that the tirade her husband had been on was over.

"Nope."

She was running out of questions. She was running out of time, too, if she was going to escape. They were almost at the last little hall.

"I had no idea The Lemonade Stand was one of your charities. Makes sense, with the association between your brother and Brett Ackerman, but you weren't involved with the last fund-raiser..."

"It's not one of my charities..." Too late she realized the answer could lead to questions she wasn't going to answer. "I'm not on the board." She scrambled for an answer that held the truth, but also protected her. "I'm a volunteer."

Beyond that, he didn't need to know. Their

worlds, his so unfettered and free, and hers crippled by angst and mistrust, were total opposites.

"That's how you came to meet Joy?"

"Yes."

They'd turned the corner, were heading toward the big double swinging doors that led to the kitchen. Doors that were currently open.

She could still leave. Could still...

Then she saw Joy. The little girl sat unmoving on a stool, her arms clutching one of Julie's books to her chest, staring at a huge bowl of cookie dough in a commercial-size mixer. There was no expression on her face.

Not sadness. Or fear. No contentment or longing, either.

Sara had slowed, which brought all of them close together.

"Is that her?" Edward's voice was a broken whisper.

"Yeah," Lila answered, looking at him. Julie figured Lila was assessing whether or not she felt Edward could keep it together long enough to see Joy without alarming her.

More might have been said, but the woman with Joy noticed them. Smiled. If they were going to be unthreatening, on a nonchalant tour, they had to keep moving. As a group, as though they were tied together, they did.

The others in the room faded for Julie as they

drew closer to the little girl. She could almost feel Joy's disconnect—her state of fugue—as life went on around her. Without her. Joy didn't seem to care that strangers had entered the room.

But Julie knew the second she started to care. As the five of them moved toward the counter where Joy sat, with Sara describing the coming movie night for which the cookies were being baked, Edward stepped within a foot of the child. Joy bent her head, resting her chin on the book.

"She's afraid," Julie whispered. If she spoke any louder Joy would hear, and having attention drawn to her could have an adverse effect. Julie didn't know that because of any studying she'd done regarding the kind of feelings Joy might be experiencing. She knew because she'd lived them.

"Cookie dough!" Hunter moved to stand beside her, startling her. "That's what Edward here was hoping to see," he said, pushing to the front of the group. Then, before Julie had any idea what he'd been planning to do, he stuck his finger in the big bowl of dough, came up with a glob and thrust the whole thing in his mouth. "He's just too polite to do this," Hunter said, his words garbled around the dough.

Julie would've smiled but was too worried about the little girl. About doing more harm. Sending her further away from them, deeper into her mental hell. She glanced at Joy—and stood there, openmouthed.

Joy was watching Hunter. Holding her breath, Julie watched as Hunter stuck his finger in the bowl a second time and offered the glob of dough to Edward who, without losing a beat, took it in his mouth.

"Mmm, that's good," the doctor said with his mouth full.

Joy looked at the older man. Studied him.

"Anyone else want some?" Hunter asked, putting his finger back in the bowl of now-ruined dough. He held out his finger to Joy, but didn't keep it there when she didn't react. Instead, he moved around the group, first in front of Lila who shook her head, and then Sara, who did the same. When he got to Julie, Joy was watching her.

She did not want Hunter Rafferty's finger in her mouth.

Didn't want the cookie dough, either, for that matter.

But Joy was watching.

Opening wide, Julie took in the entire glob of dough. She tried to pretend she hadn't felt Hunter's finger against her cheek from inside her mouth. Tried to pretend she hadn't liked it.

"Over here is where our team of mostly volunteer cooks prepare all the salads…" Sara had moved on. So had Edward and Lila. Hunter put a hand on Julie's shoulder and she moved, too. Away from him.

Away from Joy.

But when, with cookie dough still on her tongue, she turned back for one last glance at the little girl, Joy was watching her. And continued to watch as the group moved away. Julie smiled at her. She didn't get a smile in return, but she believed that Joy had found comfort in her presence.

And was thankful she hadn't run home to hide.

CHAPTER NINE

HUNTER HAD TO rearrange some things, delegate some tasks early Saturday. Edward had received a call indicating that he and Hunter were welcome to stop by the small art room where Julie would be working with Joy that morning. Lila and Sara would be there, too. The same group from the day before.

He'd been invited specifically because of the way he'd stuck his finger in the cookie dough the other day. They believed Joy would welcome him more than Edward at this point. Or be more open to having Edward in the room if Hunter was there with him.

So fitting. Some guys did heroic deeds. Hunter ate cookie dough.

There were no immediate plans to tell Joy that Edward was her grandfather. They were taking things one step at a time—but trying to take those steps as rapidly as possible, in case she could give them some information about her mother.

"There's been no activity on their credit cards," Edward was saying as Hunter drove the two of them from Edward's hotel to The Lemonade Stand. "No money taken from their bank accounts."

"They've been gone a week," Hunter said, telling himself he was *not* looking forward to seeing Julie Fairbanks again. Sure, he'd thought of her in the hours they'd been apart, picturing her with Joy, using her art therapy to draw her out. That was because of Edward, he told himself. And, of course, the little girl. "How could they not have used any money?"

"Shawn could have a place somewhere, ready for such an instance. Could be holed up with a friend. Or he could have had cash on him enough to pay for a seedy motel somewhere where there'd be no record and no questions asked."

Or Cara could be with him willingly. They could've made plans together. Hunter knew it was a possibility. Didn't see much point in bringing it up to Edward again.

"They could be clear across the United States by now. Or even in Mexico. From what friends told the police, Shawn used to like it down there." Edward frowned and Hunter felt for the guy.

It'd been good the night before, having Edward with him at the medical fund-raiser. He'd seen a different side to him. The professional, confident side. The group had taken in almost double what they'd hoped for. He figured Edward's working the room accounted for at least part of that.

"They've gone through all the records for Amos Surfing," Edward continued. He'd had a conversation with the Ventura detective in charge of his daughter's case early that morning, but most of what he was saying now they'd already discussed. "There's nothing amiss. He just finished a hugely successful summer."

"Maybe he goes down to Rocky Point to teach when it gets too cold here," Hunter said, mentioning a vacation town an hour across the US border. He knew Edward was talking because he needed to. Knew that Edward needed more than that. He just had nothing to offer that would do any good. Except what he was doing. Accompanying him on this visit with his granddaughter.

"The police are in touch with the Mexican authorities. So far, nothing."

"What about their house here?"

"It's in Mary's name." Right. His dad had said something about that.

"Any change in her condition?" He should have asked the night before. His mind had been on other things.

"The swelling hasn't gone down enough for them to start waking her up."

Edward had been to see her, though. Every day.

The more time Hunter spent with the guy, the more he liked him. Not just as a favor to his father.

It was good to know his dad had married into a decent family.

Something he might've known sooner if he'd accepted any of the myriad invitations he'd been issued over the years. Instead, John and Betty had to come visit him. Not easy for a dedicated doctor with a thriving practice.

These weren't thoughts Hunter generally entertained.

Edward had the passenger door open before Hunter had pulled his Cadillac Escalade to a stop at The Lemonade Stand. The SUV's flashiness, while important to his job, seemed embarrassingly out of place in the small, unadorned parking lot.

"Lila said she'd be meeting us inside," the older man said.

Hands in the pockets of his beige chinos, Hunter followed Edward. He'd purposely chosen the purple shirt with the sleeves rolled up because purple was a kid color. Seeing Edward in his suit pants, white shirt and tie, he wasn't sure which of them was inappropriately dressed.

"Thank you so much for doing this," Edward said, his speech a little rushed as they entered the nondescript waiting room. Lila McDaniels, in what looked like the same gray pants, shirt and jacket she'd worn during one of their previous visits, didn't seem to notice anything amiss as Edward shook her hand. But then she probably dealt with emotionally charged situations on a regular basis. Everything about her was contained. From the serviceable flat shoes to the gray bun at her nape.

Admirable. Taking life in stride. Just like he did. She was bolder in her approach than he was, however. She actually saved lives while he planned parties to help people make the money to save lives.

Hunter's work mattered. He knew that. He just liked to keep himself in check. It told others not to expect more than he could deliver.

All his life, his parents had looked to him for their happiness. He'd never quite succeeded in delivering that, either.

They'd entered the same hall he'd been down before on the way to Lila's office. Women milled around in small groups, but as usual, he didn't make eye contact. The majority of them were there because they'd been abused by a man. Hunter wasn't sure his masculinity would be welcomed. And didn't want to invade the peace they were struggling to find.

Although the hall was wide enough for the three of them, they'd take up most of the space if he walked with Lila and Edward, so he fell just behind them, content to be invisible.

Instead of heading into one of the rooms along that hall, as he'd expected, they reached a glass door and went outside. To one of the most beautiful resorts he'd seen on the California coast. From impeccable landscaping, with flower-lined walkways and lush green grass, to a wooded garden off in the distance, the place was elegant. Beautiful. Filled with peace.

Bungalows dotted the walkways in a neighborhood kind of setting, three or four to a circle. Lila was telling them about the pool that was just beyond a hill to the left, and the private beach on the other side of the woods. Residents had to have a key to get through a locked gate between the woods and the beach, but the beach was only accessible by water or through the private Stand entrance.

"It could seem prison-like," Lila was saying as Hunter came up beside Edward on the sidewalk. Glancing around, he didn't think so.

"But our residents aren't locked in. Danger is locked out."

He liked that. Even as he thought about it, he was keeping an eye out for Julie Fairbanks. She'd be at the meeting. And while his first priority was being there for Edward and facilitating his meeting with Joy in any manner that would help, he was very much looking forward to seeing Julie.

She worked practically full-time for no pay. He'd had to spend half an hour on the phone rearranging schedules and organizing deliveries just so he could afford to be there that morning and not lose a paycheck.

Their worlds were miles apart. He still wanted to take her to dinner.

Just once.

So he could move on.

JULIE HADN'T HAD to wait for Joy to pick up the pencil that morning. As soon as Sara had walked the silent child into the room where Julie already had their easels and chairs set up, Joy made a beeline for her pencil. Black again. And she'd taken her chair. She didn't draw, though.

Not until Sara had stepped out—to wait for Lila and Edward and Hunter—and Julie had picked up her own pencil, did Joy's small hand rise to the page.

Unlike other days, Julie wasn't drawing Amy. She was working on a big ice cream cone floating in the sky. A stuffed toy puppy would be next. And then maybe a beach ball. Under Sara's directive, she was to draw "fun things" that a seven-year-old girl would love. The idea was to create an atmosphere of nonthreatening fun before bringing in their visitors.

The only thing Joy seemed to be relating to so far was Amy and, through Amy, Julie's drawings. So they'd use the drawings to assure her that everything was fine. That was the theory, in any case.

"Amy loves chocolate ice cream," she said, something she'd already mentioned to Joy. "And she looovvves sugar cones," she said, drawing the pointy tip of the waffled cone in a light brown. "Do you like sugar cones?"

With the page in front of her still blank, Joy was watching Julie's page. She didn't respond. So Julie kept talking. And drawing. Adding dimension to the ice cream.

Joy's pencil finally began to move. Making a V shape. With a circle on top. It wasn't symmetrical. And all in black. But Julie's heart started to pound.

Had Joy just told her that she liked sugar cones, too?

Miraculously Julie's pencil didn't falter. As soon as she'd finished the single scoop, she changed pencils, switching to a light blue, and outlined the clouds in the sky in which the ice cream cone was floating. Sara had told her to do what came naturally, as though she was in her studio working. When emotions got intense, she moved to more ethereal things. Or detail that was uneventful.

She wanted so badly to free this little girl from the internal chains that were keeping her captive. She'd been there. She knew how horrible it felt to be locked up inside. To fear speaking out. And for the first time since she'd been so brutally raped, she felt…not like a victim in recovery mode.

More like a survivor with something unique and valuable to offer.

She started in on the puppy. Brown with floppy ears. She was fully aware of the big brown eyes watching her. Aware, too, of the adults who'd soon be joining them. She hoped their arrival in the room wouldn't rattle Joy to the point of no longer being open to the work they were quietly doing there.

As usual, while she drew, she talked. Un-coached by Sara. The therapist had told her to draw happy childhood things. She hadn't told her what to say.

She'd said that Julie's own words, through her stories, were what reached the child. It had to come from her.

So…

"When I lost my mom and dad, I wanted a puppy," she said. *Lost.* To an adult that meant death. But to a child whose parents were missing? She hoped Joy had only "lost" her mom and would soon find her again. Alive and able to heal. From what Julie had been told, the police had no reason to believe otherwise at that point. But she didn't ask questions.

"And even before that, I wanted grandparents." Her neck felt tight. Maybe she was pushing things.

"Amy wanted them, too," she said, continuing to add detail to the puppy. He had big brown eyes like Joy. His little pink tongue lolled out of the side of his mouth. He looked like he was smiling. And prancing.

"I don't remember my grandparents," she continued, "but my friends all had them. Do you know what grandparents are?" She paused for an answer, just in case, but didn't look at the little girl. She didn't want to put her on the spot. "Grandparents are your mama's and daddy's mamas and daddies," she said. Amy called her mom "mama."

"And the magical thing about them is that they love grandkids as much as kids love ice cream and puppies."

She put the finishing touches on the puppy. Then she began outlining a beach ball. Sitting in the sand. Next to what was going to be a sand castle. She left detail and color to fill in as time allowed.

"Grandparents bring you presents and they almost never get mad at you," she said. "Unless you do something dangerous that could hurt you. Then they'll get upset, but mostly they just smile and hug you and love you…"

Even as she heard herself pouring it on thick, she knew Amy would've loved hearing those words.

No. Wait. Amy *would* love hearing them. Her next Amy story was going to be a grandparent book.

And maybe Joy could be a source of inspiration for her? Joy and Edward?

She talked about how Amy wanted to go to the beach one time, and her friend's grandparents took them. A happy childhood memory of her own.

Amy's book would be about the different grandparents she met in her life. And how they loved other people's kids, too...

She was so deeply involved with Joy, the drawing and Amy's new book that she'd forgotten they were going to have visitors until a knock sounded on the door.

She'd forgotten to worry about what was coming in Joy's world. Worry that the child would reject the love that was awaiting her. Or be unable to access it.

And worry about seeing Hunter Rafferty again. After the night before, watching him dip that finger... She'd even dreamed about him. The man was rattling her, and that didn't fit with her world. When Julie got rattled, she retreated. That was just the way it was.

CHAPTER TEN

"MIND IF WE come in for a second?"

Hunter could only see the back of Sara's head as she peeked past the solid wooden door she'd just opened. Behind Lila and Edward, he was content to simply hang out, not get in the way.

But he was eager to see Julie. And her drawing therapy. Although he wasn't quite sure what it meant, exactly, or how it worked, he was intrigued. In part, because Julie was doing it.

"Hi." He heard her voice in response to Sara. "I don't mind if you want to come in. Do you, Joy?"

Startled, he listened. He'd understood the little girl to be mute since the incident. She certainly hadn't spoken last night. Had she begun speaking since then?

After a brief pause, he heard Julie's voice again. "We're just drawing, aren't we, Joy?"

Hunter was in the room at that point, following Sara and the others to a spot along the side wall. He could see the easels, and Joy, but only at an angle.

"I'm working on the beach ball, but a sand castle is coming," Julie was saying as she continued to draw as though nothing unusual was happening.

Transfixed, Hunter watched. With brief strokes she added colors, dimension, a hint of sunshine. She made it look so easy.

"We were talking about grandparents. I never knew mine," she said. "Joy didn't say whether or not she has any…" Chat. Pencil stroke. She didn't miss a beat.

His heart did when Sara said, "She does."

What the hell? There'd been no plan to out Edward yet. This was supposed to be a quick non-threatening getting-to know-you visit. What if the girl was afraid of her grandfather? What if…

The potential for out-of-control drama was huge. He wasn't prepared.

Edward wasn't prepared. No way was the kid prepared.

Was Julie?

Joy gave no indication of hearing Sara's announcement or of understanding its significance.

He'd learned from Edward that Shawn and his sister, Mary, grew up in foster care. Which left only Edward, not that Joy knew this.

A sand castle was appearing on Julie's page. "I used to love playing in the sand when I was a kid," she said, and it took him a second to realize this was her art therapy, not a group conversation.

She talked about a time when she was little and her friend's grandparents took them to the beach right there in Santa Raquel.

"Wow, that's good," Lila said, watching Julie draw. Lila looked at Sara, who nodded, and then asked, "Is it okay if we stay a few minutes and watch?"

"It's fine with me." Julie's reply was easy. Calm. Soothing.

"What about you?" she asked the girl at her side. Joy's gaze was focused on the sand castle.

The two women took seats at the table behind the easels. Edward half sat on the table. The doctor was sweating. There was a twitch at his temple.

Hunter was here to…he didn't know what. But his job had always been to ease the tension. He had to do *something*.

"Can I draw, too?" he asked.

"Sure," Sara answered, and Julie's voice followed, telling him to look in the cupboard for another easel. Hunter wasn't convinced, when Sara settled his easel next to Joy's, that she'd made the right choice. This wasn't cookie dough. And he had no "troubled kid" training at all.

"I'm not as good at drawing as Julie is," he said as he picked up a purple pencil and took his seat. Joy had an ice cream cone on her page, clearly not drawn by Julie. He didn't know if Joy's drawing was a significant breakthrough, but he noticed

Sara looking at the rudimentary drawing and then at Julie, who nodded.

If they wanted the child to relax, they definitely needed some lightening up here.

He didn't want to interrupt Julie's art therapy. He preferred to leave it up to the professionals, who knew what they were doing. But they'd asked him to be there…

He started to draw—all in purple—doing his best to badly emulate the lines and shadows on Julie's page. His beach ball looked drunk. One cloud, in exactly the same place as on her picture, and approximately the same size, was sticking out its tongue.

Her voice faded, and he made a "phhht" noise with his teeth against his lip. Several times.

Joy turned her head.

Julie spoke again, and he remained silent. She wasn't looking at him. He wasn't even sure she wanted him sitting there. But he found a kind of rhythm in the soft cadence of her voice as she described playful memories of her childhood, interspersed with his random noises during her silences.

A wicker picnic basket appeared on her page. A purple box on his.

Joy appeared to be watching both of them. If she was aware of the people behind them, she didn't show it. Certainly there was no sense that she felt concerned.

Which was the point. To slowly initiate Edward into her presence, without threat.

He had no idea how long art therapy lasted. He'd been drawing and making noises for a good fifteen minutes.

Julie flipped her page over, leaving a clean sheet on her easel.

He did the same.

Joy didn't touch her page. Nor did she let go of her pencil.

"I used to imagine what my grandfather looked like," Julie said then, and Hunter went on red alert. The woman who seemed to have some kind of crazy power over him started to draw, and he had to figure out how to ease the tension in the room.

The face she'd sketched was basic, a beginning outline. But already he could tell it was a man. With a face shaped like Edward's.

"Aw, come on, Jules," he said in a whiny voice. "I can't draw thaaaat." His up-and-down cadence could have been a tune. If he'd been a singer.

"You don't have to draw what I draw," she told him. "You can draw anything you like."

When he'd seen Joy's ice cream cone, he'd assumed the task in art therapy was to draw what the instructor drew.

Julie talked. He went back to making little

noises. Drew a stick figure. Joy seemed content to sit between them, her head turning from one to the other. If he wasn't feeling the tension from the "gallery" behind him, he wouldn't have known anyone else was in the room.

"I can't do it," he finally said, with a teasing whine. "Joy, let's see what kind of grandpa you can draw."

She didn't raise her pencil, but she looked up at him. Straight at him.

He had to sneeze. At that exact, completely incredible moment, he felt the sneeze come on. And being Hunter in a potentially intense moment, he didn't just sneeze. He did it up big. Really big. As in spewing all over the stick figure he'd drawn.

Joy laughed.

JULIE COULDN'T GET the morning out of her mind. All day Saturday, as she drove to LA to attend an afternoon rummage sale at one of the children's homes supported by Sunshine Children's League, she thought about Hunter Rafferty and his effect on Joy.

He was a charmer all the way and yet…he'd made an intrinsically mistrustful and frightened little girl laugh!

She could still feel the thrill of that sound. And felt tears spring to her eyes again, as she remembered the moment.

Sara had called a halt to the exercise shortly after that. Maybe for Edward's sake. So the doctor could collect himself without alarming the child.

She was thinking about Hunter again, about his instinctive—almost gifted—way with a damaged and terrified child, when her phone rang on the drive back to Santa Raquel. It was a few minutes after five that evening. Even if he hadn't been in her contacts with all her other business acquaintances, she would've recognized his number.

She pushed the button on her steering wheel—and ignored any thrill she might've felt at the sight of his name. Determined to decline whatever invitation he was about to offer, just as she'd done with all the others he'd issued over the past few months, she said, "Hello?"

"I have a favor to ask."

This was a new approach. If it had been anything to do with Joy, the request would have come through Sara. Or Lila. Her connection—and work with—the child was at their request.

"What?"

"I need you to accompany me tonight. Can you be ready in an hour and a half?" She was ten minutes from home. And he had a political fundraiser, a roast. He'd wanted her to try the desserts because the same company was serving at her gala on Thursday.

"Of course not. Hunter, I already told you—"

"I know." He cut her off. "I'm not asking you to go so you can try the desserts, although that'll be an added benefit and will help me make sure you're pleased with next Thursday night's event. The reason I need you to come is because I'm truly in over my head with this Joy thing and now that we're all meeting again tomorrow, I just need to talk to you. Seriously, Julie. I throw parties for a living. I don't work with troubled kids. You're so good with her. So calm and confident. I sneeze all over a paper and eat cookie dough. I want to help Edward. I need to help him. But I'm…please, tonight's event is the only chance I'll have to speak with you. I'm there out of respect, not to work, unless something goes wrong, of course. So I'll have time to talk. I do have to be there, or I'd meet you somewhere else, anywhere else."

She couldn't go to a political fund-raiser in Santa Raquel.

He'd have no way of knowing that.

She didn't want him to know that.

But she couldn't go.

Still, it was for Joy.

"Julie?"

"I'm here."

"So…will you come? I can be at your place in an hour."

"You said an hour and a half."

"I can give you that, too, but then I'll have to send a car for you."

She wasn't going.

"Are my brother and his wife on the guest list?" She should already know. She remembered they were going out that night; she just hadn't paid attention to where.

"Yes. Is that a bad thing? Because I can make sure they're seated far—"

"I can't go, Hunter. But if I could, having Colin and Chantel there would be a good thing. I adore them both."

Why had she told him that?

"So I'll have them seated at our table."

A political event. In Santa Raquel. Her worst nightmare. The perpetrator wouldn't be there. David Smyth Jr. was in jail for many, many years. But his parents might be present. Now that the ex-police commissioner had left town, David Smyth Sr., his former best friend, had started showing himself around town again. He'd made amends. Made his son take a plea agreement that sent him away for a long time. Delivered a load of mea culpas.

But his money was still powerful.

"I need your help, Julie. I swear, I'll let the whole room know that it's not a date if you'll agree to sit with me for half an hour. Just long enough to tell me what's going on in your mind when you work with Joy."

"You could ask Sara."

"I've already spoken with her. Edward and I had a meeting with her over lunch today. She suggested I speak with you."

Sara had sent him to her? An extra weight on her shoulders.

"Is Leslie Morrison on the guest list tonight?" Leslie had been Julie's mother's best friend, a woman who'd also been a victim of Julie's rapist, although no one had known that—including Leslie's husband—until Chantel had come bursting into her and Colin's lives, an undercover cop, and figured out that a woman she'd thought was being abused by her husband had issues horrifyingly similar to Julie's. Her refusal to back down on her investigation had nearly cost Chantel her life. Her job, too. But she'd persevered and exposed the commissioner, who'd taken money to protect his best friend's son.

"The Morrisons sent a refusal."

She wasn't surprised. Like Julie, Leslie was living with years' worth of self-flagellation. In some ways, the effects on Leslie were even worse because, while Julie had been a teenager when she was raped by one of the town's richest sons, Leslie had been an adult, unable to protect herself against the child of one of her husband's peers.

She'd been shamed and bullied into saying nothing. Smyth had threatened to say that the sex was not only consensual, but that Leslie had come on to him. He'd threatened to claim statutory rape.

At least Julie and Colin had tried to expose the creep. Until the evidence, her hospital rape kit, had mysteriously disappeared and her doctor had moved out of state.

She was almost home. Saw Chantel's car in the drive. And remembered how her sister-in-law had put herself in the fiend's hands, literally, in order to trap him into confessing—for Julie's sake.

Joy needed her. Julie wondered if she could handle attending this evening's event—for Joy's sake.

"What do you say? Can I pick you up?"

Colin would make a big deal of it.

"If you can arrange a seat for me at my brother's table, I'll ride with him and Chantel."

She couldn't go out with Hunter Rafferty.

She couldn't attend a political event with him.

But for Joy she could ride to a venue with her brother. And have his car as an escape hatch when she needed it. Because she would.

Julie had absolutely no doubt about that.

CHAPTER ELEVEN

It took a little last-minute scrambling, but Hunter got himself and Julie seated at a round table for eight that included Colin and Chantel Fairbanks. Edward had elected not to join him that evening. Hunter, in his newest black tux, was waiting near their table, admittedly watching for his guest's arrival, when Julie entered the room with her brother and sister-in-law. He had a couple seated on either side of Colin and Chantel—couples who'd already been assigned to their table—which left him and Julie across the table from them. On their own.

In a long black gown, stunning in its simplicity, Julie moved slowly, but with her usual quiet confidence, as she crossed toward them. With his own movements perfectly timed, Hunter stepped forward just as they reached the table, pointing out her brother and sister-in-law's seats before leaning toward Julie. He'd intended to take her hand, to lead her around to their chairs.

And somehow, once again, he missed. He was beginning to realize that his inability to touch her was no accident, but before he could react,

Chantel had grabbed Julie's attention, telling her to come and sit beside her. With glossy nails, the detective scooped up name placards and moved the new police commissioner and his wife into the seats reserved for Hunter and Julie. She didn't ask if he minded. Julie didn't look at him, either.

What the heck?

Hunter recovered almost immediately—not that anyone was paying enough attention to him to notice—and walked around to stand behind his seat. He held Julie's chair for her, breathing in a scent of flowers and femininity that made him horny. Yeah, that was the word for it. He asked if everyone was comfortable, took drink orders himself and went to the bar. His palms were sweating. Getting through dinner was going to require a bourbon.

JULIE MADE IT through the first course. The one glass of white wine she'd allowed herself had helped. She'd been out in the evening on a few occasions since her first foray into the adult night-time social scene a year and a half before. That had been a fund-raiser for the new library in town. And the night she'd faced her fears enough to help Chantel capture the man who'd raped her.

The night he'd finally been forced to start paying for his years of sexual predation.

But being seated among the town's elite—with

everyone wearing their public faces and some pretending to be things they weren't—made her tense. Uncomfortable. She didn't like it. And she didn't have to do anything she didn't like anymore. Not unless she chose to. She'd chosen to be there. For Joy.

Sitting there, between her sister-in-law and Hunter, she almost relaxed. Until Hunter laughed at something the police commissioner had said and she felt herself warming in the way a woman warmed toward a man she was dating. Hunter was charming—which was what made him good at his job, she reminded herself.

And it also made him dangerous to her.

Yes, he was having a wonderful effect on Joy. Yes, he had a gift when it came to putting people at ease.

But he also had the ability to hide his real feelings. To convince others he was anything he wanted them to see.

And that she couldn't abide. Because you never knew what lurked beneath that surface. You couldn't know. Couldn't see if there were demons, waiting to pounce.

Between the salad and the main course, while Colin was busy speaking with the man on his left, a wealthy client of his law firm, Chantel, Julie and Hunter spoke about Joy. As a Santa Raquel detective, Chantel was familiar with the case.

"As you know, I have no experience with children," Hunter told them both, and yet Julie felt as though he was only aware of her.

How did he do that? David Smyth Jr. had the same talent. For a time, Julie had basked in the feeling that she was the only girl he noticed.

"Walking by her, observing an art class, okay, but now with us taking her to breakfast tomorrow… We're all going to be sitting at a table, looking at each other…" Hunter was still talking.

Sara had called Julie earlier, after a meeting with Edward and Hunter, and asked if she'd be willing to join a group taking Joy to breakfast the next morning. At a place in Joy's old neighborhood, close to LA. A place neighbors had said her mom, Cara, used to take her sometimes. A place that would be familiar to her. More easing into the process of introducing Edward as family to the little girl. But it was also a move designed to help break through to her, in the hope of finding out what she did or didn't know about her mother's disappearance.

Sara wasn't going to be present this time. But Lila would be there.

And a couple of police officers would be close by. Just in case. No one was going to put Joy's life at risk. But if her father was in the vicinity, if he was watching for her, and saw her, maybe he'd make a mistake. Make himself known.

Tomorrow's breakfast was why she was at tonight's fund-raiser, she reminded herself. Because Hunter needed to talk about Joy. The fact that he was also a charmer was irrelevant.

"Just be yourself, Hunter. She likes you," Julie told him, even as she doubted that she, or anyone, would ever know his true self. People like Hunter, the charmers, the fun guys, they seemed to live two lives—the one on the surface, and a different one underneath.

"I have no idea how you talk to a child," he said now. "I'm guessing golf scores aren't going to do it. And probably not surfing, either." His chuckle made her smile. Which sent warning notes through her. She was not going to soften toward this man.

Some man. Someday. Sure. If she was attracted to one she felt she could trust.

But not this man. Not a charmer.

"You talk to her like she's a person but with limited experiences," Julie said. "I remember back to when I was a kid, and pull from that."

His attention, fully on her now, warmed her all up again.

She was there to help him for Joy's sake. She had to get it done.

And get out.

So, CLEARLY, HE wanted more than just one dinner with Julie. His words to Brett Ackerman about "just one" had been erroneous. One wasn't going to be nearly enough.

Really, he didn't know why he was bothering with his pursuit of this woman.

She was infuriating in her guardedness. He wasn't Bigfoot. Or the Abominable Snowman.

And yet, the very second their dinner plates were cleared, he knew she wouldn't be staying for the evening's roast. She'd been looking over at the door for a good fifteen minutes. And he knew she wasn't expecting anyone. She'd picked up her purse earlier to get a contact out of her phone for her brother, and had left the purse in her lap.

"I ordered six desserts for you," he told her, deliberately trying to keep her there a bit longer. And feeling no shame whatsoever for doing so.

After his failed attempt to take her hand, he'd been very careful not to touch her. Some people didn't like casual touching. He got that.

She leaned over to tell him quietly, but firmly, "I am not going to eat six desserts,"

"Six bites. That's all. Six bites. Doesn't even equal a full dessert."

He leaned in, too. Almost brushed his nose against her ear. Felt her shiver. And had his very first glimmer of hope where she was concerned.

If he wasn't mistaken, she'd just responded to him. Sexually.

Not since his first year in business had he been

concerned about his clients being pleased with whatever food he brought in for them. He knew his stuff, and he had a top-notch list of caterers who were always happy and eager to give him whatever he asked for.

Julie's nod gave him a respite before her imminent departure.

Who knew a mere whisper by her ear was his ticket in?

He'd barely had a chance to celebrate his good fortune when the desserts were placed in front of them. But before he could make some clever comment about the chocolate on her fork, his attention was summoned. Kyle, tonight's event manager and his most trusted employee, needed him. They had a problem. The—until that moment, unknown—mistress of the man being roasted had just shown up at the door. With a few quick confirming nods, letting his next-in-command know that his plans to handle the situation were spot-on, Hunter sent Kyle to deal with it.

By the time he turned around, Julie was gone.

SHE MADE IT out to the valet stand at the private-event venue on the ocean, just outside Santa Raquel. Intending to order a cab and text her brother and Chantel once she was gone, so they couldn't decide to leave early and take her home themselves, she hadn't yet spoken to anyone when Hunter suddenly appeared.

"I don't get it." His first words were so startling, she forgot for a second that she was on the run. Back to her studio. To her comfort zone.

To the place she needed to be so she could spend her days giving all her energy to other people and to the causes that benefited the most. To her personal work. Her books. She had one due in a couple of weeks, and because of the extra time she was spending with Joy, she was behind.

"Don't get what?" There was no chill in the air, but she shivered anyway and gathered her light wrap around her mostly bare shoulders. How much longer was the valet going to be talking to the older gentleman with the Continental? Couldn't he see he had a customer waiting?

"What is it about me that you find so reprehensible?" He could have sounded angry. He didn't. He almost seemed to be teasing her. Almost.

"I don't find you reprehensible."

"As soon as my back was turned, you walked out."

She would've left anyway, but his…interruption had made it easier. She hadn't had to deal with him.

"It sounded as though you were going to be involved for a while. And you're working tonight. I understood that from the beginning."

She'd liked that part of the plan. It couldn't be

even halfway considered a sort of date if he was working.

"My staff's handling tonight's event. I was there to put the icing on the cake. So to speak."

"And yet, when there was a situation, they came right to you." That actually impressed her, the fact that he had people who relied on him.

The valet turned, saw Hunter talking to her and continued his conversation with Mr. Continental.

"What are you doing standing here anyway?" he asked, his hands in his pockets now.

She could've asked the same thing. The roast had to be starting. And he was outside with her.

She didn't ask, though. She didn't want to hear his answer.

"Getting a cab." She told him the truth.

"A cab? You came with your brother." He glanced toward the door that led to the ballroom holding their event. "Do you need me to speak with him for you? Are you feeling sick?"

"No." She might have smiled. If she'd been her seventeen-year-old self. Now she calmly said, "If you speak to him, he and Chantel will be out here calling for their car. They'll miss the rest of their evening out. Colin not only enjoys a good roast, he has a lot of clients here tonight—and potential clients, as well. He needs to stay."

Pulling keys out of his pocket, Hunter said, "Then I'll take you home."

She wasn't going to ride alone in his car in the dark with him. She just wasn't.

Not because of some fear for her physical safety. Ironically, at the moment, that wasn't even an issue. He was far more of a threat to her emotional equilibrium than her physical safety.

"You're working," she reminded him, taking the obvious way out. And she was going home to work, too. Not that she'd tell him that.

Because his inevitable question would be to ask what kind of work she was doing at nine o'clock on a Saturday night.

And her books were her secret. Hers and Chantel's and Colin's. And Sara's and Lila's. And now, Joy's and probably her housemates'.

"I don't have to be here. And it'll only take half an hour to get you home and return… I'll be back before the roast is over."

Other than the tension that was building in her, Julie had been feeling fine. But a headache was coming on. She couldn't let it. She wouldn't get enough work done if she was hit with a migraine.

Hers were caused by tension. Which Hunter was creating. Inadvertently, but still…

"Was it the desserts?" he asked next. "Because I guilted you into tasting all six of them?"

"I didn't taste all six of them," she told him.

"Colin and Chantel did. Both of them. All six. I trust their judgment."

What on earth was she doing? Flirting with him?

Of course not!

But what if he thought she was?

The headache he was giving her had dissipated for the moment. She took a step toward the valet, whose back was to her so he didn't notice.

"Have dinner with me sometime." Hunter hadn't moved, so he was one step behind her.

"We just had dinner."

"I mean some *other* time. Right now, let me take you home."

"I'd rather get a cab." She'd never met a man who took a hint worse than he did.

Well, yes, she had. And that was part of the problem. More than ten years ago, she'd fallen for a man who not only didn't take a hint, but wouldn't take no for an answer. And she had ended up forever changed.

She'd just never met a man who attracted her so strongly even when her mind told her to get away from him.

Usually her mind and emotions went hand in hand. They were in complete agreement, always gave her the same message. With David Smyth, they'd both told her to grab hold and never let go. And with every man since, the message had been the complete opposite. *Get away.*

"But you don't want me to go get your brother."

"No. I'd stay here at the event first."

"Okay then, stay." Well, she'd walked into that one.

"I don't want to stay." Now she sounded petulant.

"Why not?"

"Because…I don't like crowds." True enough. But not the real reason she needed to go.

"Ahh…so that's why you left so early?"

Okay. If it pleased him to think so.

Julie might've felt bad, misleading him, if she wasn't so absolutely certain that there was nothing wrong with protecting herself. Keeping her secrets to herself.

She didn't like crowds. But she hadn't left the event because of them.

"So, let's sit," he said. "Over there. On the benches." She told herself not to look.

She did anyway. There were four benches. They were surrounded by flowering shrubs. Subtle landscape lighting completed the decor. But the best part was the view. The benches faced the ocean.

Of course, at night, there'd be no view.

"If you sit with me for a few minutes, I won't tell your brother you're leaving before you have a chance to get away. If you insist on calling a cab, I'm going to get him right now. According to you, that'll take him away from his clients, since he'll insist on taking you home himself."

Julie actually found herself calculating her chances of having a cab called and arriving in the time it would take Hunter to bring Colin out. When she pictured herself falling into the cab and slamming the door just as Hunter came running back outside, her brother at his heels, she almost smiled. As if she'd really run amok to that extent! Trying to race him…

She suppressed her smile and turned to him instead. "Why?"

"Why what?"

"Why are you doing this? Pursuing me like this? I've made it perfectly obvious that I'm not interested."

The suddenly serious expression on his face etched itself in her mind. "I don't know," he said.

She couldn't tell if he was charming her. Or being genuine.

It felt…unlike him. So, genuine?

"There's something about you. It's like you're a witch and you've cast a spell on me and if I could only have dinner with you, the spell would be broken."

Probably one of the least charming things a man had ever said to her.

"Your goal is to break the spell?"

"Yes."

"Then what?"

"Then I don't have to keep asking you out and getting turned down."

The boyishly pleading look on his face had her almost smiling again. Pretty sure now that he wasn't being serious at all, she was surprised to find that she'd lost her immediate need to run.

"Okay, I'll sit with you. But only to break the spell. Since we've already had dinner." She hadn't talked nonsense in…far too many years. She felt awkward.

But she followed him to the bench.

And prayed she wasn't making another big mistake.

CHAPTER TWELVE

HUNTER COULD HARDLY believe that Julie Fairbanks had just agreed to be alone with him. As he led her to the bench, he half expected whatever spell she had over him to dissipate by the time they got there. She'd finally said yes. A few minutes to talk to her. To figure out what it was about her that attracted him. So he could distance himself. Walk away.

Just like he always did.

He waited for her to sit—she chose the bench closest to the building—and then, remembering how many times she'd avoided his touch, sat on the other end. There was enough room for a third person to sit between them.

For a rich woman, she didn't wear a lot of jewelry. A single gold chain with an angel charm on the end. Gold and diamond studs in her ears. In triplicate.

Odd, he'd never noticed before that she had three piercings in each ear. He liked that hint of the less traditional in a woman so clearly conservative.

She was fiddling with the onyx and diamond

ring on her right hand. And then, when she caught him looking at her hands, they suddenly stilled.

"So this is it? Just sitting here on a bench is the spell-breaker?" she asked. She might appear timid, but she had enough fight in her to win her battles. That much he knew.

"I'm not sure," he told her. "Maybe if you told me a little bit about yourself, that would do the trick. Other than the things I already know. Take away the mystery."

"Like what?" She was gazing out toward the ocean. He could see a couple of lights in the far distance. A commercial ship? Military?

"You told Joy you don't have any grandparents. And it's just you and Colin and now Chantel at home. Where are your parents?"

What was he doing? He didn't need to know those things to get her out of his system.

"Mom died of hepatitis when I was fifteen. Dad of a heart attack when I was sixteen. Colin was in law school, and it's just been him and me and Louisa, our housekeeper, ever since."

"What happened to your grandparents?"

"Mom's parents divorced when she was young. I only ever knew her mother, who died of an overdose in Hollywood when I was little. I never knew Dad's mother. She was gone before I was born, but I have vague memories of his dad. My grandfather built the house we live in. He started Fairbanks and Fairbanks, as well."

The lucrative law firm her brother now ran.

"He was killed in a car accident when I was two."

She wasn't helping him get rid of the spell. As a matter of fact, the damned thing didn't seem to be fading at all. Time to change tactics.

"Why won't you go out with me?"

"We're back to that *again*?"

"Just tell me why. Maybe that'll end this." He knew Brett was wrong; this wasn't simply about her saying no. As if he was a guy who couldn't accept a turndown. He wasn't. And could. All he needed to know was why this particular woman kept turning him down.

"Well, then, that's easy," she said. Her tone was calm. Congenial. Businesslike. And yet…she was still looking out at the ocean. As though…there was something she wasn't saying. "It has nothing to do with you. Like I've told you a number of times, I don't date."

He stared. Started to make a joke. And then stared some more. "At all? You don't date at all?" Yeah, she *had* told him that, but… The woman was drop-dead gorgeous. Smart. Caring. Intriguing. And…rich. Not that he gave a hoot about her money. He had more than enough to keep him happy. And not enough to weigh him down. But her money would mean some less ethical guys might want to exploit her. Was that it? She was afraid of being used for her money?

"That's right. I don't date at all."

"As in never?"

"For now." And there it was. That hint of intrigue. Maybe that was all this was. She sent out mixed messages. And he was picking up on them.

"What does 'for now' mean?"

"Nothing. I don't date."

"But you might in the future?"

"I… Someday. I'd like…to have a family."

"And in the past?"

She shook her head.

"You've never been on a date?" He couldn't keep the incredulity out of his voice. Where had she gone to school? A convent?

"I…dated. It's been years."

Brett's warning came back to him. She'd been badly hurt.

He wanted to know what had happened. Based on his intimate knowledge of the evening's schedule, he gave them another hour outside, at the most. If she was willing to stay there that long.

"He must've really done a number on you." He put his observation out into the air—not directing it at her. As if that somehow made a difference.

"Who?"

"Whoever put you off dating."

She let the statement lie there, and he wondered if she was reneging on her agreement to help him get rid of the "spell" in exchange for not telling her brother she was leaving. If she did try to get a cab, he was going to follow through and tell Colin Fairbanks that his sister was on her way home before she could make it into the cab.

Because he didn't feel comfortable *not* doing that. Hunter might not have a clue how to be a good thing in Julie's life, but Colin would know. And by putting it in her brother's hands, he could rid himself of any responsibility.

"I have an inability to trust."

Her words fell like rocks at their feet. The waves weren't all that far off. The surf should've been calling to him right about then.

She didn't turn it into an issue with the guy. Whoever he was. Didn't even mention a guy—other than not refuting his assumption that her lack of dating had to do with one.

"Well, you don't need to worry about me," he said. "I don't get tangled up in making promises, which is how trust is broken. Broken promises and all that…"

Smoothing the waters without a lot of forethought. Yep, that was his way.

He was usually better at it.

"You date, but don't make promises?"

"Yep."

"Do the women you're with understand that?"

"Yep."

"What about a family? Kids?"

"They're great. Just not for me. I'm not the guy who's good at having other people rely on him for their happiness."

"Happiness comes from within."

He liked to think so.

"Besides, you're talking out of both sides of your mouth, don't you think?" she added. He wanted to believe that it was a hint of lightness he heard in her voice. Maybe even teasing.

"How's that?"

"You make your living by showing people a good time. If you weren't able to keep them happy you'd be out of business pretty fast."

"Ah, but there's a difference between showing someone a good time for an evening, and being responsible for their long-term happiness. Hence, my no-promises philosophy, and my only-asking-for-dinner strategy. I know my strengths. And my limitations."

He was glad they were finally having this talk. Yeah, getting it out was good.

"People are responsible for their own happiness," she said. "In any relationship, they're as tied to your happiness as you are to theirs. You contribute to a happy life for each other—or not—but the ability to be happy? That comes from within."

Her words set him on edge. In a curious, not

angry, but definitely uncomfortable way. "For someone who doesn't even date, you sure have a lot to say on the subject of relationships."

"I'm single. Not ignorant." Shifting, she drew attention to the straight set of her shoulders. The fragile-looking neck. And nicely ample breasts that her black dress highlighted—and hid, as well. While current California female fashion seemed to lean toward daringly low-cut cleavage, her high-necked yet sleeveless dress was far sexier.

"Besides, that goes for any relationship, not just couples," she said.

She was also pretty damned sure of herself. A turn-on. Damn it.

"So you don't look to your brother to make you happy?"

"Of course not."

"But there are things he can do that make you happy?"

"There are things he can do, or not do, that please or displease me, but those are momentary reactions. Having him for a brother is a happy part of my life, but for a lot of years, I had him, and I was still unhappy."

Definitely surf time for him. And yet, there he sat.

Knowing that she'd been unhappy for a lot of years. Wanting to know more.

Not wanting to think about what he knew about obligations to your loved ones and their happiness.

Not wanting to disengage her from her views on the subject.

"Anyway, you should think about kids someday," she told him. She was apparently on a roll now that he had her talking. Getting way too intense for him. Normally he'd be heading out by that stage of a conversation. But he still couldn't leave her to get a cab on her own.

"And why is that?" he asked, in spite of his certainty that he didn't want to hear the answer. Curiosity won out.

"You're so good with Joy. Exactly the kind of dad a kid needs."

She'd had a good father. He couldn't blow off her opinion based on a lack of experience on her part. No matter, he had another way to defuse it. "I stuck my finger in cookie dough. And sneezed. I'd hardly call that being 'good' with her."

"You seem to know when her tension's starting to overwhelm her."

That was stretching the truth. A lot.

"And she's comfortable enough with you that she responds when you distract her."

He ate cookie dough. And sneezed. Hunter didn't get what she wanted from him on the whole Joy thing. He'd already agreed to tag along the next day, and had in no way indicated that he'd back out. As long as Edward wanted or needed him, he'd be there. He'd given his father his word.

She didn't have to build him up, or make his contribution look like more than it was.

"I'm just glad I can help." The words were inane. He didn't want to think about Joy. Or Edward. Or the young woman who was missing from both their lives. Or the aunt in the hospital, either. He didn't want to think about the man who was a surfer, just like him, beating up on his wife and sister. He couldn't do a damn thing to fix any of it.

"So…did this do it? Is the spell gone?"

She'd turned her head, was actually looking at him as she spoke. He couldn't see as much of her expression as he would've liked. The moon was out, but not shining directly on them.

Nothing pithy came to mind. Nothing to lighten the sudden band of emotion that had him by the throat. "I don't think so," he told her, adding a grin and hoping that he came off as teasing.

"There's absolutely no future in it," she told him so matter-of-factly that he almost did laugh. As though she could dispel any attraction he might feel for her, any malady of the heart that could befall a guy where she was concerned, just by saying so.

"Ah, but that's the thing about spells," he said. "They aren't about the future. Or the past. They just…are."

When she turned her head back out toward the sea, he knew his remark had hit home.

And he was glad.

CHAPTER THIRTEEN

IT WASN'T THAT the night was unseasonably warm. Sitting out on that bench with Hunter, knowing that otherwise he'd carry out his threat to let her brother know she was leaving, Julie should have been pissed. At the very least. Instead, she felt... warm. From the inside out. In places that had felt cold for most of her life.

She couldn't explain the sensation. Not to herself, and certainly not to anyone else—therapists included. For the moment, she just experienced it.

He'd seated himself at a safe distance.

And conversation-wise, she was holding her own. With a man. In the dark.

Not talking business.

The realization was heady. Invigorating.

So was the fact that she wasn't afraid.

Maybe she should have been. If she'd been afraid a little sooner in the past, she might have saved herself from the most heinous life-changing event. But maybe not.

She was a hell of a lot more aware now than she'd been back then. She and Hunter were completely alone—but they also weren't anywhere he could do anything to her. The valet wouldn't be able to hear their conversation, but he could see them. And unless Hunter planned to drag her across the large expanse of grass to the beach and ocean beyond, there was nowhere for him to take her but back toward the valet. The other direction led to a ten-foot-high privacy wall surrounding the property.

All information she'd taken in before she'd agreed to sit with him.

He was doing her a favor, really. Providing the means for her to enjoy the night air, the slight scent of ocean beyond. The moon.

Rather than feeling claustrophobic and tense at the event…

And his silly talk about a spell was oddly engaging.

No different than cookie dough and sneezes. Hunter was an entertainer. Just not one who needed a stage. She was curious about him. The real him.

"Are you pretty close with your dad?" she asked. He'd said he was helping Edward at the request of his father.

He shrugged. "We see each other once or twice a year," he said.

"What about your mom?"

"She visits more often. I call her once a week. She calls more if she needs to talk."

He was close with both of them. That was nice. He was lucky.

"Did she remarry, too?"

"Nope. Mom says once in a lifetime was enough to convince her that once was enough."

He had a grin on his face, which was shadowed. She couldn't tell if he was teasing or not, but figured he was—and that there was also truth in what he said.

"What about siblings? You have brothers and sisters?"

"Nope."

An only child of divorced parents. Who both visited him. A picture was forming in her mind. Still vague, but there. Kind of like sitting in her studio and letting the image appear one stroke at a time.

"I'll bet you were popular in high school." He was the type.

She'd been popular, too. Outgoing and social like her mother. She'd had her pick of dates. And, like more than half the girls in her class, had fallen for the most popular, outgoing, good-looking guy. Unfortunately, he'd gone for her, too.

Shivering, she pulled her thin wrap from her elbows up over her shoulders. She wasn't going to visit that memory again this evening. She was enjoying the night air. The moon. Being away from the people inside the building in her peripheral vision.

"I knew how to have a good time," Hunter said with a casual shrug that looked…sexy in his tux, taking her mind off herself. "I fancied myself as a surfer dude."

A vision of a younger, seminude Hunter, his blond hair windblown and maybe a little longer, superimposed itself on the image she was forming of him. "Were you good at it?" she asked, her artistic eye approving the vision.

"I won some competitions."

Of course he had. Just like another young man she'd known. David Smyth had been a competitive surfer in high school. Maybe they'd even competed against each other.

Another shiver. She waited for the aversion to come. The moment she knew she was going to run at all costs—when her studio called out to her so strongly that she couldn't deny the summons.

"A boy of privilege…" She said the words aloud. She wasn't sure why.

Not only was the boy who'd stolen her trust and happiness, her ability to have normal relationships, a charmer like Hunter, he'd also been a surfer—like Hunter.

And yet, here she sat.

"You've got the wrong guy." His words inter-

rupted the cacophony in her mind. "I do okay
for myself, but don't mistake me for one of your
crowd," he continued. "Not there and I don't want
to be."

One of her crowd? He was confusing her. Until
she thought about her last comment. *A boy of privilege.* She'd been referring to David.

Not that she'd ever tell Hunter. Or mention
Smyth Jr. at all.

"Your father's a doctor," she said inanely.

"And yours was a lawyer. They've had vastly
different clientele. Don't get me wrong, I'm not
complaining or judging. I had a great childhood.
I just don't want you to take me for something I'm
not. I work in your circles, Julie. I don't live there."

What was going on here? What was he doing?
Warning her off?

Being honest?

To what end?

What did he want? Or hope to gain?

"I'll bet you were the model son, too." David
Smyth Jr. had been. On the surface.

"Not hardly." His chuckle had her looking at
him again. Shaking her head.

"What?" he asked, his face turned in her direction in the darkness.

"I'm trying to figure you out," she told him. No
finesse. Merely talking out loud.

"I could take that as a sign that you have at least a smidgen of interest in me."

He was teasing her again, and she gave it right back to him. "Just passing the time, since I'm required to sit here."

"I actually got into some moderately serious trouble my senior year of high school," he told her.

David's age. When he'd...

"And your dad bailed you out." She heard the bitterness in her tone. Wanted so badly to take it back. She couldn't afford bitterness. It could consume her.

Again, she marveled that she was still sitting there.

"Nope. He made me work my ass off to pay my fines and to pay for all the damages, too. I'd been partying with friends, and things got way out of hand. Some public property was damaged. I ended up in jail and was too drunk to get my own number right for the one phone call I was allowed. Lucky for me or not, I was a minor, so the cops called my dad."

"I can just imagine that car ride home."

She couldn't, though. Had the vehicle been filled with stony silence? With harsh words? Or a more understanding attitude that "boys will be boys"?

"There wasn't any ride. Not that night," Hunter said. "He told the police that he wanted my ass right where it was. The place I'd earned the, uh, *honor* of being."

Her mouth fell open. She noticed immediately and closed it. She wished she could see his face. He had to be putting her on. He must somehow have heard her story and was trying to...she didn't know what. She'd made clear that she wasn't interested in him. That she didn't date. He had to realize there was no reason to do a number on her.

He *couldn't* know her story. Only a handful of people did. Some suspected. Some surmised parts of the truth. But...

Brett Ackerman. He and Hunter were friends. Longtime friends. Had he told?

He wouldn't. Julie damned her untrusting nature. Brett was one of the truly good guys. She would not allow David Smyth Jr. to taint that.

"Your dad didn't have your back," she finally said because it felt as though his statement required response.

"Yeah, actually, he did. The next day, he bailed me out. He stood beside me in court. He taught me how to be accountable. And then told me he was proud of me for doing that. He also told me if I loved partying so much, that was fine, but somehow I had to turn it into a positive."

Her body tingled. From a breeze she was unaware had passed through? The low timbre of Hunter's voice? She didn't know.

"He sounds like a wonderful man," she said. Because they did exist. More often than not.

"He had his moments." Hunter looked out to sea. So she watched him. "He worked long hours, wasn't around as much as Mom needed him to be. Which was probably why I got into partying to begin with, according to her."

"Is that what you think?"

"I think I was turned on to marijuana by a friend and got hooked on the high."

Who said things like that? Was he trying to shock her? To what end?

So…she refused to be shocked. "Do you still?"

He turned back to look at her. "Smoke pot? You kidding me? I haven't touched anything, except an occasional alcoholic beverage, since my one night in jail. Quit it all. Cold turkey. Of course, it helped that my dad was a doctor and had me seeing someone."

Wow. For a fun guy, Hunter was…deep.

Or he was working her. To get something.

"You aren't getting in my pants." She'd probably be horribly embarrassed by that statement in the light of day. She had to cooperate with him on fund-raising projects. See him again. At the moment, she didn't care.

She was still sitting there. And didn't understand why.

"Thanks for the confirmation," he said. "I'd

kind of figured that one out, but it's good to know for sure."

He was teasing her again.

And, in spite of herself, she grinned.

HIS LIFE WAS an open book. Hunter had nothing to hide. No deep waters to slow him down. As long as he kept things light, he wouldn't be a letdown.

Like his father had taught him, he did what he knew he was good at.

And something else he'd learned from his father, although inadvertently, was never to let others depend on him for their happiness. Never to promise anything he might not be able to deliver. John Rafferty's one mistake had been marrying a woman who'd needed things he could never give her.

He was a great doctor. A great man. He just hadn't been a great husband for Karen Rafferty.

Usually, when Hunter sought his own personal fun, he ended up with similar kinds of people.

Yet there he was, sitting outside on a Saturday night with a beautiful woman who was much too deep for him, when not far away he had the opportunity to observe the fruits of his labor, enjoying the way his guests were enjoying themselves.

Not that he was seeking personal fun at the moment. Trouble was, he didn't know what he was seeking.

He just knew he had at least another fifteen minutes before the event started to break up. At least a quarter of an hour before her brother would be ready to leave.

"I'm surprised Colin and Chantel haven't come looking for you."

"They're used to me slipping out."

"So they knew you were hailing a cab?" Then why was she sitting there with him? His blood started to heat up.

"No. Usually I wander around the venue. Find a quiet place to sit."

Whoa. "Usually? You do this a lot?"

"Only when I'm required to attend a social evening function."

She'd said she didn't date. Some guy had ruined her trust in men. Must've been unfaithful to her. Or lied to her to some atrocious extent. Hunter wasn't good at figuring out the drama. But…

"Which is pretty much all the time, right?" he said. She had the gala on Thursday. And, he assumed, other functions on a regular basis, based on how many boards she sat on.

"Almost never. Colin and Chantel handle the socializing part of our obligations."

Hunter was truly shocked. And…something more. It wasn't as though he had enough of a personal investment to care. But a guy could feel concerned for a fellow human being.

And then something else hit him. "But tonight you weren't finding a quiet place to sit. You were actually leaving. Why?"

"You."

"Me?" When he heard his voice reverberate around him, he consciously took a deep breath. Quieted his tone. "What on earth have I done to you? Why would I drive you to the point of needing to get a cab?" He was the guy who made everyone comfortable. He'd always been that guy.

"You're the only reason I was there," she said. And he wondered if she was backtracking. Or if he was missing some crucial fact. "Or rather, your need for reassurance where Joy was concerned. We were finished talking about Joy, so I wanted out." She didn't sound like herself.

"You said I was the reason you were leaving."

"Like I said, our business was done. It was time to go." She paused. "I don't get you. I don't get what you're about."

"You don't get me?"

"You...keep pursuing me when..."

"When what?"

"You're gorgeous, successful, charming...not the type of guy who needs to pursue a woman. Any woman. And especially not one as backward as I am."

Backward? Had she looked at herself? Heard herself in a meeting? Seen herself with Joy?

"I told you, it's the spell." He had no other answer for her.

She grinned again. And he felt like he'd hit a home run.

CHAPTER FOURTEEN

JULIE DRESSED WITH Joy in mind Sunday morning. The little girl had been in jeans and T-shirts every time she'd seen her. And because she knew they'd brought Joy's clothes from home and that she was choosing what she wanted to wear, Julie figured jeans and T-shirts were what made her comfortable.

She only owned two T-shirts.

The one she chose was old but hardly worn—because, technically, it wasn't hers. She'd purchased it for her mother as a Mother's Day gift the year she'd died. White with pink and purple glittery hearts across the front, it read Best Mom Ever. She'd chosen it because she and Amy and Joy all missed their mothers. And because the only other one she owned had been a freebie, advertized a local winery and was extralarge.

The jeans were her own. Skinny jeans. Cut low on the hips. The ones Chantel had given her for Christmas.

Pausing with her brush halfway through her long dark hair, she stared at the mirror in her bathroom suite, wondering if she should take off the makeup she'd so carefully applied. She always wore some. But only when she went out to a function did she bother with her eyes. Breakfast with Joy wasn't a function.

And she hadn't put on the makeup with the little girl in mind, either.

Was it wrong to be dressing herself up because of a man she had no interest in encouraging?

Was it wrong to want to feel good about herself?

Hunter desired nothing from her but a flirtation. He'd made that quite clear. Just as she'd made clear that she wasn't interested.

With that honesty between them, was there any harm in enjoying a bit of nonthreatening banter with him? Since they were being thrust together for Joy's sake. And then at Thursday night's gala.

Yanking the brush down, she winced and put it away. No time now to pull her hair back into her usual careful ponytail.

Out of the house before Chantel and Colin were up and could comment on the makeup and lack of ponytail, she breathed a sigh of relief. She didn't like that reaction and felt a little guilty about it. She loved her family. Trusted them. More than anyone.

If she felt she had to hide something from them, that something was not good.

Determining that she'd talk to Chantel about the whole situation when she got home that afternoon, Julie turned her car toward the highway.

HUNTER MADE EDWARD change his clothes. Who wore a suit and tie to breakfast with a child on Sunday morning?

Not anyone he could think of. Not if the guy wanted the child to warm up to him. Or find him in any way playful.

Playful. Wasn't that what seven-year-old kids wanted? Julie had said he should try to remember himself at that age. But he wasn't sure he remembered seven any differently than nine or eleven. It had always been about the fact that his folks got mad at each other, and he made them both happy. But he remembered wanting to have fun. And doing dumb stuff to make them laugh.

He'd loved it when his parents laughed together. Which they did if they were having fun.

Things were bad when the fun stopped.

Now, as he waited for Edward in the hotel lobby, he directed his attention to a thirtysomething blonde woman who was walking toward the reception desk. In wedge heels and a short dress, she looked a bit too done up for Sunday morning, too.

But attractive. She might be fun for a night of clubbing. If she was single.

Hunter always drew the line at married women. Or engaged women.

A glance at his watch told him they were losing the fifteen-minute window he'd scheduled into their travel plans that morning. He'd wanted to be at the restaurant first, ahead of Julie Fairbanks. He wanted to be certain he had a chance to sit beside her.

The time he'd spent with her last night had left him craving more. And feeling weirdly confident that with her nearby, he'd do just fine with Joy. Maybe because he was convinced that if he screwed up, she'd kick him under the table to keep him in line.

Gently, of course.

"This better?" Edward stood there in khakis and a long-sleeved plaid button-up shirt, looking like something out of an elite men's magazine.

"Much," Hunter replied, pulling the keys out of his jeans pocket and heading toward his SUV. They could still be first on the scene.

But they weren't. Lila and Joy were already seated at a round table for five in front of a window by the time Hunter followed Edward into the restaurant. Still, things worked out fine when Edward took the seat next to Lila rather than the one next to Joy. Leaving Hunter to snag the one beside Edward for himself without drawing attention to the fact that Julie, when she arrived, would be in the perfect place, next to him and next to Joy, too.

He didn't even have to worry about entertaining the child until Julie got there because Lila was asking Edward what he thought of Joy's T-shirt.

It had some colorful character on it. He wasn't up on kids' wear. Edward seemed to recognize it, though. He was a general practitioner, so he probably saw some kids. Maybe even had kids' stuff in his waiting room.

Bottom line, Hunter was off the hook. Which was pretty much the way the whole breakfast went, even more than he'd intended. Sitting next to Julie didn't go exactly as he'd hoped. Focused as she was on Joy, she was turned away from Hunter through almost the entire meal.

She'd said hello when she arrived. He thought she'd smiled, but she'd turned toward Joy so quickly, he wasn't completely sure.

Her leg bumped into his under the table once. He liked that. In a pathetic kind of way.

A guy who took undue notice of an accidental leg bump needed a head adjustment.

The good news was that Edward was actually getting to talk to Joy. She wasn't responding, but there was nothing wrong with her hearing. He wasn't saying much. Answering questions that Lila was posing to him—or rather, following her suggestions.

"Tell Joy about your house," she was saying as their waiter, Tom something, laid a plate of huge pancakes in front of Hunter. And a plate of similarly thick but smaller ones in front of Joy. Julie's toast and fruit seemed tame in comparison.

"It's right on the beach," Edward said, looking directly at the girl. "You finish your lunch and you walk outside the door and play in the sand. Or go for a swim."

Hunter had no idea if Joy liked to swim. But living in Ventura, she'd be familiar with the beach. The ocean.

From what he'd been told, though, her home, on the far inland side of town, had been about as far from the ocean as you could get.

But with a surfer father…

"Wouldn't that be fun?" Edward asked. "Spending part of every day on the beach?"

The girl's expression didn't change. Hunter just caught the slight flinch because he'd been staring at her. Looking for any sign of softening for Edward's sake.

Surfer father. Abusive father. Kid might not love the beach.

Hunter tipped over his glass of orange juice. Choosing it rather than the water he wasn't going to drink because the water glass was completely full and the orange juice mostly gone. Jumping up, he mopped with his napkin at the little puddle he'd made.

He noticed Joy watching him, as he'd hoped. He made a goofy face for her benefit.

"I'm sorry," he said to the table, then quietly sat back down.

Julie was putting syrup on Joy's pancakes. Edward and Lila were eating their eggs. Joy glanced at Hunter again. Like she wanted something from him.

Like he was supposed to know what to do.

Or maybe she just thought he was nuts.

Maybe he was.

Snatching a couple of grapes out of Julie's bowl of fruit, he shoved them deep into his pancake, giving it eyes. Joy was busy eating, but glanced over once.

A stolen strawberry became a nose.

"I intended to eat that," Julie said dryly.

"You want it back?" He dug it out of the pancake, catching a finger full of dough, and pretended he was going to plop the whole thing back in Julie's bowl.

"No, thank you," she said, covering her bowl with both hands.

Shrugging, he put the glob in his mouth. Not bad. Would've been better with some strawberry syrup to go along with it.

"I thought maybe we could go to the park up in

Santa Raquel after breakfast," Lila said. It was so far from Ventura that even if Shawn Amos was looking for his daughter, he'd be unlikely to go there.

Edward enthusiastically concurred.

"What do you think?" Julie turned to Joy.

Hunter took advantage of that to steal another strawberry out of her bowl, dropping it in the nose hole on his pancake.

Joy glanced at it.

He snatched up a bottle of ketchup and made a straight line for a mouth. Looked at the little girl, then scrunched his nose and wiped the red off his pancake, licking the finger with which he'd done so.

"I think going to the park's a good idea," Julie said. Hunter couldn't tell if she was purposely ignoring him or was simply unaware of what he was doing. But Joy was relaxing the rigidity that had appeared in her shoulders when Edward had mentioned the beach.

He wanted to tell her how cool surfing was. How he'd found his lifeline in the waves and she could, too. How your stomach jumped as if it was on a carnival ride when a wave hit you just right.

Instead, he grabbed the syrup and drew a squiggly line for a mouth on the pile on his plate. He was getting kind of hungry, but he was a bit too keyed up to eat. He'd hoped to have a minute or two to speak with Julie that morning.

To undo whatever he'd done the night before, whatever had made him think of her more rather than less. If not today, he'd have to wait until Thursday's gala and he didn't like the thought of that.

"Have you ever climbed a tree?" Julie asked the girl.

Joy glanced at his plate again.

Hunter cleaned the syrup off his pancake with his cookie dough finger and licked it clean.

"Amy learned to climb trees when she was little," Julie was saying. Hunter didn't have a clue who Amy was, but he figured Joy must know. Probably a little girl at the shelter. Or maybe someone from Joy's school.

Pulling a glob of syrupy pancake out of the stack, he left a hole for the mouth.

"She thought trees were a good place to hide, high above everyone else, and read," Julie was saying. "When we go to the park, we can see if there's a tree with a low enough branch for us to sit on."

When Julie reached over to cut a piece of pancake for Joy and hand her the fork, he grabbed some lettuce off her plate and dropped it quickly above the eyes on his. Green hair.

Joy laughed out loud.

Edward froze. Lila stopped, fork suspended, and stared at the little girl.

"You want to climb a tree?" Julie asked.

Hunter snatched a piece of cantaloupe and stuck it in his mouth.

"Yes," Joy said. In a little girl lisp. And then, as though she hadn't been mute for more than a week, added, "If you take me and he comes, too."

She was pointing at Hunter.

He'd been caught. Mid-chew.

CHAPTER FIFTEEN

OF ANY SESSION for Sara to be absent, this was the worst. Heart pounding, Julie drew on more than a decade of calming her own fears and keeping up appearances. She smiled at Joy, who'd finally gifted them with the sweetest little voice, and hoped she was hiding the fact that the world was shifting.

"I can certainly go with you," she told Joy, pretending to herself that they were in their small art room, in front of a pair of easels. "But Ms. McDaniels wants to take you there..." She tried to recall everything Sara had told her.

They didn't want Joy to be afraid or feel as though she was in prison. And yet, they couldn't insult her intelligence, either. She was observant. And living with other victims.

Sara had also counseled her on how to handle things in the event that Joy spoke for the first time while alone with Julie.

They weren't currently alone. Julie looked at Lila.

"How about if Julie rides along with us?" the

older woman asked Joy, with her hint of a smile. She could've been talking to any of the residents' children, in any situation. Lila was the same with all of them.

Instilling a confidence that couldn't be shattered.

Joy turned to Julie, who nodded.

The child remained silent. But looking at them, rather than down or vacantly away. That direct look was something Julie had begun to recognize as acquiescence.

There was so much they needed the child to tell them. As soon as possible. And yet, to push her, to instill any kind of alarm, or even drama, could force her back into her shell.

Hunter, calmly eating his pancakes beside her, was the perfect antidote to the urgency Julie was trying hard to contain.

She glanced at Edward. The older man's eyes glistened. He'd been counseled, too. And Lila had leaned over to speak quietly to him.

Still, Julie felt it was time for them to get out of there.

Edward might need a little while to collect himself.

THEY FOUND A TREE. At the park not far from The Lemonade Stand. Lila's choice. She'd wanted to be close, just in case.

Julie didn't want to think about "in case" of what. But she knew Lila was concerned about Joy's emotional and mental state. And that she wanted to be close to the Stand because Sara was there.

Edward had driven Julie's car, with Hunter's Escalade behind him.

From her perch on the long branch that hung low, propped up by an equally thick branch behind her, Julie peered over at Edward and Lila, sitting on a bench, wishing the other woman was within hearing distance.

She glanced down at Joy. Felt a tremendous tug at her heart. And knew she was getting in deep.

"I've been telling you so many stories about Amy, I was thinking maybe, while we're way up here in one of Amy's special places, you could tell me a story," she said, an arm around Joy as the child sat tucked between Julie and the tree trunk. The small girl with her big brown eyes asked for so little, and yet compelled Julie to give her everything she had.

Since that one sentence at the table over breakfast, Joy hadn't said another word.

Hunter stood just beneath them. He'd said it was because he was Joy's ladder. She figured he was there to catch her if she fell.

But she had a feeling he'd deny that if she called him on it.

"Just a quick story?" she asked. "We're safe up here. No one can hear us."

Joy looked down at Hunter. He started to whistle.

"Then tomorrow when we do our drawing, we can draw about today," she continued. She couldn't push too hard. Or be too obvious.

And yet, if the little girl knew anything about her mother, if she could tell them anything at all about the day her battered aunt had taken Joy and run with her...

If only Julie could find a way to help her divulge whatever secrets she held so deeply inside. Hunter's whistling grew louder.

While his nonchalance took her aback, it also eased some of her tension.

He began to circle the tree, walking in beat with his tune. One she didn't recognize.

She would've felt utterly ridiculous out in public, circling a tree while whistling, but Hunter made it look natural. And enough fun that she almost wanted to join him.

At least *fun* was the reason she gave for her sudden desire to be down on the ground with him.

Joy moved, and the weight of her little body brought Julie completely back to the moment, up in that tree.

"There was a monster in the house." Joy's unexpected whisper, complete with the lisp and *r*'s that sounded like *w*'s, spoken close to Julie's ear, spread chills down her spine.

Joy had a speech impediment. Sara would want to know that. And she'd probably draw some conclusions from it, too. Like…could it be a sign of long-term insecurity? A hint of the life Joy had been living?

Was Joy telling her a made-up story? Or something real? Either way, a monster in the house wasn't good.

Hunter didn't miss a beat, either with his walking or his accompanying whistle. Julie wasn't sure if he knew Joy had spoken again.

Mentally she was back in her studio. Seeking Amy's help.

Does this monster have a name? she wondered.

"He hurt Mommy and Aunt Mary."

The babyish *r*'s broke her heart. No, it was the story that was doing that. The *r*'s just emphasized the sweet innocence that had been so horribly violated.

Did he hurt you, too? she wanted to ask, but was afraid to interject.

Whenever Julie told her stories, Joy listened intently, looking at her the whole time. So now she looked at the little girl. And waited to see if there'd be more.

"Mommy told Aunt Mary to take me and run and she did 'cept we didn't 'cause we hid 'cause

Aunt Mary didn't want to leave Mommy with the monster in the house."

Joy was speaking as though she was reading from a book. There was emotion there. Yet, Joy seemed removed, too.

Julie's palms were sweaty. She wanted help.

But she *was* the help.

And so far, Joy hadn't given them much more than they already had.

Hunter stilled beneath them, no longer whistling. The air grew quiet. And so did Joy.

Tense, feeling she had to control every nuance of the situation so as not to shut Joy down, she started to panic. They couldn't stop here.

Because Joy had more to say. Even if it was just a need to express the fear the monster must have left within her.

"Amy hid in the closet," she said. Joy carried that book almost constantly when she was at the Stand. Amy, afraid of her shadow, thinking she was escaping it, only to have it suddenly appear again, someplace it hadn't been before.

Hunter started in on another tune. Changing his course but walking once again. His hands in his pockets, it was as though he didn't have a care in the world.

But he did care. Julie was certain of that now.

He cared about Joy. And Edward. About doing what he could to help a frightened little girl.

And maybe about the causes that were his clients?

"Aunt Mary hid me by the dog wall that doesn't have dogs no more and maked me put my hands over my ears."

Julie's thighs were going numb. She wondered how much longer Joy would be content to sit on the limb with her. How long Lila would leave them up there before she had to get back to work.

"Amy did that sometimes," she said. "You know, put her hands over her ears. It was so she wouldn't hear things that scared her." Thank God for Amy. That was another book, not the one Joy carried around. But there were copies of it at the Stand. Chances were that someone had read it to Joy over the past week. Particularly since she was so fond of Amy's shadow book.

"I heared," Joy said softly, in her almost-whisper while Hunter changed tunes yet again. "Mommy screamed." It came out "sqweamed." And the words made Julie squirm inside.

All the Amy books were at the Stand, So why was the shadow book the one Joy carried around with her? What was it about that particular story?

Joy had heard Cara scream.

That wasn't good, to say the least.

Neither would it be good for Edward to know what his granddaughter was telling her. The older man was watching the tree; Lila was, too. They were conversing, and Julie hoped that Lila could give the doctor words of comfort. She had a feeling he was going to need it.

The whistling stopped again. All was quiet, and Julie's tension grew. Lila could stand up at any minute. How could she signal the director not to interrupt, without distracting Joy? And possibly ending this "story" time?

She heard humming from directly below her. Hunter was on to another tune, but he'd switched from whistling to a quiet hum.

"I seed a shadow."

That was when she knew.

Why that book, the shadow book. Amy was afraid of shadows.

So was Joy.

"Amy sees shadows," she said with growing conviction. And confidence. "She talks about them, huh?"

"She hides."

"Yes, but she tells us about them and that's what makes them not so scary to her." Experience was talking now. Speaking through Amy had been the means by which Julie had begun to heal.

"Mommy told me 'be quiet, Joy.'"

She watched the girl, tried to determine from that mostly expressionless face what was going on. Had her mother spoken to her when she'd been in hiding with her aunt? Or before? That day? Or another day?

"Ssshhh," Joy continued, putting her finger to

her lips. She leaned forward, and Julie grabbed her waist, holding her in place. When Joy didn't flinch, she left her hand on the little girl's side.

"Be quiet so the monster can't find you," Joy said.

"Amy was always quiet when she was hiding," Julie told her.

"'Good girl,' Mommy said."

Because Joy had been quiet?

While she was hiding by what she called the dog wall? As she pictured this sweet child who'd locked herself away in silence, hiding by a wall, another thought occurred to her.

A woman who was screaming couldn't tell her daughter "Good girl."

Joy was talking about something that had happened before that last day when Mary Amos had taken her niece and run. Cara telling her to be quiet so the monster wouldn't get her? Had Shawn beaten Cara on a regular basis?

Like Amy's shadow. Always showing up.

Joy had been a "good girl," so did that mean the monster didn't find her? Had the little girl been saved from the monster's wrath?

The photo she'd been shown of Cara Amos sprang to mind. The woman had been screaming that last day she was seen.

And there'd been that shadow.

"Maybe it would help Amy if you talked about

the shadow in your story," she said now. "If you tell me, I could tell her."

Joy knew that Amy lived inside Julie's mind. Kids accepted things like imaginary friends. It was only when you grew older that analyzing your feelings robbed you of the comforts that were meant to see you through hard times.

Joy looked down at Hunter, who was humming quite steadily, but again, Julie didn't detect an actual tune.

"It was Mommy's," Joy said. "Mommy's shadow. The monster was pulling her hair so she goed with him. But 'shh.'" The small finger went to those rosy lips one more time. "You can't tell because the monster will hurt her more."

Where'd they go, Joy? Someone had to find Cara Amos before it was too late.

Unless it was already too late.

She gave herself a mental shake. Negative thinking served no purpose. Helped no one.

"Amy wants to know what you did after the shadow was gone." Amy's shadow always left when she hid.

"Aunt Mary taked me next door and then we goed to the hospital."

Joy's face grew sad, but she didn't cry. Instead, she quietly laid her head against Julie's shoulder.

And fell silent once again.

CHAPTER SIXTEEN

HUNTER HAD A late-afternoon/early-evening fund-raiser on a yacht scheduled for Sunday. The change from breakfast jeans to off-white pants and blue blazer had been rushed, but he got to the dock with the half hour to spare he'd allotted himself. Time to shoot the breeze with the man who'd captain the boat for the three-hour dinner cruise. Time to chat up the caterer while her crew finished last-minute arrangements and set tables. And to greet the two of his three employees who were scheduled to oversee every minute detail of the event, one on each deck.

As he did his job, his mind constantly wanted to take him back to Julie Fairbanks. To Joy Amos. To a morning that had been way more intense than his life supported.

There'd been a voice mail from Mandy—his long-time, no strings attached "girlfriend" to hang out with on occasion. He'd listened to it after dropping off Edward. She had something going that night and wanted him to be her date. A perfect solution to how the day had left him feeling.

He hadn't called her back yet.

Not a big deal. Last minute was typical for them.

She could look on his website and see that he had a function that afternoon.

"Tablets are all checked and operational upstairs." Trina Matthews, the employee who'd been with him the longest, came up behind him as he stood by the rail on the ship's top deck, staring out at the ocean.

When did Hunter Rafferty ever just stand and stare at the ocean?

He turned to the fortysomething divorcée. "Have you talked to Kyle?" Kyle had the main deck because he was the one who handled things like Hunter would. And because the "good old boys" who were guests at the political fund-raiser tended to get a bit rowdy the more they drank, and all of them were seated on the main deck.

"I just texted him," Trina said. "Haven't heard back."

The tablets were relatively new for him, an investment that he'd debated making for a good six months. But the payoff had already been phenomenal. Donations were made using credit cards and bank accounts while people sat at the tables. Much more efficient than pledges or checks.

Much more lucrative, too.

"Opening the gate to the dock in ten," Trina

said. It wasn't until he actually noticed the oddly assessing look on her face, the concern in her green eyes, that he realized he wasn't behaving like himself. Being in place to meet guests was a priority from which he never strayed.

"I'm heading down now." He gave Trina a killer smile and started acting like the Hunter Rafferty she knew.

He was definitely going to call and accept Mandy's invitation.

He needed a night out.

JULIE WAS UP in her studio Sunday night, working on storyboards for a new Amy book or for various Amy books to come, when her phone rang. She wasn't going to answer it. The emotions battering her would conquer her if she didn't get them out. Deal with them. And her stories were how she did that.

After the park, she'd gone with Lila to The Lemonade Stand. Sara had met them and asked her to sit in on a session with Joy. Now that they had confirmation that Cara had been forced to leave with her husband—being pulled out by the hair made that pretty clear—the sense of urgency had ramped up even more. Lila had immediately advised the local police, who'd called their Ventura counterparts.

Her phone rang again. As though the caller

had hung up and was trying a second time. Colin and Chantel were downstairs, enjoying a quiet evening watching television. Now that Chantel was pregnant, Colin was more protective than ever of his energetic and sometimes-too-daring-and-determined wife. They were all safe. Joy was safe and with professionals trained to care for her. Julie didn't have to worry about the phone.

She didn't need to worry, period. Worry served no purpose. Except to drain energy that could be better spent elsewhere.

Amy had both hands over her mouth. She'd been yelled at by a bully at school. Julie had no idea where she was going with this one. She hadn't planned to write a book about bullying—although the idea made a lot of sense.

It was just that, so far, the Amy books were all about living with the demons inside, in a very upbeat, cute, little-kid way. About the doubts and uncertainties, the fears, that plagued most kids in some fashion.

Her phone rang a third time. A vision of Joy popped into her head, a Joy who would speak only to her, and with fear slicing her heart, she pulled her cell out of the back pocket of her jeans.

Hunter. Not The Lemonade Stand.

"Hello?"

"Thank God! I've been trying to get hold of

someone, and no one's answering." He sounded...
unlike Hunter.

"What's wrong?" she asked, instantly tuning
in. He'd been so effective with Joy over the past
few days. He had a way of sensing when people
were starting to go downhill and then bringing
them back up. He wasn't friend material for her,
but if he was in trouble...

"Nothing," he said, his voice still curt. "I just...
Edward wasn't answering his phone and—"

"I think he's at the Stand," she told him.

"Is something wrong?"

"Not that I know of."

"But when I left... What about Joy?"

Right. They'd ended up playing musical cars
that afternoon. When she'd had to ride back with
Joy, Edward had driven Julie's car to The Lemonade Stand, so she'd have it later. Hunter had
gone on to work.

"That's why you were calling Edward," she said
now. Because he'd been worried about Joy. You
wouldn't know it, the way he'd walked around
whistling and humming, acting as if the afternoon had been nothing more than a Sunday stroll
in the park.

But she'd sensed that he was aware of everything going on.

"You knew she was talking to me," Julie said,
taking her phone to the couch in her studio and

curling her legs beneath her. "You started whistling so she'd talk to me."

"I didn't know she'd talk to you," he said. "I just figured that if the idea was for her to feel she couldn't be overheard, I shouldn't be down there listening in."

"Could you hear what she was saying?"

It wasn't as though they could talk about Julie's time in the tree with Joy while the little girl was standing there with them. Edward hadn't been told about Joy's speaking until they were all back at The Lemonade Stand and Joy was in a private session with Sara.

Lila had taken Joy to use the restroom as soon as they got back, which had given Julie time to fill Sara in. It wasn't until Joy was with Sara that Julie had a chance to tell the director why she'd asked her to call Sara and have the counselor meet them at the Stand.

"I could hear her lisp. I couldn't make out words," Hunter said.

Julie told him what Joy had revealed during their time in the tree. "Lila told Edward about it later, while I was in with Sara and Joy. Sara tried to talk to her alone, but Joy just kept looking at the door. Sara decided Joy wanted me with her and called me in to join them. She relaxed a little, but didn't speak again. I even took her in to draw. She stayed close to me, held my hand as we walked, which is a new thing. But she hasn't said a word since I handed her out of the tree to you."

"What time did you leave the Stand?"

"Around five." Joy had fallen asleep with her head on Julie's shoulder, and her house mother had carried her in to bed.

"So we're back at square one."

We're. He wasn't on this journey just because Edward had asked for moral support. Maybe it had started out that way, but...

"The police went back to the Amos home this afternoon." Julie told Hunter the rest of what she knew. When he wasn't coming on to her, or being the charming host, he was actually an easy person to talk to. "They found a dog pen with a cement wall and another cement wall behind it. There was about a foot between the two walls. They're pretty sure that's the hiding spot Joy referred to."

She was sitting in her studio, talking on the phone as though she had a close friend. Speaking with a man she couldn't get out of her mind.

So much was happening. Her quiet life of charity work, their little family, was imploding on her. First Hunter, the charmer, not leaving her alone. Then Chantel's pregnancy. Joy reacting to Amy so strongly. And consequently needing Julie.

"They know what time Mary and Joy showed up at the neighbor's—it was late morning—so they're going back tomorrow morning, to re-create the scene and see where Cara would've had to be for Joy to see her shadow. They're hoping to determine which direction they went."

"What would it matter? We know they're gone."

"They can pull surveillance footage from surrounding areas, which they've already done to some extent. But if they can determine which direction Amos took, they'll know better where to search."

"Maybe they could tell whether or not he took her through the yard or out to a vehicle," Hunter added.

"He might've had a friend who lived close by who helped him out, too. If so, there's someone who knows something, someone the police haven't found yet. Someone who lent him a car."

Since the family van was still parked in their driveway.

"With luck, they might find some evidence of her having been at least partially dragged, now that they know she was."

"I know they're looking for a ponytail holder," Julie said. "Apparently she always wore her hair in a ponytail. Maybe, if he was pulling her by that, it came loose."

Julie didn't know if Edward had heard the news in the same way she had—she'd gotten it from Lila just before she left—but her understanding was that the police were more worried than ever that Cara Amos was in immediate danger.

And that she could already be dead.

"Mary Amos took a turn for the worse this afternoon, too," Julie continued. Edward would be telling him this when they spoke. Better that Hunter be prepared to lighten the other man's load.

"I thought they were going to start bringing her out of the medically induced coma?"

"They were. They did. It didn't go well and they had to put her back in the coma."

She didn't know the particulars. Neither did Edward. They weren't Mary's relatives.

"How are you doing?" Her feet hit the ground at his question. A personal question. Out of the blue like that.

"I'm fine." She gave her rote answer. One she did so well, had been giving for so many years, she could probably do it on her deathbed. "How about you?"

It was polite to ask. And it took the pressure off her. Also a rote response.

"I'm... Have a drink with me."

Not that again.

"Hunter..."

"Just a glass of wine. You and Edward and Lila, you all had a chance to debrief. And you all have way more experience with this kind of thing than

I do. Edward's not directly involved with domestic violence situations, but as a doctor I'm sure he's seen his share."

Was he working her? She thought so. But there was truth in what he said, too.

Of course that was what made manipulation so successful. The grains of truth that were embedded in what was invented, the put-on. Or truth that was twisted until the meaning changed and it was only truth in disguise. She'd been worked by masters—not only Smyth Jr., but his father and his father's rich and powerful cronies, who all insisted that the sex had been consensual. They'd shut her and Colin down fast.

"I don't drink and drive." She finally said the one thing that came to mind while she tried to sort through the myriad thoughts and feelings arguing inside her.

Another upsetting occurrence. Generally Julie was at peace with herself. She knew who she was. She knew what she wanted to do with her life. And she knew her limitations.

"I didn't ask to be involved in all this," Hunter went on, as though he hadn't heard her. "I'm not complaining. I want to do anything I can to help. But like I said before, I'm in way over my head. All I'm asking for is a little time."

She recognized truth in his words. She didn't

think it was disguised. But there was no way to be sure. "I don't drink and drive," she repeated.

"I can pick you up."

She wasn't going to ride alone in a car with him at night. She was rational enough to understand that she had nothing to fear from him. And yet… she was also injured enough to know she'd be quivering inside if she got in a car with him. "I…" Before she could form whatever refusal she'd been about to come up with, he interrupted her.

"I called Edward first. I'd have taken him for a beer. He's not available."

He wasn't hitting on her, she decided. He really just wanted a drink. A chance to debrief and to unwind from the day's events.

Hunter didn't have a studio to escape to. Or an Amy.

He didn't have years' worth of experience in dealing with emotional trauma.

He was helping them save the little girl from the demons inside her. Helping her to help them find her mother.

If Joy could climb trees and talk about her terror, surely Julie could get in an Escalade and ride a mile to the closest beach bar…

"How far away are you?"

"I'm actually parked outside, on the street, in front of your drive."

He was outside? Hand to her throat, she thought

about him sitting there in his car. So close. Her heart was pounding, but, strangely, not with alarm. Not yet.

If she wasn't mistaken, she might even be feeling some anticipation. She couldn't remember a time she'd been excited about something. Really, truly excited.

Well, she could. But not in the past ten years.

Not that *excited* was the right word. How could it be when what he needed was to discuss the day's trauma. But the anticipation, the first step to unbridled excitement—it had been so long since she'd felt it.

She didn't want to get in his car and lose that feeling.

And yet, she owed it to Hunter to see him. Or owed it to Joy.

Okay, she *wanted* to see him.

But she didn't want to be completely alone with him.

Colin and Chantel were downstairs. In the TV room with the door closed for the best surround-sound effects. But still there.

"How about if we just have a drink here?" she asked him before she could change her mind. "I can open a bottle of wine, and we can sit out by the pool." It was a little breezy. "We have a gas fireplace out there."

She crossed over to the door that led to the bathroom in her suite. Frowned at her hair. Her lack of makeup. What she'd applied that morning had, of course, worn off.

The T-shirt and jeans she'd worn all day.

She wanted to look better for him. There wasn't time.

"You're on," he said. Through her upstairs window she saw his lights turn into their drive.

She wasn't going to make more of his visit than there was. Hunter was not a relationship type of guy. She had nothing to fear.

Energized, she hurried downstairs before he could ring the bell. The last thing she needed was her big brother making a big deal out of a little glass of wine.

CHAPTER SEVENTEEN

HUNTER HAD JUST turned off the Escalade's engine in the driveway round in front of a set of massive front doors when his phone vibrated, signaling a text.

Hey, hot guy, you standing me up?

Mandy.

He'd forgotten to text her. Had forgotten that he'd planned to tell her yes, he'd be her date. As soon as he'd said his goodbyes to the last guest off the yacht, he'd phoned Edward. Who hadn't answered…

Shooting off a quick Sorry, sexy, tied up with business tonight. Rain check OK? he put his phone away, telling himself he'd call her as soon as he was done with his glass of wine. If it wasn't too late, maybe he could still catch up with her.

One glance at Julie, looking almost fragile as she stood framed by the huge doors of the family mansion, and he knew a glass of wine wasn't going to be enough.

He wasn't sure what would be. He just knew he needed to find it.

Fast.

He would've liked to see more of her home, thinking maybe he'd get some kind of clue to the mystery that seemed to surround her—whatever it was that wouldn't let go of him—but she whisked him through a foyer and outside before he'd done more than notice that she hadn't changed her clothes from that morning.

Even in jeans and a T-shirt, she looked like she belonged in her elegant surroundings. She also looked like they were swallowing her up.

Which made no sense at all.

He must be more tired than he'd thought.

"Red or white?" She'd shown him to a table out by an impressive, even by Santa Raquel standards, swimming pool. Right beside the table was the fireplace she'd mentioned.

She'd failed to say it was a piece of art sculpted out of a combination of marble and river rock.

She was currently standing under an awning that housed an outdoor kitchen more lavish than his indoor one, looking into a refrigerator.

He wasn't really a big wine drinker. "White," he said, because that was what she'd ordered at his function the previous night. He could tolerate either.

She uncorked the bottle like a pro, but he

thought her hand was shaking as she poured, which was why he watched her hands when she set his glass in front of him.

Definitely a tremor there.

So she was feeling something, too.

Thinking that maybe together they could figure it out and get rid of whatever it was, he raised his eyes to hers.

She met his look. Unflinching.

Her silent communication was about as personal as a tax collector's.

Until he held up his glass for a toast. She blinked then. And there might have been a hint of more than he was supposed to see in those blue eyes. The dim lighting—track lighting around the pool and patio area—made it a little hard to tell.

"To us," he said, more out of habit than anything else.

At work, he toasted to success. Out with friends it was always "To us." Simple. Nonthreatening. No need to get inventive.

"To finding Cara quickly, alive and well," she said. "And to Joy. She has no idea how much rests on her shoulders right now, and I hope she doesn't find out anytime soon."

He preferred "To us." But toasted anyway. He needed a sip of the wine.

"So, what did Sara say about Joy? Is she discouraged that Joy quit talking?" He'd said he was there to unwind. Might as well do it.

If it would keep Julie sitting there next to him, alone with him and the fire and the pool and the wine…

"Not at all." Julie's words surprised him. Pleased him quite a bit, too.

He didn't have any personal investment with the little girl, but a guy would have to be a real ass not to care.

"She compared the situation to a clogged ketchup bottle. Said that once you've let in some air and punctured the clog, a little bit of ketchup starts to come through, and with that air hole, it's only a matter of time before more ketchup pushes through and opens the hole even wider."

"Unless too much comes out at once and clogs it back up again." He might not know emotional trauma, but he knew his ketchup.

And remembered a few things from his psychology courses, too.

"Exactly. That's why, even with Cara's life possibly at stake, we can't pressure her. The hope is that sometime within the next twenty-four hours, she'll have a complete breakthrough."

"I'm guessing that might come in the form of a breakdown," he told her.

"Which is why Sara's sleeping at the Stand tonight."

"I'm surprised you didn't stay."

Her shrug wasn't nonchalant, but he had a sense that she'd wanted it to be.

"Lila told me to go home," she said. "They want me back there first thing in the morning, but I'm not Joy's caregiver. We can't have her relying only on me." She took a sip of wine. And then another. "If, as a therapeutic artist, a friend, I can help her open up, then that's what I need to do, but there have to be boundaries." Her voice didn't quaver.

"You're okay with that."

Her shocked look told him a lot—and unsettled him, too. "Of course."

"But it's obvious how much you care for her. Not just as a professional. You're giving your heart to that little girl."

"I'm not a professional."

That wasn't his point.

"So how do you give your heart and not have a problem with being turned away during what could be one of the most critical nights of Joy's life?"

Her second shrug didn't do any better than the first. She shook her head. "Life isn't always easy, Hunter. You do what you have to do. You're right, I'm not Joy's caregiver. It would be cruel to let her depend on me alone, to have only me saving her from her demons, and then have me desert her. The boundaries are for her sake. Not mine. She needs them. How could I possibly care for her and not do whatever I can?" Sinking a bit lower in his chair, he raised a hand to his chin, watching her. She was a complete dichotomy. Living in a protective bubble—and yet strong as steel. Refusing him so much as a pity date, and willing to sacrifice her own feelings, to expose her heart to pain, in order to do what was best for a little girl.

Fascinating.

Intriguing.

He dropped his hand and took another sip of wine.

"YOU DID GREAT TODAY." Julie's voice had changed. It was warm, filled with compassion, as she looked over at him. Their glasses were more than half-empty. But he was nowhere near ready to leave.

"I didn't do anything," he told her. He most certainly didn't need to waste time talking about himself. "I walked and whistled and played with my food. You...you knew just what to say to reach her."

He wasn't a counselor. Nor did he consider himself any good at the emotional stuff; a lifetime of heading in the other direction when emotions got tough was proof of his abilities on that score. But he'd studied psychology. He could discern when someone *was* good at it.

"You read her, Hunter. Like you were in her heart. You seemed to know every single time her emotions were reaching a critical level, and you defused it. Every time. Without that, nothing I said would've done any good."

She was making too much of his contribution. Clearly. But it felt so good to have her praising him that he didn't argue.

Damn pathetic party-thrower. That was how he saw himself. How he was comfortable seeing himself. It left little room for expectations that couldn't be met. Let him off the hook.

Not feeling all that fond of himself he tried a different direction. "You said you attended UCLA. You have a degree?"

There. A nice, first-date question. Or a going-out-to-dinner-to-figure-you-out kind of question.

"Yes." She sipped wine. Looked into her glass. Almost...shyly?

"In what?" His easy tone came naturally. Putting people at ease was what he *was* good at, after all.

"Art and finance, with a minor in child development."

"A double major and a minor?" He wasn't surprised. Impressed. But not surprised.

"Art was a given. With only my brother and me left, it was imperative that I understand finance."

"And child development?"

A shadow passed over her face. Not literally. He saw it all the same.

"I like kids."

He didn't doubt the truth of her answer, but knew there was more. It was always like that with her. She gave you what you asked for, but withheld so much.

Somehow he had to figure out what that "more" was, so he could ask for it and be done.

"What about you?" She turned the table on him. Again. Julie might be a mystery in many ways, but in this, her social skills, she was a member of the trained elite.

"I went to Southern Cal."

"Did you graduate?"

The question insulted him. Which made no sense at all. Even friends from high school asked it. People who knew him. He wasn't the college grad type.

"Yes."

"What was your major?"

He grabbed the bottle of wine without asking. Topped off a glass that should be emptied and done. For both of them. She could have stopped him; she didn't.

"Psychology."

"You have a degree in psychology."

"I know, right?" He didn't even try to pretend offense at that one. "How someone can study enough of the subject to get a degree in it and still treat life like one big party must be hard to fathom. Believe me, I've had this conversation more than once." Usually while drinking.

Alone. The only time he really ever let himself look too deeply into his own psyche.

Not that he was going to share that point. With anyone.

"No, Hunter." She put down her glass. "It makes total sense."

He scoffed. He might not have illusions about himself, but neither did he need or want her pity. A pity date, maybe. But...

"It does *not* make sense," he asserted with more firmness than he normally used. "If a moment gets even a hint of emotional drama, I stick my finger up my nose." Okay, that was an exaggeration. But not much of one. If breakfast had gone on much longer that morning, he might have resorted to the tactic. "And to be clear, it's only a BS degree—take that for the acronym if you choose—which makes it particularly useless. You can't do anything in psychology with only a bachelor's degree."

"You have a gift, Hunter. I think I've already mentioned that. You sense emotional trauma and ease it enough for the person experiencing it to gain control."

He wasn't open to this discussion. But Hunter wasn't ready to leave, either. He had almost a full glass of wine to finish. So he let her think what she wanted to think.

As long as it kept her sitting there.

Letting him sit there with her.

CHAPTER EIGHTEEN

HUNTER RAFFERTY OBVIOUSLY didn't think highly of himself. Sitting outside in her backyard, in an atmosphere meant for entertaining—and one in which she hadn't entertained since high school—Julie sipped wine.

And took it all in. Without discomfort.

In fact, she was enjoying herself.

Not because her companion didn't see his worth, or even that she did, but because he was... genuine. Charming, yes. But genuine. At least, at this moment.

Unless...

She waited for the doubts. They didn't come.

Hunter really didn't have a high opinion of his ability to handle emotional crises.

She'd known many charming men. In polite, moneyed society they were bountiful. She'd fallen in love with one. And found that beneath the charm lay selfishness. Rotten eggs on a heart of ice.

But Hunter... She kept picturing him with his hands in his pockets walking around a tree and humming. And felt herself smiling from the inside out.

For the first time in a very long time.

They talked some more about Joy. A little about Edward and Lila. About his fund-raiser that evening. And then Joy again.

"She needs to have fun at the beach," Hunter said, after Julie expressed disappointment that she'd been unable to get the girl to speak again once they came down from the tree.

"At the beach?" she echoed.

"Edward's talk about his house being on the beach didn't make her happy."

She'd noticed, of course. Had suspected that he had, as well, based on his pancake art and food-stealing.

She'd been hesitant to believe that he'd really discerned Joy's discomfort. She was always hesitant to believe. That came with having trust issues as high as the Empire State Building.

It felt good to know she'd been right in her first assessment. Hunter had played with his food to help Joy.

"Her father was a surfer," she reminded him. He was close enough that she could smell a hint of musk. And yet, she didn't feel threatened.

A moment to savor.

To give her hope.

He nodded. Watched her in a way that was personal. But she was okay. No need for her studio right now. It would come. The need. Her studio would be there waiting for her. And she'd go. For now, though…

"I surf." Why did it seem as if there was so much more to those words? His expression wasn't smiling. Or charming. It was…serious. About surfing.

"You've mentioned that before."

"The feeling you get, when you catch a wave just right. If she knew that feeling…"

He stopped and Julie straightened. "What?"

He shook his head. "I'm not good at this."

"At what?"

"The emotional drama. I'm the guy who checks out."

"I don't see you that way."

"You don't know me well enough. Trust me. Or ask my father. Or my mother, for that matter. They'll tell you. The going gets tough, I go surfing."

He was touching something deep inside her. Nudging the heart she kept so carefully protected. Just as Joy had.

Because of Joy? Was she at risk with Hunter because her heart had to be open to help Joy? Was she entering a minefield she'd promised herself she'd never get close to again?

He walked around a tree and hummed. For as long as it took.

But maybe he really didn't get it. Didn't see his abilities to empathize, to recognize when someone was in trouble and step in to lighten the load long enough for them to find their own emotional strength?

Maybe she was making him into what she needed him to be in order to sit outside by the pool and drink wine with him.

"What's the feeling you get when you hit the wave just right?" she asked.

His assessing look gave her pause. As did the bit of a smirk on his shadowed face. He sipped his wine, then held his glass suspended as he said, "It's like that dip in the roller coaster, the carnival ride excitement you felt as a kid. It's all about the fun. But it's also about the rush of fear, facing it and ending up safely on shore."

He took another sip of wine. "But if Shawn forced Joy on to a board, or pulled her underwater to teach her to get used to it…"

She'd been wondering about that. Wondering what it was about the beach that Joy didn't like. If she really didn't like it the way they were assuming.

Lila had told Sara about Joy's reaction, minute as it had been. So it wasn't a question of Julie seeing things that weren't there. Or Hunter.

"Maybe he deserted her on the beach at some point. Or she saw him hit her mother there," she suggested.

"But if she learned to surf now…"

"What? What's this great thing that makes you such an advocate of a dangerous sport? What do you get out of it?"

"Strength."

He said the word like a challenge. Then he stopped, shook his head again. Sipped wine.

"Strength." She gave the word back to him, with a challenging tone.

She wasn't like him. Wasn't good at letting go when emotions surfaced. No, she glommed. Because she knew that the only true way to emotional freedom, to possible happiness, was to deal with them.

"Clearly you've never been on a board."

"I've never mastered the art of surfing, no."

"But you've tried?"

"No."

He nodded, and seemed to relax again. Then he said, "When you hit the crest of a wave, when you ride it in, you're on top of the ocean. One with it. Part of it. The ride itself is fun, but it's that ability to stand up to it, with it, to glide to shore and hop off. If you can do that, you know you can do other things, too."

Like facing whatever had sent him surfing to begin with?

The man was an enigma. She didn't get him. Wasn't sure she'd have a chance to understand him before their brief association ended. But she knew she wasn't going to forget him, either.

"So...you think we should propose a trip to the beach? With Edward and Lila along, of course?" She didn't see that one flying—a trip to the beach in the middle of a busy weekday? But she didn't hate the idea...

So she told him, "Sara says we need to instigate safe feelings of family in whatever way we can. We need to not only bring out of Joy whatever she's hiding, but also to help her see Edward as a safe figure in her life before they tell her who he is."

"If Cara isn't found..." He stopped, and she wondered if he'd avoided saying, "or found alive." "Edward will be her next of kin. Chances are he'll get custody of her."

Down the road. If things didn't end as well as everyone wanted.

Worst-case scenario, Joy would be loved. She'd have security for the rest of her growing up, including Edward's financial security. She'd have family, starting with his sister, who was married to Hunter's father.

"You're her cousin, you know," she said aloud now.

"What?"

"Cara. And Joy. They're your cousins."

"By marriage only."

"Marriage has been making families since the beginning of time, Hunter. Parents are only related by marriage, and yet parents are the backbone, the basis, of all family."

When he sat forward and grinned, she felt a little foolish. She'd always had a tendency to be passionate in her delivery.

It had been a while since she'd delivered anything from inside herself to anyone but Chantel or Colin.

"Go out with me."

At that moment, she wanted to.

She wouldn't. Couldn't.

But, miracle of miracles, she felt the desire to date.

"I…"

It wouldn't last. This crazy sense of going back in time. Of being like the girl she'd been before David Smyth Jr. had asked her to date him exclusively.

"I know it's crazy," Hunter said, leaning closer to her, almost close enough for his hands to touch her knees. "We're so different. You're rich, I'm a working man. You dedicate your life to seeing the world's ailments and fixing them, and I'm great at helping rich people forget their troubles and feel good about themselves. You've told me about a million times that you don't want to go out with me…"

"You said you aren't the type of guy who dates seriously."

"And you said you don't date, period. I know."

Right. Okay. Back on an even footing.

"Well?" His look was so expectant, she wanted to come up with just the right thing to say. To impress him. Because he probably already had an answer on the tip of his tongue. Some light and airy comment, letting them both off the hook.

"Well?" she echoed. She'd let him do it for them.

"So will you go out with me." It was more statement than question this time. More like confirmation of something that was a foregone conclusion.

Except it wasn't.

Confused now, Julie could feel herself getting upset. No. She didn't want to be afraid. Didn't want to be injured.

Or act weird.

She was in control. Capable. Successful.

He was watching her, that half grin on his face. As if in slow motion, she could feel the panic, the tornado rising up within her.

She looked at Hunter, and the vision abated. For a second. For two.

"I can't."

The words brought her calm.

Relief.

And a surprising wave of disappointment.

"Why?"

She was wringing her hands together when what she wanted to do was pick up her glass of wine. Take a sip. Say something sassy.

"What's going on, Julie? After the past few days…everything with Joy…being at The Lemonade Stand…" He reached over and took her hands between his.

Julie jerked back. Forcefully. She hit her elbow on the metal arm of the chair so hard, it brought tears to her eyes. Pushing the chair back, she stood, took a step away. She needed some distance.

A few minutes to calm herself. Regain control. Make the next choice because she had that right. And because she wanted to be happy.

Because she liked him.

"Julie?" He was coming toward her.

No! She could feel the pounding of her heart. Hunter was the one who didn't push. Who ran when pushing happened, according to him. He was the one who knew when someone was in trouble and lightened the moment.

She needed him to lighten her moment.

No. She needed to do that herself. To be okay.

She backed up. He stood a couple of feet away. She wanted him to stay there, and kept backing farther away until she was up against the fire-place. His hands reached out, but he came no closer.

Tears spilled from her eyes.

"Get away from her!"

Julie's arm stung where it hit the edge of the fire-place as she jumped at the sound of her brother's voice.

Colin?

"If you ever lay a hand on my sister again…"

An arm wrapped around Julie's shoulders. Feminine. Familiar. Chantel was there, too?

"Hunter? Hunter Rafferty?" Colin's tone held confusion now, along with aggression.

"Whoa, wait a minute here!" Hunter's hands were in the air, as though Colin was holding a gun on him. "I'm not… I don't know what I'm not, but…really?" He looked at Colin, frowning.

And then at her. His glance finally rested on Chantel. A Santa Raquel detective.

Julie pulled away from her sister-in-law's comforting hold.

"I'm sorry," she said, addressing Hunter first. Approaching him. She didn't reach out. Didn't touch him. But she stood next to him, facing her brother and his wife.

"He wasn't hurting me."

"You were crying." Colin's adrenaline rush had clearly not abated.

"You were backing away from him and he stood his ground, forcing you up against the fireplace." Chantel's tone was a mixture of conciliatory, explanatory, and...embarrassed.

"I was crying before Hunter came toward me. He came over to find out what was wrong."

She could feel him next to her. Figured he was watching them all like they were some kind of freak show and waiting for a chance to make his escape without losing potential clients. After all, Colin, and now Chantel, were lucrative donors.

"I think I should leave so you can work this out."

He wasn't stepping away from her, though.

"You sure you're okay?" Colin didn't seem to know what to do with himself all of a sudden.

She nodded.

Her brother stared at the glasses on the table for a few long seconds, and then back at her, while Hunter stood there, doing nothing about leaving. "You were out here drinking wine."

She nodded again. He'd know the significance of that, far more than Hunter Rafferty ever would.

"And I just made a fool of myself," Colin muttered.

Where were Hunter's jokes? His silly antics?

Approaching Colin, Chantel slipped her arm

through his. "I think we should go back inside," she said.

He took a step with her, then looked back at Julie. "You swear you're okay."

She wasn't, of course.

But this situation was hers to deal with. However it turned out. She couldn't be a complete person, independent, living a full life, until she quit leaning on Colin and faced her own issues. Took them on instead of hiding from them. Or giving in to them. Learned how to coexist with them.

She'd been telling him so, with Chantel's help, for more than a year. And yet she relied on him for rides home from evening events. Went to these events with plans to hide out in his car. Her mixed messages weren't fair to him.

To any of them.

"I swear," she said. "I invited Hunter in. I should've told you, and I apologize for that."

"Oh, God." Colin looked at Hunter again. Hung his head a second and then stretched out a hand. "Sorry, man," he said. "I...don't know how to salvage this one. I'm sorry."

"Just don't tell anyone I made a lady cry," Hunter said with that half grin. "It'd be bad for business."

Julie wrapped her arms around her as the night's chill seeped through her T-shirt and into her soul. She watched her brother and Chantel head back inside. Moving to the fire once again, to get warm, she listened for Hunter's departure.

CHAPTER NINETEEN

"NORMALLY, YOU COME out here alone. Sit by the fire alone. Have a glass of wine alone."

Hunter didn't know why he was still there. The Escalade wasn't far. He had the freedom to walk through the Fairbanks mansion to get to it. He had the keys. But his feet hadn't moved since Colin had stepped away from him.

Julie's nod didn't satisfy him.

Or give him the go-ahead to take off.

Her brother hadn't been surprised to see Julie outside. He'd become unhinged when he'd seen a man outside with her.

It was that unusual for her to be with a man.

Any fool could figure it out.

Julie was lucky to have such a knight in shining armor in her corner. To have that kind of familial protection. Support. Security.

Yet she'd sent her brother away.

And Colin had left.

Colin was overprotective. But he respected her judgment.

Again, Hunter knew he was only coming up with the obvious.

"I'm sorry." Her words were soft.

Apparently her apology hadn't been what he was waiting for, either. In fact, it kind of pissed him off. As pissed off as he ever got in personal relationships. "For what?"

With the fire at her back, her face was in shadow. She'd pulled the ponytail holder out of her hair. He preferred it down. But would've liked a better look at her face.

"Colin. The way you were treated. I should've told him we were out here."

"That I was here, you mean."

"Yes."

"So why didn't you?" That was it. He just needed to know why. Then he'd get the hell out of there.

Maybe take a drive by the beach on his way home.

Or call and see if Edward wanted to meet for a beer.

"I didn't want him to make a big deal out of it."

Because she didn't have men over for glasses of wine. He'd already realized that. Which meant he still didn't have what he needed to set himself free.

"You didn't think he'd notice us out here."

"He and Chantel were in the TV room." As if that explained it all. His expression must have given away at least a hint of the dissatisfaction in his thoughts because she added, "It's close to their suite. Normally they go straight to bed from there."

So she hadn't expected to get caught. And that brought up something else. "You're ashamed to be seen with me."

Was that the real reason she wouldn't go out with him? As much as it made her seem like a snob, it was also an answer he could live with.

Well, perhaps not live with, but understand.

He hadn't taken her for such a snob. If she felt that way, she should just have said so.

Maybe he could leave.

As soon as she confirmed her views. Satisfied his curiosity. So they didn't have to revisit any of this.

Her chuckle might have been right up his alley if he hadn't seen the glint of tears in her eyes. Or heard the break in her voice as she said, "If I was ever seen with you, Hunter, shame is the last thing I'd be feeling."

What. The. Hell.

It was too dark to surf. That was why he was still there.

If he wasn't getting out, he might as well sit down. Drink. There was still wine left in his glass. And in the bottle.

Wine was a party.

"Come here," he said once he was firmly in his chair, wineglass in hand. Lord knew, he wasn't going over there to get her.

No, sir. Not making that mistake twice.

He wasn't going to touch her at all. He might be unreliable when it came to emotional support, or want to think he was, but no one had ever accused him of being stupid.

When she did as he'd suggested, okay, commanded—not that he'd expected his statement to have any power whatsoever—he wasn't any more satisfied than he'd been when she'd stood over by the fire.

Having her close was harder. He could see her. Those eyes. There was a look of agony in them.

Something was eating her up. And he was still sitting there.

"I warned you to leave me alone."

Not really. She'd told him she didn't date. "I'll go now. Just say the word."

She didn't say any words at all. She took a sip of her wine. He'd noticed that their wine was still cool. The night air? Maybe the air they were creating between them, too.

"Why do you volunteer at The Lemonade Stand?" The question was an obvious one. He'd been avoiding it.

He didn't really want to know.

He didn't want to lead her on, didn't want her

to assume he was the type of guy who'd be there for her if she confided in him. He'd rather not put that kind of pressure on himself.

If he was even half as decent as he liked to think, he'd get up and leave. With a knock on her brother's door to tell Colin his sister needed him.

"Same reason I sit on boards of charities. I've dedicated my life to helping others. Especially children."

He believed her. And knew he'd received the keeping-up-appearances version of her life. That was where he lived, too.

"How did you become associated with them?" What was it with his mouth? His foot was bobbing so fast he was going to get a cramp. A sure sign he was ready to go.

"Through Chantel."

At least she wasn't crying. Or sounding like she was about to.

"Chantel? Worked a victim case, I guess, huh?"

"Sort of." Julie nodded. Then shook her head. "Yes, she worked a case. Actually, we both did."

"You were a cop?" Shouldn't he have heard something about that before now?

When Julie shook her head again, he knew he was in trouble. Her mouth started to crumple at the sides, and there was no one here but him.

He'd had too much wine for this, even though he hadn't even finished a full glass.

Okay, so he hadn't had nearly enough.

What the hell had he expected? Hanging around. Asking questions. He never did that. And this was why.

He'd created a situation with both of them on the losing end. She was putting herself out there—and she was going to need something from him.

Her mouth moved. She was about to speak. He saw it all happening in slow motion. Saw himself getting up to leave, to make it stop.

And heard a tremulous voice say, "No, Hunter. I wasn't a cop. I was the victim."

JULIE HAD THOUGHT the night she'd attended the Santa Raquel library's fund-raiser the year before, the first time she'd gone out at night in ten years, knowing that David Smyth was going to be present, had been the hardest thing she'd ever done.

But as she sat there at her pool—always a haven for her—locked securely in her backyard with the beauty her grandfather and parents had created, she realized that night, while hard, had been just a beginning.

She wasn't ever going to change what David had done to her. She'd never be the girl she'd been before she went to that party with him so long ago. But she had to be able to feel fully alive outside her studio.

She had to embrace life as the woman she was today.

She had to tell Hunter why she couldn't have a relationship with him, no matter how superficial it might be. Because she'd let things go too far not to.

He'd nearly been assaulted by her brother.

"I'm sorry," she said again, thinking of the second she'd heard her brother's voice and feared he was going to hit Hunter.

"Would you please quit saying that?"

She nodded. Wanting to give him anything he asked for, but knowing that wasn't right, either. She could feel herself slipping back into victim mode. Shrinking.

Just from saying those words.

She *wasn't* a victim. Yes, she'd been one, for far too long.

But no more.

She was a survivor.

"I was raped, Hunter."

The words were bald. Ugly. And they seemed to hang there. In her haven. She didn't want them.

But couldn't hide them, either.

Victims hid.

Survivors stood.

If her haven was going to be true, it had to include what had happened to her, had to include the ways she'd changed, had to allow them in in order to heal them.

His mouth was half-open. He stared at her.

And yet, looking him in the eye, she didn't feel like a freak.

She was a strong, competent woman who lived with emotions that made it impossible for her to do certain things.

Like date.

Or...other things.

Not all rape victims were the same. While many of the emotions they shared were similar, they all dealt with them in different ways. Some of the scars they carried were the same; some were different. Even with a crime as horrible as rape, they were all individuals.

Hunter was still staring.

Then it hit her. He had no idea what to do. Or say. He was like the proverbial deer in the headlights. And her heart opened. Not wide. But enough. Some vestiges of strength dripped through.

They were only going to do this once. She might only *ever* do this once, so it had to be complete.

"Not just one time," she admitted to him. It was something Colin didn't even know. "In an hour he raped me three times. He was my date. We were at a party, and he put some kind of drug, probably

Rohypnol, in my drink. Pushed me into a room. Locked the door."

She was back there for a second. In the opulent home with its soundproof walls. The silk-covered down bedding and five-thousand-dollar mattress.

She'd revisited that place, that night, many times in her memory. She was through with trying to push it away because it didn't leave. It only lingered in the dark, to batter her down. So she'd learned to light up that room. To look at it.

And she'd learned that while the sight still stopped her breath, it wasn't killing her anymore.

"I screamed, but the music was too loud." Both in the room and outside it. Not that it would have mattered. She'd screamed until her throat was burning and raw. He'd laughed and stripped off her underwear anyway. Done what he was going to do.

When he was finished, her skirt had fallen over her hips, covering everything. She remembered noticing that her shirt was still tucked in. David hadn't bothered much with breasts.

At least not with hers.

"There's nothing I can say that's going to make this better for you." Hunter's first words in minutes didn't tell her much. They spoke to her, though.

"I know."

"I'm an ass for pushing you on this."

"You had no idea."

"You tried to warn me."

"I invited you over for a glass of wine."

"Yeah. Why did you do that?"

She was the one without an answer now. Hunter leaned forward and reached out a hand. "May I hold your hand?" he asked. He was close enough to take hers, but he didn't.

Not until she gave it to him.

Then he held on, passing the warmth from his body to hers.

"There's more," she told him. "I'm okay if you need to leave now. If you've done all you can here. For the rest, I have a support system."

He nodded. She didn't know if that meant he wanted to hear more or was confirming that he'd done all he could. Taken all he was equipped to take.

She knew differently. Hunter was the most empathetic man she'd ever met. But he had to see that for himself, just as she'd had to accept certain things about herself.

"We aren't doing this again," she said. And then, when she heard her own words, was afraid he'd think she meant they weren't going to talk alone again, or share a glass of wine at her pool. Maybe they weren't. Probably they weren't. But she didn't want to make that decision right now.

"Talking about it, I mean." She stumbled a bit over the clarification. Aware of her hand still held between both of his. Liking it there.

Wanting it there.

"So…if you want to know the rest, now's the time."

Prepared for his rejection—actually kind of hoping for it—Julie was surprised when her heartbeat accelerated as Hunter said, "I think I need to know the rest."

She met his gaze. Wondered what they were doing. And why.

But she didn't want to hold that thought long enough to find an answer.

One thing at a time. One step at a time. That was the way to climb mountains.

She thought about Colin inside with Chantel. For so long, she and her brother had held their secret, only the two of them. And then Chantel had burst into their lives, and Julie had seen how her life, her secrets, had kept her brother in prison, too.

No more. She had to set Colin completely free.

By owning her life.

Why it hit her just then, she didn't know. But once she'd gained the awareness, there was no going back.

Hunter was a moment in her life. But he was there for a reason.

And maybe she was in his for a reason, too.

With that in mind, she found her voice.

CHAPTER TWENTY

I THINK I need to know the rest? What the hell was that about? *I think I need to know the rest?*

He was playing with fire, and he wasn't the only one who'd get burned. What was the matter with him? He didn't lead women on.

Didn't promise things he couldn't do. Or provide.

The noise in his brain was so loud he almost missed her first word. He caught the second. And was locked in place by the third.

"You know them."

He did?

Not for long he wouldn't.

He'd kill them.

Them?

When she'd talked about the rape she'd said *he.* "There was more than one of them?" Hunter wasn't a violent man. He avoided fights, walked away. Turned his back.

Which was why when his mother had accused his father of domestic violence, almost killing him and his career, Hunter had been unable to testify, unequivocally, that his father had never lifted a hand to his mother.

He'd never seen him do it. Had never seen bruises or been witness to more than a raised voice. And he'd certainly never been on the receiving end of anything but respect from the elder Rafferty.

He hadn't stuck around. When the fights started, he got out. And according to his mother, that was when the hitting began. In places he wouldn't have seen any bruises, she'd said. And now he was thinking he'd go after "more than one of them"? If what she was saying was that he knew her rapist and "he" was a "them"...

He wasn't himself. And yet he still felt a heavy anger brewing inside him.

"You know the family," Julie said. She was choosing her words carefully. That much was obvious. It was taking her a long time to get them out.

Too much time. Giving his mind a chance to ramble unrestrained all over the place...

Messing him up.

Beautiful, kind, sweet Julie had been raped? As a teenager? By someone she knew and trusted. Someone *he* knew.

The next question waited for him. He was avoiding it. What was he going to do with the answer?

But he had to know.

"Who?"

Her gaze met his, and Hunter's mind raced, thinking of everyone he knew among Santa Raquel's elite. Not one of them came across as even partially criminal to him. They were decent people. Pretty people. The ones he associated with anyway. They gave generously to charities.

He couldn't imagine wanting any of them dead.

His foot began to tap. He still held her hand. Both hands now. He wanted his wine, but couldn't let go of her.

"The Smyths."

Hunter stared at her. She couldn't be serious. The businessman was one of the richest men Hunter knew. And the most private. He didn't involve himself in gossip. He and his wife kept to themselves in their lovely home.

Hunter had been there for dinner several times in the past year because they preferred to donate privately. He'd only recently had some success in cajoling them into joining some of his parties.

"It was kept out of the news." Julie was speaking again. "They pretty much own the media around here."

Yeah, he'd had luck getting good press through someone Smyth knew. But...

"This doesn't make sense."

She pulled her hand away, and he had to let her go. No one was ever going to use physical force of any kind on Julie again, not if he had anything to do with it.

Yeah, and what *would* he have to do with it?

Hunter took a sip of wine. A small sip. He needed his faculties completely clear.

"The Smyths only have one son," he said. "He's married and has kids and lives on the East Coast."

Her eyes filled with tears. He wanted to wipe them away. To get up and take her surfing.

"His wife took their kids and moved home with her folks," she told him. "She's from New York. He's also on the East Coast. Part of his plea agreement. So that they can visit him if they ever decide they want to. But he's in prison. He was charged with kidnapping, among other things, and for holding his victims hostage. I was underage, too, so those are federal crimes, which means he can serve his time in any federal prison the judge deems appropriate. From what I understand, he's in one of those minimum security places for the rich and famous."

So Hunter wasn't needed. The man had already been put away. No killing necessary.

His thoughts were growing increasingly bizarre. Still, he sat there. So that was it. The "more" she'd had to tell him.

His mouth fell open. He stared at her. What an idiot he was!

"So when I was asking you to go with me to the roast…"

Smyth Sr. had been there. She must've realized he could be. And she'd gone anyway. For Joy. To help him. His incredible respect for her grew.

The woman had courage. Backbone. Strength.

More than any woman he'd ever known, his own mother included.

Not that David Smyth Sr. had been her rapist. On the contrary, the man had obviously stood aside while his son was prosecuted. Someone with his kind of money could have covered up the crime, could have conspired in making it look consensual. They'd been on a date, at a party. She'd gone there willingly. Not that he doubted Julie for one second. But he knew what money could do. How the system worked.

He'd lived in California his whole life. He read the news. And…

"Wait. He's married. Has kids…" That didn't fit with a high school girl on a date. "When was this?"

Julie stood. Wineglass in hand, she moved back to the fireplace. Hunter followed her again. He took her hand and sat on the hearth to the right of the fire. Looked up at her.

She could go. Tell him to go. She'd already said they were never going to speak about this again after tonight. She sat, too.

"The rape was ten years ago."

He realized it had to be about that. She'd moved on with her life. Graduated from college. Held charity board positions.

And she'd never dated.

Things dawned on him slowly sometimes.

This was why she wouldn't go out with him. She didn't go out with anyone.

"I came home to Colin right afterward. Told him what happened. He called the police, took me to the hospital. They did a rape kit. And they called the police, as well."

Right. He was aware of the general process. TV and all.

"Next thing we knew Colin was called into the police commissioner's office. He was barely out of law school, just taking over the family firm due to our father's unexpected and very premature death."

He was getting the picture more quickly now. Definitely wanted to take her surfing. And wanted to barf up every bite of food he'd ever eaten at the Smyth home.

But their son was in prison, so...

"David Smyth Sr. and Commissioner Reynolds had known each other all their lives. They also knew just about every lucrative client the law firm had. They said they could easily paint a picture of consensual sex. That I liked it rough, so the rape kit would only appear to confirm their theory. That they weren't even sure the rape kit had ever made it into evidence. Or if it had, that it was still there. They insinuated that it wouldn't be. They said they'd ruin my reputation and that Colin's clients would leave him." She paused, took a breath. "Everyone knew I'd been after David, that I'd had a crush on him all through high school. When he started asking me out, that was all I could talk about."

He got the picture. Had bile in his mouth. What he didn't grasp was how they got from there to now. With Smyth in jail.

"You said you and Chantel worked a case. And that's how you became associated with The Lemonade Stand."

He was in way over his head, and not for the first time, either.

But he wouldn't listen to his better judgment and leave.

Not until this was done.

And where he went after? Physically or emotionally? He'd figure that one out later.

"Chantel was new to the force, working undercover, posing as a member of an elite East Coast family. She was at an art auction and met Colin. He asked her out. She saw that as her way in to our crowd and accepted. Except that she fell in love with him."

Nice. But it had nothing to do with what he had to know.

"She was there to investigate allegations of domestic violence against a member of our social group."

"Smyth."

"No." Julie shook her head. "James Morrison. He and his wife, Leslie, were my parents' closest friends. After my mother died, Leslie became like a second mother to me. James was a great help to Colin as he took over the firm."

Hunter was more confused than ever. On edge. Sipping the wine he'd carried over with him. Feeling he was sinking deeper into a place he definitely didn't belong. And yet he couldn't *not* sit there. Holding her hand in his, resting their joined hands just above his knee.

Nothing made sense.

Including the way his heart was continuing to bleed for the woman next to him.

"There's this High Risk team here in Santa Raquel. It's made up of police, school and medical personnel and provides a means by which all these professionals come together with reports of possible domestic violence. Their hope is to prevent domestic violence deaths."

He'd heard of the team through Brett Ackerman and would soon be working on a fund-raiser for a new computer program that would give minute-to-minute mobile updates to all the team members.

"Over the course of a couple of years, Leslie had been in the hospital for injuries that drew concern. Their son was struggling at school."

Oh, God. Not Morrison, too. He was watching his donor list crumble. Not just Morrison and Smyth, but all of the people the two of them knew.

How could he take money from them, regardless of the charities and causes? How could he invite them to parties, knowing this?

How did Julie live with it all?

He looked over at her, saw the pain in her eyes. And...

Needed to give her the crest of a wave.

"I didn't know what was going on, but I was absolutely sure that James would never hurt Leslie."

Hallelujah. Hunter felt like dropping to his knees. A gesture that was far too dramatic for him. Unless he happened to be licking the floor to get a smile out of Joy.

"She wouldn't talk to Chantel, but she talked to me. Her injuries were truly accidents, but self-inflicted ones. Her psyche's way of punishing her for what she believed she should have prevented. She'd been raped by David Smyth, too."

"She didn't know about your..." He couldn't finish the sentence.

Julie's nod had his stomach lurching again.

"She knew I'd been raped. But she didn't know it was by him. Not until afterward, when he told her. She'd offered to give him a ride home when he was stranded, never thinking she'd be in danger with him."

"And by then he was already married with kids."

She shook her head. "He had just started college then. Leslie didn't tell a soul. He told her what had happened with Colin and me when I tried to claim he'd raped me. That's when she found out who my rapist was. The Smyths and the commissioner made a powerful team. The Morrisons are rich, but only because people like the Smyths and Reynolds keep their money in Morrison's bank. She knew that if anyone found out what had happened, they'd be destitute. More than that, she knew her husband would end up in jail because he'd kill Smyth himself. She also knew that coming forward, blowing her family's lives apart, wasn't going to change anything. And she couldn't face the humiliation of admitting she'd been raped by a college boy, the son of a friend of theirs. David would say it was consensual, just like he did with me. That she'd propositioned him. There'd be people who'd believe him…"

"So the two of you held on to your secrets?"

For the first time in a while, Julie's eyes filled

with tears. A small smile tilted her lips. Not with humor, but with…something.

"Chantel wouldn't let us," Julie said. "She was a junior officer and took on the police commissioner. She devised a plan to trap David into attempting to rape her. But she couldn't do it without Leslie's and my help."

"You helped her catch him."

"Yes."

"All those years later."

"I wanted to get out of my prison."

He looked at the grounds, at the mansion beside them, and understood. She'd been held hostage by lies. And fear. For more than a decade.

"I also knew, as Chantel did, that there had to be more victims. That if David had done to Leslie what he'd done to me, then he hadn't learned his lesson, despite what his father had promised us. There had to be others in between."

"Were there?"

She nodded.

"And none of this made it to the papers?"

"One thing did. Commissioner Reynolds's resignation. Chantel had a list of demands she made in order to keep her mouth shut. That was one of them. And David was charged with a laundry list of crimes. His father managed to convince him to take a plea deal so his family could be spared the publicity. Victims were paid off, and it all went quietly away."

"I'm glad it was kept quiet."

"Me, too," Julie said. "The thought of everyone knowing what I've just told you…"

"The thought of you having to go through that…"

They were looking at each other. Their faces so close.

Hunter squeezed her hand. She squeezed his.

And let go.

CHAPTER TWENTY-ONE

JULIE ALMOST DIDN'T make breakfast Monday morning. It would've been a first, but Colin and Chantel would have understood. She'd had a man at the pool.

Major life change.

She didn't want to face their questions.

Or their concern.

But when she considered the alternative—avoiding them, hiding out in her studio—she went downstairs as usual. She made fruit crepes and fresh-squeezed orange juice and had the table set by the time they showed up in the breakfast room.

"This looks great." Chantel was in the pants and jacket she wore to work now that she'd made detective. Her gun strapped at her waist used to make Julie uncomfortable. She was accustomed to it now.

Colin had his tablet on the table, open to a news source.

"You okay?" Chantel asked, just as Julie, staring at the tablet, noticed that her brother hadn't scrolled down the screen since taking his seat.

"I think I am," she said, and then to Colin, "You can relax. And...I love you."

He looked at her. Assessing. Because he would always be her big brother, watching her back.

"Thank you," she added.

He nodded. Ate his breakfast.

And not another word was said about Hunter Rafferty. Or her highly unusual night by the pool.

FOR THE FIRST TIME since his business opened Hunter was missing an important function. The Monday-night toy auction in Santa Barbara was a yearly event. In its third year with The Time of Your Life. Kyle was handling it for him. Happy to, actually.

His second-in-command had been champing at the bit to take on more responsibility. They could do twice as much business if there were two of them who could host. They'd have to hire another event manager to take Kyle's place.

Hunter wasn't ready for that. His business was built on his reputation, and his events all had the hallmark of his personality.

Or maybe he was a little too full of himself.

Or...afraid to find out that he wasn't as necessary as he thought he was. Maybe he didn't want to know if things went on just as well without him as they did when he was in attendance.

On his way to pick up Edward for a light picnic

dinner at the beach with Julie and Lila and Joy, he thrummed a quick beat on the steering wheel.

Other than the fact that police had been able to determine a direction in which Shawn had dragged Cara, based on Joy's account of seeing a shadow the morning her mother disappeared, there'd been no progress that day.

They'd discovered signs in the dirt of a struggle not far from where Joy would've seen her mother. But the sidewalk had been just past that, and the trail was lost. They'd called in dogs, but again, the trail was lost. Police were canvassing neighborhoods. Anyone who knew anything wasn't saying.

Julie had had an art session with Joy that morning. He'd been hugely relieved to hear Edward's report that Julie was carrying on as normal.

Although why he'd thought she might not be, he didn't know.

The rape and all the ensuing misconduct, the wrongdoing, had been news to him. She'd lived with the crushing effects of it for more than a decade. For her, nothing had changed.

For him, the entire world seemed to have shifted. It wasn't that he was an idealist. Or at all naive. He knew that where there was money, there was a good chance of corruption. Knew that American politics had its share. He worked with political campaigns, with candidates, with PACs. They were some of the clients who hired him.

He just hadn't realized that the men and women in this small town, some of the people on his donor list, the ones he'd grown to trust, in a business sense, had harbored an actual criminal.

Other than Brett Ackerman, who was more of a recluse than not, Hunter didn't have personal relationships with these people. They were a list of invitees. Period.

How many of them knew about the Smyths? Commissioner Reynolds? All of them, he'd bet. They could keep it out of the news, but their gossip, among themselves, was a beast of its own.

One that ate well.

According to Edward, art with Joy had not gone well that morning. Nothing bad had happened. From what he'd said, Joy had been happy to see Julie. She just hadn't said another word. Or revealed any more clues that could help them find her mother.

Which was why they were having a picnic at the beach. After a discussion between Julie, Sara and Lila—at which Julie had made the suggestion, based on her conversation with Hunter—it was determined that a trip to the beach was their best bet.

They'd all seen Joy's reaction to the mention of Edward's house by the ocean. While going to the beach might not be immediately pleasant, it would be familiar. She'd be with people who made her feel safe, and if she was frightened, maybe she'd open up to Julie again.

Over the past week, they'd been giving Joy a sense of family.

Lila and Sara felt that they needed to tell her that Edward was her grandfather. To reinforce a sense of security. She needed to understand that she had someplace to go. Family to look after her.

They also needed to prevent her from forming too close an attachment to Julie.

Bottom line, they needed Julie to continue to give her all to the little girl. But to do that knowing she was expendable. That at some point, and the sooner the better, Joy would no longer need her.

Or be in her life.

They were asking a hell of a lot from Julie, in Hunter's opinion. But if anyone could handle it, she could.

They were also attributing far too much importance to his offhand suggestion of a trip to the beach. Maybe the visit would be enough— through fear or familiarity—to trigger more information from Joy. Maybe it would just be about the sand and the water.

If their excursion sent the little girl further back into her shell, a possibility that had been discussed at length, he'd been told, he'd have more proof that he needed to stay out of the emotional arena.

A couple of blocks from Edward's hotel, Hunter's

phone rang. He pulled it out of his pocket immediately. Julie might need to—

Mandy.

He let it go to voice mail. He'd texted her earlier that day to apologize for the night before. Told her he'd make it up to her.

And he would.

She'd know he had a function tonight if she looked at his website. Which she usually did when she wanted to hook up. He'd try her later.

He'd been waiting all day for Julie's call. Thinking she'd want to check in after their time together the night before.

He was new to this…emotional…thing and had guessed wrong. He hadn't heard from her.

Told himself that was good. That he had no reason to be disappointed.

He'd never even kissed the woman. So why did he feel as though they were intimately involved? As though he was in a relationship, a committed one, for the first time in his life.

He'd been to bed with women and not felt that way.

Uncomfortable with the certainty that he was going to let her down sooner or later, he knew he had to see her.

To set things straight.

He needed out.

She hadn't called.

THEY WERE MEETING at The Lemonade Stand and would walk through the back of the property, through a locked gate to the private beach. It was down a fairly steep path, which was walled off from the property on either side of the Stand. Property also owned by Brett Ackerman. Most times the beach went unused. As a general rule, residents at the Stand preferred to stay close to the buildings, with security nearby. They held their water parties at the lovely pool on the premises, or in the Garden of Renewal. But they'd had a beach party or two.

While Joy was with her house mother, changing her sandals for tennis shoes that also went with the jeans and red short-sleeved shirt she'd chosen that morning, Julie had gone in to see Lila.

She'd been at the Stand for most of the day—minus a couple of hours for a lunch meeting to discuss final plans for Thursday night's gala—but had been busy with Joy, or discussing Joy, most of that time.

She would've liked to change from the brown pants and tailored cream shirt she'd put on for her business luncheon—and to have something other than the matching leather loafers to wear down to the beach. But she hadn't had a chance to run home and put on something else.

Her loafers would slip off easily. She'd been walking barefoot in the sand since she was a kid.

It was too cool for shorts. And her only pair of jeans was in the wash.

Lila was in jeans, which Julie had never seen her wear before. They were fairly formfitting and looked…really good. They were gray—Lila always wore brown or gray—but she'd topped them with a lighter-colored short-sleeved cotton shirt. And tennis shoes. Stunned, Julie stared for a moment.

And then grinned. "You look great."

"I look like I'm going to work in my garden," the older woman said as they entered her office, and Lila locked the door behind them.

"I didn't know you had a garden," Julie said as they settled on the couch. They were meeting Hunter and Edward in the lobby out front, but had a few minutes. Sara would be bringing Joy to them shortly.

"At my condominium. It's small. Tomatoes. Cucumbers. That's it."

Julie couldn't imagine gardening. Or imagine Lila doing it, either. For a while she'd been feeling as if she and Lila had a lot in common. They were both accomplished, independent women. And they both lived single lives, dedicating themselves to charity work, with no immediate families of their own.

Lila had always seemed content. Complete. Peaceful.

Exactly what Julie wanted to be.

"I'd like to talk to you for a second," she said now. They didn't have much time, at least not for personal conversation. And she had to speak with Lila. Not Sara, or Bloom Larson, her therapist.

"What's up?" The other woman's immediate attention was a balm, but it made her nervous, too.

"I need your opinion on something."

Lila nodded, her hands in her lap. "Fine."

"Do you think that everything's possible for every person? That traditional choices, societal norms, are the best way to happiness?" She held her breath. Not sure what answer she wanted. Just knowing that she couldn't let hope be born where it didn't belong.

Lila studied her as if they had all day. They didn't. They only had a few minutes and...

"I'm not clear on what you're asking me," she finally said.

"I'm talking about relationships. Personal partnerships. Do you think everyone has to have one to be happy?"

Lila didn't have one. Julie needed to know if she was happy.

Because after the night before with Hunter...

She couldn't afford to waste her limited ability to hope on something that wasn't right for her.

"I'm confused...by some of the things I see and hear that don't seem to go together. We talk about healing with our residents, talk about hope for the future and the happiness that awaits them. We talk about everyone having the right to find their own happiness. But…are we being fair? I mean, what if a partner relationship *isn't* what's best for someone, isn't that person's way to happiness?"

Lila's expression was serious as she answered slowly. "Sometimes, things happen to people that change them. Or things *they* do that change them. Sometimes, because of things that have happened because of them or to them, even things done by them, people can't be in partner relationships. It doesn't mean, however, that they can't be happy. It just means they have to find another path to that happiness."

Julie swallowed. Because she knew Lila was right. She was describing Julie as well as if she was inside her mind. Her heart.

"But…" Her voice broke, but she pushed forward. "What about healing?"

That was where her confusion lay. Sara and Bloom Larson—Chantel's psychiatrist friend to whom she'd referred Julie—talked about the next phases of her life. Everything that came after healing.

Bloom was a former victim. And she probably had the happiest, sexiest relationship in town to hear Chantel talk about it. Many of the Stand's residents had moved on to find truly happy lives.

And there were some people, like Julie, whose

psyches had been so damaged they weren't equipped to be healthy partners in a relationship. Her own psyche had been broken not only by the rape, but by the death of her parents shortly before that, and then ten years of being a virtual prisoner because of the lie she lived and her constant fear of running into the man who'd raped her.

"You've come to me because I'm alone." Lila was looking her straight in the eye.

Julie gave her the same respect, holding her gaze. "Yes." Julie needed to know if she should be, too. And if it was better for her to stay alone, could she still be happy?

"I'm happy, Julie. Maybe in ways you can't understand. Ways I never thought I'd be…"

Lila's voice faded as voices sounded in the hall. The older woman smiled, and said, "Trust me, my dear. I'm happy."

Julie wanted to believe that and to be happy for Lila. To feel good about accepting the other woman's answer. To take hope that one day she'd understand. And that she'd be happy in ways she'd never thought she would be. Instead, as Sara knocked and entered with Joy, Julie was left with an overwhelming sense of sadness.

CHAPTER TWENTY-TWO

HUNTER AND EDWARD talked about golf all the way to the Stand. Golf courses. Golf scores. Golf clubs. Golf games between Edward and John Rafferty. Edward had found his match in John. Hunter wasn't the least bit surprised to hear it.

Edward was about to be introduced as grandpa to his only grandchild, and he talked about golf.

A man after Hunter's own heart.

You'd think they were related by blood, not just marriage.

As usual, he hung back as the party gathered and headed toward the grounds, through the garden and woods beyond, to the gate that led down to the beach. If not for the security guards around the place, and the surveillance cameras and security lights he saw mounted even on trees in the woods, he could be forgiven for thinking he was at an expensive, private resort.

Julie had smiled in his general direction when they met in the lobby. But with Joy attached to her hand, she'd been otherwise engaged.

Giving Hunter plenty of time to watch her.

And to hate himself for finding her backside so attractive in those pants she was wearing.

The last thing Julie needed, or would want, was a guy lusting after her.

Because Joy was going to be told Edward was her grandfather, Sara had opted to join them at the beach. Hunter liked the counselor.

But he didn't like how she monopolized Julie whenever Julie wasn't speaking directly to Joy. It wasn't as if he'd expected to have any kind of personal…moment with Julie, but a meeting of the eyes would be nice.

Something to acknowledge that they'd become more to each other last evening than they'd been the morning before.

They were just approaching the beach when it occurred to him that maybe Julie was avoiding any contact between them.

That maybe she was regretting the night before.

He told himself he was glad about that and tried to focus his mind on being the life of the party. He hadn't even gotten a start when they stepped onto the sand and Joy stopped in her tracks.

Meaning that Hunter, who'd been behind them, nearly ran into her. He leaped around her instead, lost his balance and somersaulted in the sand. After that, he danced around like a crazy fool, trying to get the sand out of his shirt and pants.

"It tickles!" he exclaimed, dancing backward on to the beach.

"You like sand in your clothes?" he asked Joy, who was watching him—and letting Julie lead her closer to him.

She looked at Julie, who then looked at him. Finally.

Joy followed her lead.

"You know what I hate most? Sand in my shoes." With that he kicked off one of his deck shoes, backward, so that it flew behind him, and he caught it over his shoulder.

A stupid trick he'd practiced for months during his partying years in high school. The guys had always been drunk enough to find his pranks funny. And he'd always had invitations to parties.

The movement of Joy's head followed the line of his shoe as it landed in his hand. He kicked off the left shoe. It had taken him a lot longer to perfect that one. Thank goodness he'd gone to so many parties. When he caught it, the little girl laughed out loud.

GRANT AND DARIN BISHOP had set up the picnic for them. They were brothers, one of whom—Grant, a local landscape artist who also maintained the grounds at the Stand—was married to the resident nurse. The other, Darin, had suffered brain damage and lived with them, together with his wife and child on the property. The picnic dinner came complete with table, tablecloth, a basket filled with plastic dishes and food, and a cooler with drinks. They'd be down later to carry everything back to the Stand.

Joy sat in the middle on one side of the plastic folding picnic table, with Edward directly across from her. Lila and Sara flanked Edward. Julie and Hunter were on either side of Joy. Sitting across from Lila, Julie took strength from the older woman. Absorbed her calm. The plan was to tell Joy about Edward as soon as dessert was served.

Chocolate cupcakes. Joy chose them any time she went through the cafeteria line.

Sweets to go with sweet news.

They hoped.

But first…

Sara was running the show. Julie felt confident that things wouldn't deteriorate to disaster level mainly because Hunter was there.

She hadn't wanted to tune in to him. To have him stand out from the rest of the people present. Hadn't wanted to feel anything at all where he was concerned.

There was no point.

Then he'd gone and flipped on the sand—and her heart had flipped right with him.

Sara talked about when she'd been little and had a picnic with her family at the beach. Edward, speaking to Sara, related a time he'd taken his little girl snorkeling. Hunter talked about surfing, about what a blast he had whenever he went out.

His litany had been planned, as had all of theirs. They were attempting to shine a light on things that might be lurking inside Joy. A safe, secure light. Clearly the little girl trusted Hunter. She didn't seem disturbed by the fact that he was a surfer, too.

Until it was her turn, Julie mostly held her breath. And pretended to eat the club sandwich and fruit on her plate. Joy, on the other hand, had her sandwich almost gone. Her legs were swinging beneath the table. She'd glanced at Julie's full plate at least three times.

"Amy doesn't like club sandwiches that much," Julie said, feeling inane. Joy knew that Amy was really Julie. Just a younger version.

As far as Hunter and Edward were concerned— Amy was merely a character in a book Joy had become attached to. And that Julie was using the Amy books in art therapy. The distinction, the reminder that Hunter didn't know, was important to her.

She took a bite of her sandwich and tried not to think about what was coming.

She didn't want Joy hurt. Upset. Scared. But the little girl couldn't continue to live in limbo, either.

And if Joy could help her mother…

The tide was coming in. Waves lapped more loudly against the shore. Julie watched them, wondering what it would feel like to ride one. Her stomach jumped. She had a hard time swallowing the food in her mouth.

Sara and Lila both glanced at her.

Her stomach jumped again. And seemed to lodge in her throat. It was her turn to speak.

"Joy, you remember yesterday when we were at the park and you told me some secrets?"

The little girl stared at the middle of the table.

"It's okay, sweetie," she continued, knowing that it was the right thing to do. That there had to be some pressure applied to this wound now. And that the person who stood the greatest chance of stopping the bleeding was her. "You're safe."

Sara had said to get that point across over and over. Because Joy's life had clearly not left her with a feeling of security, and to a seven-year-old, safety, security and food were the driving forces.

Taking a slow breath, she thought about Amy. Trusted Amy. Put herself in Amy's shoes.

"Do you remember the story where Amy made a choice to eat all that candy without permission? She felt sick to her stomach and thought she might throw up, but then she told her mom about it and her mom gave her something to drink to settle her stomach, and it turned out that just telling her mother made her feel better. Because it was really the secret that was making her feel so bad."

Julie had read the book to Joy. A couple of times. Joy hadn't seemed to respond. But it was about Amy, and that was the best Julie had.

"Secrets do that," she went on. "They stay inside and sometimes they get bigger and eventually they can make you sick. So I'm glad you told me what you did yesterday."

Amy always wanted to do the right thing. She'd wanted to be good for her mother because it made her mother happy when she was good...

"And you remember the mommy book?" she said now, going with the flow in her mind. The ocean was there, in the distance. The sun's heat was still potent enough to warm the sand. The others at the table were completely supportive, completely focused, and yet, they faded, too.

"Amy always tried to do what her mommy wanted because she loved her so much, and she wanted to make her happy."

Joy looked at her.

"Your mommy told you to be quiet."

Big brown eyes wide, Joy stared at Julie.

"She told you to hide."

Amy was afraid. And she hid from her own

shadow. Something that kept following her. Popping up in different places.

"But she didn't tell me to be quiet or to hide," Julie continued. "And I told these people about what happened. About your mommy being taken away by the monster. And they've spent all day trying to find her. To help her."

The girl's lower lip started to tremble. Was it because she felt betrayed? Or grateful?

"You did the right thing, Joy. You did what Amy would have done. You're such a brave, strong girl, and we all love you."

She rambled on. The words were tumbling out almost faster than she could speak them. Julie didn't question her comments or her insights. She glanced at Hunter once.

He sat there quietly, his expression serious. He wasn't joking. He was supporting her, supporting Joy and Edward.

Feeling stronger, she resumed speaking. "Right now, your mommy needs your help." Julie was finding words she'd been afraid wouldn't come. "She needs you to tell us anything you can that might help us figure out where she is. That way we can save her and bring her here, so she's safe from the monster, too."

Not take her home. Home was where the monster came back. Again and again.

"Can you do that, Joy? I know Amy would try. Will you try?"

Still staring at her, only at her, the little girl nodded.

Julie felt tears coming but shoved them away. Now was not the time. "Do you know where the monster would take her?"

Joy shook her head.

"Is there any place he used to take both of you? Any place he liked to go?"

She shook her head again.

Julie had been told what to ask. She so badly wanted to get the answers the police needed. She felt Edward across from them. She didn't hear him breathe, didn't sense any movement at all. But she sensed him there. Willing his toppled world upright again. Needing to do something to help his two girls.

"When you saw the shadow, did you think about where it might be headed?" It was an Amy question, not a Julie one.

"To Dan's."

"Dan's." She forced her voice to remain calm while her heart started to pound.

Joy nodded.

"Who's Dan?"

This time Joy shrugged.

"Is he the monster's friend?"

She nodded. Her gaze hadn't left Julie's face.

Hunter remained still on the other side of her. "Do you know where he lives?"

She nodded again.

Julie wanted to look at Sara, at Lila, for direction. But she didn't dare lose Joy's complete focus. She could see Hunter behind the little girl. He wasn't sending any signals.

Or putting an end to the moment.

She wasn't going to ask Joy to take them to Dan's. Maybe Sara would do that. Or the police. Julie couldn't. It felt like a betrayal of the trust Joy's sweet little heart had placed in her.

But…

She pulled a small sketch pad out of the bag she'd carried down. The pad wasn't there for the picnic. It was there because Julie never went anywhere without the means to access Amy.

"Can you draw it for me? Show me how you'd go from where you saw the shadow to Dan's?"

A first name might be enough for someone to figure out who the man was. Where he lived. That wasn't Julie's call. All she knew was that she didn't want to repeat this exercise a second time. She had to get what she could from Joy now and then simply be her friend. Her grown-up Amy.

Someone just to be there.

Joy looked at the pad. Julie set a pencil down on the table, then held her breath until Joy slowly picked it up.

The drawing was crude. Boxes and lines. With a couple of stick trees. It might help, though. And it might be completely illegible. Julie's heart swelled almost to bursting at Joy's effort.

"Okay," she said, leaving the paper to sit there. "That's so good, Joy. Your mommy's going to be so proud of you."

She blinked away tears. "I'm so proud of you."

Joy was staring at her again. Shutting the others out. Julie followed her lead, ignoring everyone else at the table. A hurting heart had its limits. She understood completely.

"One more thing," she added, "then I think Amy would want some dessert, and I do, too, because I like dessert better than club sandwiches…"

This wasn't part of the script. It was coming straight from the heart of one who knew what it felt like to keep the monster secret.

"Do you know the monster's name?"

Joy nodded, her face wearing a terrified expression.

"If you tell me his name, thinking of him won't be so scary." *Trust me, sweetheart*, her soul implored. *This is one promise I can make you.*

Joy's hand crept to Julie's lap, sliding under her palm.

Julie covered it more completely, wrapping her fingers gently around that little hand, vowing she'd do whatever it took to make sure that Joy would not spend a decade—or even a month—locked in the hell of her own memories.

"Do you trust me?" she pressed.

Joy nodded again.

"Can you tell me the monster's name?"

Joy nodded. Frowned, her eyes stark with fear. With doubt. And then she took a breath and opened her mouth.

"His name's Daddy."

CHAPTER TWENTY-THREE

After all the buildup in Hunter's mind about the great unveiling of Edward to his granddaughter, that part of the picnic was anticlimactic. Probably a testimony to Sara and her skill at her job.

Certainly a testimony to Julie Fairbanks's willingness to love the little girl. To be her interim security.

They still didn't know if Joy's seeming aversion to the beach had to do with the fact that she feared anything she associated with her father, or if there'd been a particular incident.

Hunter hoped Shawn Amos hadn't taken his wife out to sea and left her there. And kept that supposition to himself.

"Sorry it didn't go better for you," he said to Edward after they'd covered more than a mile in silence on their way back to Edward's hotel.

There were just some things that golf talk couldn't cover up. Not many, in Hunter's life, but some.

Well, one. This one.

"What?" Edward shook his head as though

coming out of a trance. "Oh, Hunter, no, that was…she was… Did you see her look at me? Those adorable brown eyes giving me the once-over, like she was deciding whether or not I was a good guy. So discerning. Just like my Cara. She'd look at me with those serious eyes, too, even when she was a baby, and I knew I'd never be able to fool her. About anything.

"Never tried, either," he continued, a smile on his face.

What the heck.

"Edward, Joy didn't speak to you." *Great, man, rub it in.*

"No, but she looked." The man sent another grinning glance his way.

Hunter didn't get it. But he was glad Edward wasn't taking the rejection as badly as Hunter had feared. Of course, there was always the chance the older man was in denial.

Who could blame him? First, losing his daughter to Shawn, then losing her to the fiend a second time. And now, having his granddaughter show no emotion at finding out he existed?

"I was prepared for her to turn her back on me. To hide away inside herself again. Instead she stood right there and studied me. She's interested. And open to the possibility."

So, yeah. Hunter could see that.

It was just that he felt superfluous. Which

should be pleasing him. One of Hunter's avowed goals in life was to slide away from the tough stuff. So if Edward didn't need his help anymore...

He should be celebrating. Or at least feeling relieved.

The man's daughter was missing, considered to be in danger. Of course, Edward still needed support.

His name's Daddy.

Joy's words had been stabbing at him since she'd uttered them more than an hour before.

His name's Daddy.

How did things get so mucked up? A father scaring his little girl to the point that she couldn't speak. Physically abusing his daughter's mother.

And his own sister.

Mary Amos still lay in the hospital, in a medically induced coma, fighting for her life.

He had no answers for any of that.

He'd grown up with a great father. And from what he'd seen of Edward, Cara had, too. The man was ready to pop the cork on a bottle of champagne because his granddaughter had looked at him. Because she hadn't run screaming in the other direction. He'd put his whole life on hold to be there for them.

Cara had turned her back on that. Rejected a decent man for an abusive one.

And Hunter?

"I'm not good at this." He couldn't keep pretending. Not with Edward. "My father should've warned you. I don't know what you need. How to help."

Truth was, he couldn't believe he was still there. Sacrificing his party for a man he barely knew.

And at the same time, he couldn't believe there was nothing he'd rather be doing.

"You're doing just fine," Edward said, glancing at him. "This is family. I appreciate you welcoming me in."

Was that what he'd done?

"I owe my dad a lot."

"Not to hear him tell it."

Of course not. Dr. John Rafferty was too classy to trash-talk his own son. Even to family. Especially to family.

"He's proud of you."

That bounced off him. But it reminded him of Julie telling Joy she was proud of her. For a second there, he'd been jealous of the little girl. He'd wondered how it would feel to have Julie's personal admiration.

"There was a time when that wasn't the case. My dad being proud of me, I mean." What was he doing?

"You're talking about high school."

And afterward. When his father had needed

him and he hadn't been able to testify, under oath, to save him.

"He blames himself, you know."

Stopped at a light, Hunter turned to the other man. His father had confided in Edward? About him?

"Blames himself for what?" He didn't want this conversation. He was just truly perplexed. His old man had been far more patient than Hunter deserved. He'd guided him in a quest to find his own talents. And then he'd challenged Hunter to use them. Supporting his choices when they were far less worthy than medical school.

"Being gone all the time. And when he was home, he and your mother… All the fighting…"

Hunter shrugged. "They weren't well suited."

"He said they both turned to you for their happiness. Putting too much pressure on you."

He'd felt the pressure. And their failure, too. It had ended up in court with his father facing the possible loss of his medical license and maybe even time in jail.

"He doesn't have your gift…"

He shook his head, made a turn, and shook his head again. "My father doesn't doubt his own abilities."

"No, he doesn't. He knows what he's good at. You're like him in that."

Hunter agreed. Thankful that his father had

forced him to face the truth, to accept who he was. And who he wasn't.

To know his own weaknesses, to be accountable for them. And to build on his strengths.

"Your father is a great doctor. Medicine, science, the human body—he's mastered all of that. But it all came at a cost. Same with me..."

Sirens went off in his mind. Was Edward blaming himself for Cara's leaving Florida? For his daughter's captivity? The danger she was in? For the abuse she'd suffered? For what had happened to Joy?

"My father is not to blame for my choices," he said, hoping Edward would get at least a hint of the point he was making. See the truth. That Edward was absolutely not to blame for the pain in their lives.

"When I was younger, when Cara's mom was alive, I had different priorities than I do now. Everything took second place to medical school and then, later, to my career. It's not that I didn't love my wife—and Cara—more than anything on earth. It's just that I took their presence for granted. I expected them to take my love for granted, too. And I chose actions that made them feel as though they didn't matter as much to me as being a doctor did."

"I never doubted my father's affection. Or my importance in his life."

"Maybe not. But apparently your mother did. My wife was very different from your mother. Beth was independent and wanted a life outside of house and home. Your mom's happiness lay in being a wife and mother. Your father knew that going in."

Screamed words came to mind. *I needed you. You weren't here. Where were you? I called but you didn't answer.* Over and over through the years. Different renditions of the same message.

He'd hear the words and know that the emotions driving them were real. And that they were true. He could sympathize with them. Could feel his mother's pain. But he also understood that his father was saving lives. That he loved his family, was thankful they were healthy, and that he'd give every cent he had to keeping them safe and secure. At the same time, his calling was to save lives.

"They weren't right for each other," he said now. His mother's emotional neediness, her expectations regarding the role of a husband in her life, hadn't suited his father's more pragmatic outlook on life.

"The thing is, your father and I—whether it's because of the generation we grew up in, because of the emotional distance necessary to practice medicine…or just because, we don't have your ability, Hunter. We fix bodies, but…you have a way of lightening emotional trauma. Having you with me this week—and I hope in the days to come... Well, thank you."

"Just don't count on me too much. My father might not have told you, but in the end, I bail."

The look Edward gave him was piercing.

But he didn't say a word.

LILA HAD DISAPPEARED into her office to call the police as soon as they'd come from the picnic. Sara took Joy back to her house mother. Hunter took Edward home.

And Julie decided she'd earned a few hours in her studio. Colin and Chantel were spending the night at her little apartment in town, as they did on occasion when Chantel needed some down-time, so Julie planned to spend a leisurely evening once she got home. She thought about making an omelet and was staring into the refrigerator when her cell phone rang.

Hunter.

"Hi." She didn't hesitate to pick up. Not even for a second. "I'm glad you called."

"You are?"

His astonishment put a halt to her pleasure, but only for a second. "Yeah. We didn't get a chance to say hello earlier. And I've been thinking about Edward. I hoped you'd call after you dropped him off."

"You could've called me."

But she wouldn't. He probably knew that.

"How is he?"

"Surprisingly upbeat."

"I thought it went well, too. Telling her he's her grandfather, I mean."

"You did?"

"You didn't?"

"It seemed…uneventful to me."

"That's because you were prepared for drama."

When he was silent she was afraid she'd overstepped the bounds. Or that she was assuming she knew him better than she really did.

"Have dinner with me."

"What?" They were back to that again?

"You didn't eat. You must be hungry."

"I figured you'd be going to your event."

Edward had mentioned, as they were all gathering for their picnic, that Hunter had had to make arrangements for his absence from work that evening.

"Kyle wants to try and run things on his own. This was a chance to see how he does."

His faith in his employee, his willingness to let someone try, made her smile.

"So, can I pick you up for dinner?"

Her eye landed on a bowl of fruit. There was Havarti in the bottom drawer of the fridge. And her favorite crackers in the pantry.

"I don't date."

"So you've said—more than once. I'm offering to take you to dinner because I know for a fact that you didn't eat. I'm not offering to pay. Or expecting to kiss you good-night when we're through."

She could invite him over.

Colin and Chantel were gone.

"I've... I haven't...ridden alone in a car with a man since..."

Maybe he'd ask to come over.

And if he did?

Colin and Chantel were gone.

"I guess I don't have an answer to that one, Julie. Either you trust me or you don't. I'd like to come by and pick you up, go to some restaurant, talk for a while, unwind a bit about what we went through tonight, and then drop you off at your front door."

He didn't know Colin and Chantel weren't home.

And the fact that she'd even paused before saying no meant her entire life was changing. *She* was changing. Growing stronger. Learning to have courage. Refusing to settle for less. Refusing to be locked inside her own hell.

Except there was one thing that wouldn't change.

"As long as you understand it's not a date."

Like Lila, she'd been through too much to be a healthy partner in an intimate relationship.

"You're serious?"

"Yes." Being wrong was better than being afraid.

"Then head on out. I'm already here."

"Give me a minute."

"Take as long as you need. But keep in mind I'm still in my beach clothes."

So was she. And she wasn't going to change.

It wasn't a date.

Ending the call, she pushed another button on her phone. Chantel's speed dial. And told her sister-in-law what she was doing, and with whom, arranging for Chantel to text her regularly, and to come looking for her if she didn't respond.

She was finding her courage.

But she wasn't stupid. She was a woman who had to know she had a safety plan, a backup plan.

No exceptions. Ever.

CHAPTER TWENTY-FOUR

HUNTER HAD ALWAYS been a go-with-the-flow type of guy. And he'd grown into a guy who controlled the flow so that he could more easily, seamlessly and painlessly go with it.

That week, he'd scheduled time for Edward. For Joy. For a meeting with Kyle to talk about the transference of one event a week to his complete care. And time for Julie, too. There was no getting her out of his mind while they were both involved with Joy.

So he went with the flow. He didn't fight how often she was on his mind. Or how compelled he was to at least touch base with her every day. He just put it in his schedule. Monday night's dinner aside, of course. That one had been impromptu because he'd wanted to give Kyle his chance.

Because he'd been…dissatisfied when he'd dropped Edward off.

Because he hadn't had a chance to talk to her earlier that day.

Dinner had been…nice. Nothing more than

food and conversation. About Joy. Edward. About surfing.

And then, exactly as he'd said, he'd driven her home, walked her to her front door and waited on the step until he heard the lock turn.

Tuesday and Wednesday she went to the Stand to work with Joy. She saw her counselor in town, a Dr. Bloom Larson. Someone she thought he should meet at some point.

He wasn't sure why. She'd just said, when she mentioned it on the phone Tuesday night, that he might like to meet her sometime. He figured Julie saw the woman as a potential donor for his list. She drove a Jaguar; he'd gleaned that much from a story she'd told him about the therapist packing her belongings in it when she'd had to go into a safe house the previous summer.

He'd had meetings and functions—a total of six over those same two days. One breakfast, two golf dates, a lunch and two dinners. He'd made it to all of them, at least long enough to greet everyone at the door, or on the first tee, for one golf event, and in the clubhouse at the eighteenth green for the other.

Every night, on his way home, he called Julie.

Edward had told him earlier that day that the police had located "Dan." In jail. On narcotics charges. He'd been there for almost a month.

His house had been lived in more recently

than that. The trash had indicated as much. But it looked like that had been a week ago.

They'd also discovered his van was missing.

An APB was out, but so far nothing had turned up.

Joy was talking more. A sentence or two to Julie. Single-word answers to her house mother. To Sara. And Lila.

Joy had seen Edward each day. For a few minutes, with Lila there. She hadn't said a word in his presence.

On Wednesday night, Hunter was pulling into his driveway, still on the phone with Julie. His house was a lot more ordinary. But nice. With an immaculate yard, trees and a view of the ocean.

"Joy asked about you today," she said. He stopped the car on the drive, the automatic door to his two-car garage open and waiting.

He didn't know what to say at first. He stared into the garage at the '72 Jag that had been his father's pride and joy when Hunter was growing up. The old man had given it to him when his mother had dropped the abuse charges and he'd left for Florida.

"She wants to see you."

"I don't know if that's a good idea. It's not like I'm part of her caregiving, like the rest of you. She shouldn't get too attached…" He hated the words even as he recognized them as the right ones to say. He shouldn't want to see Joy.

"She's your cousin, Hunter."

He had to see this through.

"Second cousin." He'd done the math. And added, "By marriage. Which makes her a second stepcousin." In other words, he had no business getting attached. Or allowing her to get attached. "I've never even met her mother."

His first stepcousin. By marriage.

"She's still family."

He sat there, fingers drumming on the steering wheel, looking at the Jag. He'd earned a car because he'd had one conversation with his mother about how much more fun she and Hunter could have together if she dropped her charges against his father. He might've said a little more than that, but he honestly couldn't remember any details. She'd apparently admitted then, to her attorney, who'd told his father's attorney, that she'd only pressed charges because she was panicked that he was leaving her. She'd been trying to keep him in California. After talking to Hunter, she'd realized that he was going to leave her anyway and she was hurting her relationship with her son. He might have pointed out that his father would be more likely to be cooperative with settlement matters if she didn't ruin his life, but mostly he'd just talked about how much more he and his mother could enjoy their time together if she wasn't fighting with his father.

Yeah, he was always about the good time.

"You think Joy would like a ride in a convertible?"

"What? Probably. Most kids do. But what convertible?"

He just went on talking. "If Lila and Sara approve, of course," he said. "And Edward. He's her grandfather." He was merely thinking out loud, he told himself. Not babbling like an idiot.

"Would you like me to make the necessary arrangements?"

"That would be fine." He knew better. It wouldn't be fine until he was through with all of them. "You'll need to be there. I don't want to do this without you there." Julie understood how to handle the fragile little girl.

"Okay."

Wow. He'd arranged a get-together for the two of them without having to beg. What a far way they'd come.

She wasn't really a friend. Although she was closer than any friend he'd ever had. She wasn't a girlfriend. They'd never even kissed.

She wasn't a permanent part of his life.

And yet…for now, he was addicted to her.

"You still haven't told me where we're going to get the convertible. And when can you go?"

They had the gala the next night. He had yet to ask his question about that.

One thing at a time.

"From my garage. And Friday afternoon?" He'd given Kyle Friday night's event—a fashion show to raise funds for a junior dance company. He was taking both Saturday gigs.

"You have a convertible."

"It's my dad's, actually. I just have the keys to it. And it lives in my garage." Plus, the title was in his name. But it didn't feel like his. He didn't believe he'd earned it.

Now, the Escalade... That he'd worked damned hard to afford. He took complete ownership of that one. Happily. Proudly.

"I have a meeting in LA Friday afternoon, but I could be back by three," she said, giving another easy acquiescence, a minor miracle, while he was busily preening over his SUV.

She said she'd talk to Lila. He was going to mention the drive to Edward, whom he'd met for lunch that day. And who'd invited Lila to Thursday night's gala as his guest.

Since it was Julie's event, the director had told him she'd be happy to attend.

"I'm guessing you're home by now," Julie said. That was when they'd hung up the night before.

He considered pulling back out of his drive so he could tell her no.

"I'd like you to agree to let me pick you up and take you to the gala tomorrow night." He'd been thinking about it all day. Been working up to asking her.

And he felt like a teenager. Worse than he'd ever felt when he was in his teens. Nothing like the thirty-three-year-old man he was now.

"Before you say no, it doesn't make sense for Colin to drive out so early, when I'm going that way at the same time you are." And no reason for her brother and his wife to have to wait around afterward, either.

"What makes you think I'm not planning to drive myself?"

She always did—anyplace he'd known her to go. But only during the day.

"Because it's at night," he said, stating the obvious. Surely she wasn't going to pretend they hadn't come this far.

"It's not like it's a date," he continued. "We're both working…"

Yeah, he'd spent way too much time on this one. And he didn't want to find out why it mattered to him, so he wasn't asking.

"Okay."

"Okay?" And he thought he'd felt stupid before. That was nothing compared to sitting there in the dark, grinning from ear to ear.

"I…was actually thinking about the fairness of

asking you for a ride," she told him. "You're right. It makes sense. I hate to put Colin out on my account. He's got his own life and schedule and—"

"And why wouldn't it be fair to ask me?" he interrupted.

"I don't want to lead you on."

So they'd come some distance. And they hadn't. He'd known that. Disappointment consumed the air around him.

But not for long. Because he didn't know how to dwell with it. And had no interest in learning. "So... I'll pick you up at four?" Their guests would start arriving at five thirty. Which would give them an hour together before they had to kick it into gear.

"I'll be ready."

"I'm looking forward to it." There. Disappointment gone. He was going to have fun.

"Me, too." He figured she was messing with him. That this was another example of the dry humor she'd treated him to during their first encounters.

Crazy thing was, this time she'd sounded as though she meant the words. And his body was happy about that. Lead him on, hell. He'd already reached his destination.

JULIE HAD ELEGANT CLOTHES. One of her favorite semiannual events—starting from her thirteenth birthday—was a benefits luncheon that included season previews from the country's top designers. A portion of every purchase went to the chosen charity. She'd attended it with her mother the first few times. Julie loved clothes. Always had.

Most of them she donated.

But her closet was full.

Thursday night's choice wasn't difficult, though. There was one dress, black with a silvery shimmer on the bodice, that had transformed her the minute she'd felt it slide over her body. It fit to perfection, hugging her shape. The dress wasn't revealing at all, yet it made her feel attractive in a mysterious kind of way. A hint of who she'd once been.

The shoes she'd purchased to go with the dress were high-heeled. And a bit daring. They were brand-new. And had been on her shelf for months.

She'd known all week she was going to wear the ensemble.

Hunter was…safe. She could allow herself to feel pretty. To tap into a little of her quashed feminine power. Not to use on anyone. Just for herself. Just to feel good.

She added diamond earrings that Colin had given her, her mother's diamond necklace, and a diamond and onyx ring she'd purchased for herself from a shopping show on television.

Her purse, a silk-strapped evening clutch,

moved gently against her hip as she walked down hallways and through the quiet rooms of the only home she'd ever known. She'd slid down the bannisters she was clutching now as she made her way downstairs. Laughed until she'd almost wet her pants after pranking her older brother. She'd done it all. Loose lid on the salt shaker. Cellophane on his toilet seat—funny but not cool. Mocking and giggling whenever a girl called.

And she'd been the one who'd given those girls a piece of her mind, too, when one of the rejected suitors started spreading rumors about him, saying he was into threesomes.

His sexual choices mattered to her not at all as long as they were legal and he was happy. But for someone to spread lies about him…

Trying to limit his chances to find true love—at least that was how she'd seen it back then.

And right after their mother had died…

She'd written an exposé for the school newspaper about the evil of spreading rumors. She was the paper's editor that year, so she was able to get it printed. She hadn't named any names, but by describing a certain situation, she'd exposed the girl for what she'd done. And talked about the dangers of spreading trash that would ultimately hurt the person doing the spreading, too. She'd talked about bitterness and the peril of always blaming someone else.

And karma had come visiting Julie the very next year in the form of a truth she could not tell. And a lie she had to live.

She'd made some bad choices. Being so desperate to date the school's star quarterback, the best-looking boy she knew, the boy every girl wanted, was one of them. She'd let her body sail away with her heart.

No more.

Her stomach might be swarming with nerves, her heart fluttery, but her body was protected by her mind.

And her mind told her that Hunter Rafferty was not a threat.

CHAPTER TWENTY-FIVE

HUNTER STUMBLED WHEN Julie opened her door as he was approaching to knock. He played it off. Stumbled a second time and made some stupid-ass comment about a court jester coming to call on the princess. He saved the moment.

And based on Julie's eye-rolling and the grin on her face, maybe the evening, too.

And maybe he'd even saved a friendship. If they'd progressed that far.

What he didn't save was himself.

By God, she was beautiful. He'd never been so hungry for a woman.

Yet the thought of taking her back inside that house or any house, to her bed or any bed, didn't light an immediate fire within him.

Or fan the flames she'd already lit.

For the first time in his life, he didn't just want bed.

He wanted that grin. The eye-rolling.

The realization hit him like a wave he'd mis-calculated. A tsunami. Leaving him without air to breathe. Confused. His world spinning with a sickening force.

She didn't seem to notice. Talked about the upcoming evening during the drive to the private oceanfront villa with a full-size theater where they were holding the gala. The acts would be showing up at five. Each group of performers had been allotted their own dressing room. The window blinds would be pulled up during the first hour while guests mingled and had hors d'oeuvres, allowing them to enjoy the ocean view. The blinds would come down at the beginning of the salad course. The lights would dim, but not go out. And the first act would come onstage. The first paid act—requiring guests to push the buttons at their seat indicating their willingness to donate further—was scheduled over dessert. Guests who didn't choose to pay wouldn't be staying for dessert.

Most of his events had closed guest lists, but tonight's gala did not. A certain number of guests would be able to purchase tickets at the door— enough to fill the dinner theater. He could've had it filled by invite only, but Julie had wanted people who weren't on the invitation lists to have an opportunity to attend. He'd been all about the money. He could get it for her guaranteed, or they could take a chance on not filling the room. They'd compromised by leaving sixteen seats—two tables of eight—open.

Trina was his event manager that evening. She'd be handling the payments that came in to keep the evening going. As long as there was one payment, on one tablet, at one table, the next act would go on.

He'd already paid all the performers. Ticket sales had made that possible. But the tickets had been priced lower than those for most of his events. The idea was to show people such a good time that they'd pay extra to stay. And in the end, the event would make more money than a set price would've brought. It was a risk he'd taken with great success in the past.

A risk Julie had opted to take when they'd first met to discuss the types of events he could do for her.

Her willingness to take the risk had been one of the first things that had drawn him to her.

And maybe it was that willingness that still called out to him. He had the thought just after five as he watched her speak with another Sunshine Children's League board member, who'd come early to support their effort and speak with guests as they arrived. Anyone who was acquainted with Julie in her current life would probably see her as the farthest thing from a risk taker.

Knowing what he knew about her now, he could see how they could think that.

So why couldn't he accept that she wasn't going to take any big risks with her personal life?

She caught him watching her as she walked toward him—as beautiful as any runway model, yet so much more. His mouth opened for the joke that would come as she reached him. The light repartee. But it didn't happen. He noticed the glow of confidence about her as she relayed the message that twelve of the sixteen open seats were already filled. He'd suggested that instead of selling online tickets for those last seats, they only give them to people who showed up at the door, ensuring that they were going to attend the show. And hopefully spend more once they got there.

They weren't out just to sell tickets, but to have guests who'd continue to donate.

All three of his employees were working that evening. Kyle was backstage with the acts. And Bob with catering. Even after The Time of Your Life got its usual percentage, the Children's League stood to gain the many thousands it needed.

"You look great," he said to her as they moved toward the main entrance where the guests were filtering in. He worked to encourage friendship and conversation among his guests, mingling, while keeping the doorway free so none of them had the uncomfortable experience of waiting in line.

"Thank you." Her response was rote.

"No, I mean…not the dress and all…though, of course, that's phenomenal…" What the hell, again! Had he lost his damned mind? "Just…you look like you're having a good time."

She was out. In the evening. Which was generally a struggle for her.

"I am." Another polite response. One she'd offer to anyone. She glanced at him. Her eyes met his. And she stopped walking. They weren't at his goal yet—the entryway—but they were close.

"Seriously, I'm enjoying myself," she told him. "But then, I know who's not going to be here tonight."

"They could show up at the door." He'd been worried about it since they got there. Just hadn't wanted to say anything.

She shook her head and looked away. Looked… uncomfortable for a second.

"How do you know they won't be here?"

"Because I know it was…suggested to them that they make plans to be out of town for the next few days. That would explain their not being here. This way it won't become fodder for gossip. You know, people saying it's a slight on either of our families."

He didn't ask who'd made the suggestion, but he could guess. Colin Fairbanks.

Hunter did not want to be on his bad side.

"Wouldn't that suggestion be made any time

you want to attend an evening function?" he said now, a bit confused. If that was all it took...

Julie's smile faltered. Only minimally. But he noticed.

"It would be, if I allowed it," she said. "And that's been the case once or twice. I just...oh..." She looked at him. At the door. And back at him. "I just...this is the first time I've actually enjoyed myself."

Oh.

Oh!

"I'm going to be cocky enough to assume I have something to do with that."

He wanted to kick himself when her eyes lost their shine. He quickly added, "You don't have this big secret that no one else knows. Because *I* know." As she'd told Joy, secrets weren't as scary when you spilled them.

"Yes." Her smile came back slowly. So did the glow in her eyes.

He felt as though he was at the crest of a wave. Wanting to ride it indefinitely.

"Hunter?" The voice came from behind him. He recognized it, yet knew a second of confusion, too.

Because she'd never been at one of his work functions before.

She wasn't part of his professional life. And he didn't want her to be.

Why the hell was Mandy there?

JULIE WASN'T SURE what hit her first. The suggestively yet appropriately dressed beauty who'd just called Hunter's name in a tone that implied she knew him well. Or the way he stiffened when he heard that voice.

The cleavage on that glittery gold neckline wasn't the lowest in the room. The swell of breast it showed wasn't the most skin being exposed. But from her thick black eyeliner to the bright red polish on her toes, the woman oozed sexuality.

"Hunter?" She was already approaching them as he turned toward her. Julie took a step back, intending to ease away, hopefully before the introduction stage. Maybe do a last check on her makeup and hair in the bathroom. Take a breather. Have a moment to herself.

Check backstage to be certain that no one was having a problem...

"Hey, baby, I couldn't believe it when I checked the website and saw that you had tickets left for tonight. Since when do you do the ticket at the door thing?"

The woman's grin seemed genuine. But there was something about her voice, a brittleness in her tone, that kept Julie's feet in place. Weighted down.

Hunter was allowed to know women. They were allowed to know him.

Allowed? How had that word crept into her thoughts?

Expected was more like it.

The man was gorgeous, funny, successful. And incredibly popular. Of course women would gravitate to him! She'd seen the evidence herself—even with the married women on the Sunshine Board.

"Mandy, what are you doing here?"

His tone was different, too. And if her last rationalization had freed her to leave the scene, that tone kept her right where she was.

That hadn't been an upbeat, have-fun, tone. It had held...history. He knew the woman well.

It made sense that he'd know women well. The man was past thirty. He'd have a sex life. A healthy one.

But...he'd been asking Julie out.

Not to bed. Just out. He'd already said he didn't want to be exclusive with anyone.

Still...

"When you stood me up on Sunday, and then didn't answer on Monday, I figured I'd better come and make sure you weren't being held hostage or something." Mandy chuckled. It sounded sexy. She glanced at Julie, who suddenly felt stupid standing there in her straitlaced gown. Superfluous.

Until Hunter turned to her. Her cheeks flushed. Her heart opened a crack. And then he said, "Mandy, this is Julie Fairbanks. She's the one who hired me for tonight's function. She's on the board of the Sunshine Children's League."

That hurt. Mandy was clearly personal. Julie, who'd sure as heck felt personal the other night at her pool, was a client.

"Oh!" Mandy's smile seemed to relax, but at that point Julie was just as convinced she could be imagining the reaction. "Maybe you can help me then. They tell me all the tickets are gone. And here I am, all dressed up and ready to donate."

Not even Julie could miss the pouty look the woman sent in Hunter's direction. A clear mandate for him to put in a word to his client on her behalf. To do whatever it took to find her a seat.

At his table, Julie was certain. Their table.

The value of the seat Julie had at his table diminished. She was about to offer it up when Hunter said, "Sorry, Mandy, we've hit the fire code max. You know me. I never turn away money for a client if I can help it, but we've already maxed out our overage."

Julie wanted to say she'd be happy to eat backstage.

To watch the show from back there, too.

"Seriously?" Mandy looked from Hunter to Julie and back. "Wow. Congratulations!"

"It's all Hunter's doing." Julie heard herself say the words, wondering where they'd come from. It wasn't what she'd been thinking.

More like, *I'll forgo dinner. You take my seat.*

Julie had no front-and-center role in the night's event. Didn't really have to be part of it. She was background. She'd need to greet certain guests. Check in with her fellow board members. She had to be on hand to formalize and approve the final monies tabulated. But she didn't have to eat. Or sit.

"I'm sure it is," Mandy said, giving him a long look that said something. Julie just couldn't translate it.

She had a feeling Hunter could, though. And did.

Still, he'd told the woman no.

And Sunday night. The night he'd been at her pool, with her, he'd stood Mandy up.

For the moment, Julie was the chosen one. That felt good. Damned good.

Until she realized, again, that he'd obviously made a date with the woman for Sunday. How else could he have stood her up?

Which meant he'd made that date while trying to cajole Julie to go out with him, too.

He'd said no strings attached, she reminded herself. And she'd made it more than clear, over a period of many months, that she wasn't going on a date with him.

She hadn't gone on a date with him. And had no plans to. But still...

He'd held her hand. Not like a high school, he's-my-boyfriend thing. Like…way more than that. Like… She didn't know what.

And none of these thoughts were fair to him.

Precisely why she, like Lila, was not healthy material for a relationship.

"Sorry about that…" Hunter called her attention back to him. Mandy was gone. And Julie was standing there wringing her hands. Wishing she was in her studio.

But knowing she didn't have to run home to be okay. She was fine. She would eat. Converse. Clap. Show her guests a good time.

Show them she was glad to be there with them. That she thought the acts they had waiting for them were worth their time and money. Show ample appreciation for both the acts and her guests.

"Julie."

Hunter placed his hand over both of hers. She separated them. From his. And then her own hands from each other.

"It's fine," she said. "You have nothing to apologize for."

"I didn't stand her up."

She didn't want to hear. It was none of her business. She couldn't make it her business.

CHAPTER TWENTY-SIX

"SHE LEFT A voice mail asking me to meet her Sunday night. I didn't ever say I would." He'd been planning to, though. He couldn't pretend he wasn't. But he hadn't stood her up. He hadn't said he'd see her and then failed to do so.

That was important.

"As a matter of fact, I texted and told her I couldn't make it." Late. He'd texted late. After she'd texted him when he hadn't responded.

He thought about taking his phone out of his pocket and proving it to her. But he couldn't be sure he hadn't called Mandy by one of his often-used pet names for her, like *Sexy*.

While he hadn't done anything wrong—he was careful not to put himself in situations that could get messy—he found himself not wanting Julie to know about that particular nickname.

"It's none of my business, Hunter."

She was distancing herself. "I'm making it your business." He looked her straight in the eye.

Guests were arriving steadily. He pulled her to the side and let Trina greet their guests, along with a couple of the board members. He and Julie would each have to make their rounds. As far as he was concerned, they could do them together but not until he'd done everything he could to bring the smile back to her eyes.

He wasn't holding her hostage. She could walk away at any time. She didn't. She met his gaze.

"It's none of my business," she said again.

"I don't think it's a question of whose business it is," he told her. He was speaking to the look in her eyes, the change in her demeanor, not to the words coming out of her mouth. "I think that her appearance here made you uncomfortable. For whatever reason."

Hunter knew she prided herself on honesty. Pretty much anyone who came in contact with her knew that much about her.

Honesty.

If they had nothing else between them, they had to have that.

He'd learned intimate things about her. She'd shared them with him. Of her own free will. That meant something.

It meant a lot.

And it meant a lot that she was still standing there, listening to him. "I'm telling you that you've got no reason to be uncomfortable."

He hadn't stood up a woman. He didn't treat

women shabbily. Lie to them. Or in any way mis-
use them. He loved women.

He loved people.

His job was to help them have fun.

Didn't she get that much about him?

"You're dating her."

He hadn't seen that coming. Probably should
have. He'd been too busy feeling her tension. Trying to ease it.

"We hang out on occasion. We aren't a couple.
We aren't even an item. When one or the other
of us is at loose ends and wants to go out, we're
a phone call—or a text—away."

"You've had sex with her."

In that second, he wanted nothing more than to
have sex with Julie Fairbanks. And reeled himself in. Quickly. Thankful he'd worn his longer
tux jacket that night.

She was staring at him.

Honesty.

"Yes."

She couldn't expect him to have been celibate.

Julie's nod, her abrupt turn as she started to
walk away, struck him as wrong.

"Hey, it's not like I've slept with her this week,"
he said. "Not since before Sunday night." He
wanted it clear. Since Sunday night he'd thought
of no woman but her.

"So… Saturday night?" She'd turned back.

Sounded hurt. He almost grinned. She cared! Julie Fairbanks was jealous!

He'd been so busy trying to get her to see that he wasn't a scumbag male, he hadn't figured out what was really getting to her.

"No, not Saturday night, either," he said, moving in closer. God, if the woman only knew. She was the one woman in the world who had no reason to be jealous of any other woman.

That thought pulled him up short. But it didn't stop him completely.

"I haven't slept with her since I started having this...thing for you."

There was still doubt in her eyes. A different kind. A better kind. She was doubting the wisdom of this conversation.

Good.

"You remember our talk a week ago Saturday was supposed to get rid of it...this...thing. But it didn't."

She ran her tongue across her lips, and that was as good as hitting a hole in one.

"What is this...thing? You never really said."

Aha. She was curious. Julie Fairbanks, a woman who hadn't dated in ten years, was curious about him. His lower region reacted again. Just that quickly.

But as overpowering as the thought—and its accompanying reaction was—it was subdued by the one that came right after. With Brett Acker-man's early warning in the mix.

Julie's different. She'd been badly hurt. *She's not a woman a guy's going to have fun with.*

Julie hadn't dated in ten years because she'd been severely damaged. She needed a man with healing power, with staying power.

That man wasn't him.

NOTHING HAD CHANGED. Julie knew that. She had to know, couldn't help but know, she kept telling herself.

For the rest of the night, she was aware of Hunter Rafferty. Whether he was sitting beside her, which she actually enjoyed, or across the room in conversation with others, she was aware of him.

Every time she thought about the fact that she was going to be driving home with him that evening, that she was the one leaving with him, her stomach gave a peculiar little leap.

Because he knew her truth.

It was…nice being with a person who knew. She didn't have to hide.

So, yeah, maybe at some point, another stage of her healing would be to tell more people. The more she told, the freer she'd be.

The thought stopped. In most cases, when people were privy to big things, dramatic things, they gossiped.

Made assumptions.

Formed judgments.

She couldn't bear that. And she didn't have to bear it, Dr. Larson had assured her. The one blessing about the way everything had happened in the past, and again the previous year, was that it'd been kept out of the papers. To protect the Smyths. But to protect her and the other victims, too.

She wanted that protection. Needed it.

And that was okay.

Being raped didn't mean you had to wear a label.

But having Hunter know...

"When was the last time you went out with her?" She and Hunter were sitting together at their table, two acts post dessert. Which meant four opportunities to make more money still ahead.

The act was a teenage boy doing comedy. She was sure he was funny; judging by the laughter and clapping in the room, he was hilarious. Hunter had laughed to the point of guffawing a couple of times.

She might have found the humor if she could shut up her mind long enough to take it in.

To give Hunter credit, when she leaned over and asked the question, he gave her his immediate attention.

"I don't know. We had dinner. A couple of weeks ago, maybe. I don't keep track."

Her heart dropped. Without cause or justification.

"You slept with her then?"

"No." He was smiling but watching the stage now, so probably whatever had just been said was funny. No one else was laughing. But Hunter was certainly the life of the party. Good humor started with him. "I haven't slept with her since the first Sunshine Board meeting."

Since he'd met her? Was that what he was implying? Oh, God, she hoped not.

And hoped so.

That wasn't fair of her. Or right.

"You have no reason to be celibate because of me," she pointed out for both of them. Her mind knew the words to be true, so she took comfort from them.

"Who said I'm celibate? I just said I haven't slept with Mandy." His grin had expanded. And he was looking directly at her.

And that was when she understood. Hunter was messing with her. Because he knew her. He understood. And knew how to bring lightness to even the darkest moments.

Her darkest moments.

"Well, if you *don't* sleep with someone, just see that she doesn't show up and glare at me," she told him. "Because I'm not responsible for the women you don't have sex with." She was grinning.

Until he spoke again.

"The hell you aren't." The words were said under his breath. Not meant for her to hear.

But she'd heard them.

THE SHOW WENT for all ten acts. More than half the guests had remained for the last act, and a good many of them were voting for an encore that didn't exist—donating money that would bear no return. They remained at their tables. Having one more drink.

Chatting.

So Hunter made a quick decision, and set about charming the ten acts—all of whom had remained for a final bow, hoping to be noticed by at least one of the two talent agents in the audience—to come out front and mingle for another hour. To greet all the remaining guests. Chat with them.

In exchange, they'd all have a shot at meeting each of the two agents in attendance, having personal conversations with them.

Julie ended the evening with ten thousand dollars more than their estimated high. Hunter had another success under his belt, new prospective names on his client list, and additional names on his donor list—the list of those who wanted to be invited to future events.

And the night went far later than planned. It was almost one in the morning by the time he opened the passenger door of the Escalade and held Julie's hand as she stepped inside.

She had to be exhausted.

He would be, too. Later. For the moment, he was energized. His adrenaline pumping. Feeling good. What a great party.

Another success.

A great evening.

As he walked around to his side of the SUV, he started thinking about asking her out for breakfast—bacon and eggs at some all-night joint. Just to be able to sit and talk to her. To savor the success. Relive the key moments. Share the ones they'd experienced separately.

And to make sure they were okay. That Mandy's unexpected arrival hadn't damaged the tenuous relationship they'd formed over the past week.

Just because it was temporary didn't mean it had to end right now. Or before the whole situation with Edward and Joy was settled.

Before Cara was found.

And Joy had a home other than The Lemonade Stand.

At least until then.

"I was jealous of her." Julie's words greeted him as he opened the door and climbed inside. Preempting his breakfast question.

"Jealous of whom?" Playing stupid was beneath her. But pretty much on par for him.

"Mandy." Her head on the back of the seat, she'd turned to look at him. "I was jealous of her."

It wasn't any great revelation. He'd been giddy for most of the night because he'd already figured that out. Confirmation was nice.

Except it meant that now they had to talk about it. Every instinct he had shied away from even getting close to that one.

"You have no reason to be," he said, going for quick and easy. Hoping to end the whole topic and open the way for his breakfast question.

"That's kind of irrelevant, don't you think?" Her tone was lazy, calm, as she continued to rest against the seat, watching him.

No, he didn't think so. Or he wouldn't have said it. But, yeah, it could be. "How so?" His internal cringe at the question didn't stop it from happening.

"Because whether you're dating her or not, having sex with her or not, I have no reason or right to be jealous."

"I wasn't aware that reason and right were requisite for jealousy."

Proud as he was of his response, the emotion was temporary. Far too temporary. Gone in seconds. Replaced by an aching need to lean over and kiss her.

As though in that kiss, he'd prove his point.

He just wasn't clear what that point might be. So he asked, "You want to stop for breakfast on the way home?" and started the engine.

"I'd rather you let me make you breakfast," she said. "It's my specialty."

She didn't want to prolong her public exposure. He knew that. But she was willing to prolong their time together.

"What about Chantel and Colin?"

Her brother and sister-in-law had been at their table that night. Hunter hadn't exchanged more than two sentences with them. To his knowledge, neither had Julie. They'd been across the table from each other. And all of them were occupied with various other people.

Colin and Chantel had left after the last act.

And before the lights went up and the final tallies.

"They wanted me to call when I got home."

Call. It took him a second to realize that when you lived in a home as large as theirs, with suites on opposite ends of the house, it would make sense to call.

"One or the other of them will be up waiting for the call. Probably both of them. In case I need to talk."

He wondered how often that happened. Had a

feeling it wasn't all that often. But he really liked the idea that they'd wait up anyway.

Julie deserved it.

She was that special.

"You going to tell them I'm coming in with you?"

"Are you coming in?"

"If you want me to."

"Then I'll tell them you are."

And she did.

CHAPTER TWENTY-SEVEN

JULIE HAD BEEN PLANNING to make crepes. Because they were kind of hard to do, and hers were better than average. She'd wanted to impress him with one of her strengths to compensate for the obvious weaknesses. The weirdness.

Hunter wanted bacon and eggs. To be fair, she hadn't mentioned crepes to him.

"I have Canadian bacon," she said as she led him to the enormous kitchen with its professional cook station. The double refrigerators of her parents' entertaining days still graced one corner of the room. Only one of them was used for anything more than beverages. The two double ovens seemed a little like overkill, too, as she tried to see the room through his eyes.

"They're great for Christmas cookie baking." She pointed to the ovens.

He smiled, responding to her earlier comment. "Canadian bacon is fine."

He wanted his eggs scrambled, with two pieces of toast on the side. Then he offered to make the eggs, which he cracked with one hand.

She asked him to teach her how, which used a few more eggs than they'd eat, but she laughed as she tried. And she learned, too.

"I'm surprised your brother hasn't come out here," Hunter said as they settled at the table in the breakfast room with their plates of toast and eggs scrambled with onion and Canadian bacon.

"He trusts you."

"Didn't seem that way the other night."

"He didn't know it was you. And besides, even if he didn't trust you, we both know that I have to learn to trust myself. To trust my own judgment again."

Probably a little too much information, she thought—middle-of-the-night conversations tended to go that way. Whether you were twelve or twenty-eight.

"The way I figure it these days," she said, "the chance of being wrong or making a bad choice is better than not making any choices at all." She took another bite of egg, enjoying it. The taste on her tongue. The texture.

She was enjoying watching him eat, too. Hunter savored his food, seeming to relish every aspect of it. Finding fun in it, just like he did with everything else in life.

"I spent a lot of years not living at all." She'd written the first four Amy books, though. She'd always be grateful for that.

Hunter didn't know about Amy.

She didn't want him to know.

If he knew that Amy was her creation, it would be like getting undressed in front of him. They were only hand-holding friends.

Her mind flashed a memory of Mandy, looking so sexy, calling Hunter's name.

A pit seemed to open in her stomach. She felt again the whisper of body parts that hadn't whispered to her in many, many years. Just as she had earlier that evening.

Her body was confused. But her mind knew the truth.

"You have to understand that my being jealous tonight…it doesn't mean anything."

"It means something to me. That's my right. To feel what I feel. You can't take that away from me. Or control it." He was being a jerk. Challenging her with a grin on his face.

"I'm serious, Hunter. I don't want you to make more of it than it is. It's…not fair to you, my feeling that way."

"Not fair to me? Now you've made me curious."

"Because it doesn't change the fact that I'm not going to date. It doesn't change who I am."

"I think it does. People change every single day of their lives, Jules."

Jules. Sounded like *Jewels* when he said it. Another warm breeze swept through her.

"Experiences, good and bad, happen every day. Mostly little ones. But they all add on to the pile that creates who we are. They change us. We're all works in progress." His expression was easy-going. His tone, suddenly, was not.

She put down her fork, pushed her half-eaten breakfast away.

It wasn't that she disagreed with him. She didn't. It was just that… "I don't want to lead you on."

She'd already said as much.

"Consider me warned."

He wasn't getting it. "Being jealous doesn't mean I can follow through." Sitting there in her expensive, glittery gown, feeling slender and feminine, across from him in the tuxedo that made him look like the sexiest man on earth, she let the words topple out.

She wasn't sure she could have stopped them if she'd wanted to. This whole thing—him, them, Mandy showing up, egg cracking and laughter and Joy, that night by the pool…it was all affecting her.

Driving everything she said and did.

She was scared. Determined. And yearning for what she couldn't have.

Because while the mind was powerful, it didn't completely control, or have the ability to create, feelings. She couldn't wish particular reactions into being, couldn't think away the pain. She could make herself face her fears, but she couldn't take away her ability to *feel* fear.

She had to tell him. It was the only way she was going to get through to him.

"I hate sex, Hunter. The thought of it repulses me. It doesn't turn me on."

Seeing Hunter with Mandy had made her want to like it, though. Which seemed kind of cruel…

"Was the rape your first sexual experience?"

The first three experiences. They'd been awful. Humiliating. Painful beyond belief. She still woke up with memories of that pain some nights.

The tapping of Hunter's fork on his plate brought her gaze to his hands. To him. She nodded.

"Then of course you hate sex. What's to like?" Relaxed in his chair, his expression was open. And…placid. He wasn't horrified.

Or even surprised.

"You don't care." Disappointment flooded her. Another instance where no matter what the mind knew, no matter how good it was that he wasn't hurt by her lack of interest—she still felt saddened that he didn't want her in that way.

"What?" He frowned. Shook his head. "Of course I care. I'm thinking about killing the bastard. But that's not what we're talking about here. We're talking about the realities you live with."

He wanted to kill David. For her. He wouldn't, of course. And she wouldn't want him to. Hunter in jail for murder would be worse than being raped. But something small and tender came to life inside her.

And she had to stick with her realities. Just like he'd said.

"We're talking about you understanding the truth." So she could spend more time with him. If he asked.

If he even wanted to spend time with her after all this.

"Which truth is that?"

"That this isn't going to lead to anything like what you have with Mandy."

"I don't want what I have with Mandy. I already have that."

Well, that pretty much put her in her place. It relieved the heck out of her, and yet hurt her feelings.

"Good, then," she said, collecting silverware on one plate and putting that plate—hers, the one with food still on it—on top of the other. "I hate sex and you don't want it with me. It's all out in the open now." She started to rise, intending to head into the kitchen with the dirty dishes. To clean up. Say good-night. Go upstairs to Amy.

No, to bed. It was late. She needed rest.

"I never said I didn't want it with you."

She fell back into her chair, heart pounding and belly fluttering. Again. The thought of sex appalled her. Hunter wanting her…didn't.

It should. The idea of a man, any man, wanting to touch her private parts, to enter them, made her shudder. Hunter wanting her… Her belly fluttered even more wildly.

What the hell was going on with her?

"Since we're being honest here, I've got it bad where you're concerned, Jules. Real bad. Worse than ever."

He was teasing her. She could tell by the grin. But there was a serious look in his eyes, too.

He leaned forward. He didn't touch her, but his face was only inches away. "I want you like I've never wanted a woman before. When I lie in bed at night, I think of you lying there beside me. I think about touching you…"

What was he doing? What was going on? What was happening? She licked her lips. Fought panic. And more belly flutters.

Her studio was right above them. Her brother in the next wing. She didn't want to leave her seat.

Even while panic threatened to consume her.

"And now I'm going to be thinking about ways to show you that sex doesn't have to hurt. Ways to slowly introduce you to the incredible pleasures a woman's body can feel. Ways to help you relax, one step at a time. Not with intercourse in mind, just pleasure."

Her mouth was thick, and her tongue stuck to the roof of her mouth. She was tired. Mindless with fatigue. Him there, in her kitchen, the two of them talking, laughing… Her emotions were overwhelmed.

What he was saying was typical Hunter gibberish. It sounded…wonderful. But life didn't work that way. She'd been robbed of her body's ability to respond.

Just as she'd been robbed of the ability to walk into a group of her social peers at night without a panic attack or two. David Smyth Jr. had taken her capacity to trust and turned it into a need to question. He'd made her afraid of her own shadow.

"But here's the thing." Hunter rubbed the top of her hand with one finger. Slowly. When she glanced at him, he was staring directly into her eyes. "I know you don't have the same thoughts about all of this. I understand that you're in a completely different place."

She didn't want to be. Tears blurred her vision.

"And I'm okay with that as far as you and I are concerned."

Because he didn't care the way she did. She didn't say the words out loud. They wouldn't be fair. To either of them.

"I'm okay with it on one condition."

She blinked. Looked him in the eye. Wanting. Doubting him. Wanting… "What condition?"

"It's not really a condition." He sat back, no longer stroking her hand.

She missed his touch. "What is it?"

As he withdrew, she felt stronger. Needing to go to him, which made no sense, either. She didn't try to figure it out.

"What bothers me, really bothers me, is that now the gala's over, and as soon as Joy's life is straightened out, as soon as she has a home outside The Lemonade Stand, I'm not going to see you anymore."

That bothered her, too.

When she didn't say anything, he leaned forward again. "I want a real friendship with you, Julie. I want this—late-night talks about real things. Glasses of wine by your pool. I want to have you over to play video games and teach you how to surf. This is a first for me. Whatever it is. This…spell you have on me. I just need to know that you're willing to be part of my life."

There was no blinking back the tears now. They spilled over, trailed down her cheeks.

She wanted a hug, but was afraid to have his arms around her.

"I want that, too," she said.

And hoped she hadn't just made the biggest mistake of her life.

CHAPTER TWENTY-EIGHT

HUNTER TOOK THE JAG out now and then, just to keep the engine running. Keep the dust out. Make sure nothing rotted or went dry from lack of use.

Maintaining that car was a labor of love. A reminder of how he'd almost screwed up his entire life. That he probably would have if not for the father who'd cared enough to guide him in the right direction.

A reminder that just because something looked bad, because it brought trouble and pain, didn't mean good couldn't come of it. His partying in high school had been self-destructive. He'd hurt a lot of people, his parents and himself included. Led some kids down the wrong track with him.

And now his love of the party was a means by which hundreds of thousands of dollars went to worthy charities every year.

So sex was off the table with Julie. That very fact was providing the opportunity for something he'd never had before. A real friendship.

If he wasn't mistaken, she was showing him

how to have a committed relationship. And it wasn't leaving a sour taste in his mouth.

On the contrary, he felt better, more alive, than he'd felt in a long time when he backed the Jag out of the drive Friday afternoon on his way to the Stand to pick up Julie and Joy.

A feeling that only intensified as the three of them drove along the highway an hour later, the ocean on one side of them, treed hills and homes on the other, the wind in their hair, and the car's heater blowing at their feet. He took a dip in the road just right, and Joy laughed out loud from her position in the back seat.

He glanced at Julie. She was smiling at him.

That was what it was all about.

LILA AND EDWARD were waiting for them when they got back to the Stand just before dinnertime. Expecting them to take Joy into the cafeteria for dinner, leaving her to get in her own car and go home, Julie was surprised when Lila, instead, handed Joy off to her house mother and asked Hunter and Julie to join her in her office.

Edward was there, too. He sat in a chair by the desk, while Hunter and Julie took the couch. She felt as if she was in the principal's office. As if she and Hunter had done something wrong.

Slumping on the couch Julie had a moment of

panic as she wondered if Lila had guessed that she and Hunter had talked about sex.

Then she straightened up. She was a grown woman. Successful. Capable. And was permitted to do whatever she wanted in her personal life. She also knew that Lila would be the first to say so.

The older woman, in her usual brown pants and jacket, leaned back against her desk, facing them. Her expression didn't bode well.

A glance at Edward showed Julie that the other man's expression was grim.

Oh, God. *Cara.*

How could she have been so wrapped up in her own nonsensical emotions to the point of—

"Mary Amos died this afternoon." Lila's words fell like bombs in the room.

Not Cara. Julie felt immediate relief. And then sorrow. The poor woman, killed by her own brother, her only living blood relative, other than Joy.

And Joy... From what Julie had heard, the little girl had loved her aunt Mary. Trusted her enough to hide with her and not make a sound even when she'd seen her mother hauled off by the monster her father had become.

"When are you going to tell Joy?" she asked.

Lila looked at Edward, who bowed his head. "Not yet," she replied. "Not until she's speaking normally and has had a chance to adjust to having Edward in her life."

Not until they'd had more time to find the little girl's mother. If they could bring Cara home, she'd be the best person to help Joy deal with Mary's death.

In the midst of this latest reality, Julie's world righted itself again. The possibility of having sex—or not—was a small thing compared to life and death. To the raising of a child. To helping her become healthy and happy.

Hunter's silent presence beside her seemed to amplify her own thoughts. She was glad he was there, not just in this room, but with her. Committed to being her friend. With his support, she felt better able to do whatever they needed her to do in order to help Joy cope.

"So…with Mary gone, Edward and Cara are Joy's only living relatives. Close relatives. For now, social services have placed her in his care. Paperwork will follow to make him her legal guardian until her mother returns…"

Her voice trailed off. Julie knew what hadn't been said. *And in case she doesn't return.* That was a higher than ever possibility with Mary's death in front of them. Cara was with a man who'd killed his own sister. Such a fiend probably wouldn't hesitate to do the same to the wife he'd also beaten.

"You're Joy's guardian." Hunter's words reminded Julie of the other part of this situation.

Edward nodded. He had to be happy about having legal custody of the little girl. And yet, under these circumstances...

"How are you doing?" Hunter asked him next. Sounding nothing like the party man she'd met months before. But exactly like the man she'd come to know. The one who could intuitively sense when someone was struggling. And then try to lighten the load.

"We're going to be just fine," Edward said, glancing at Lila.

"Edward's leaving her here, with us, for now," Lila said. The two exchanged another glance. "We're going to continue spending time with her. We're hoping you'll do more positive grandfather work with your art sessions," she said to Julie.

"I won't take her away from here until I know it's not going to be detrimental to her," Edward said. "At least not if I can help it."

He mentioned that he was thinking of taking Joy to his hotel for dinner and to play in the games room for a little while. To get her used to being with him outside of The Lemonade Stand. "I was hoping you'd come along sometime," he said to Hunter. "She likes you."

"Of course, I will." Hunter's response was immediate. "And she likes you, too," he added.

Julie listened to the plans being made around her. She loved that Joy had so many people watching out for her. She grieved a bit, too. Selfishly. And for Mary Amos.

The woman had died alone. Without anyone who loved her by her side.

Sometimes life wasn't perfect. Far from it.

Other things were changing, too. Their plans with Joy were changing.

Julie with Joy. On her own. For art therapy.

Hunter and Edward with Joy, on their own. Solidifying the family they'd become.

Lila at the Stand with Joy.

Their foursome was breaking up.

Just as she'd known it would.

HUNTER HAD SPENT eight hours engrossed with business tasks before taking the Jag out on Friday. Much as he wanted to ask Julie to have dinner with him as they left the Stand, after saying goodbye to Edward and Lila who were going to the hotel with Joy for dinner, he knew he needed to get home. He had to exchange the Jag for his Escalade and head over to the hospital event that Kyle was hosting. Not to check up on him. Just to schmooze. The Time of Your Life was his economic mainstay. His support and his grounding, too.

He needed grounding.

News of Mary's untimely death, of Edward suddenly being the sole legal caregiver of a seven-year-old child, had brought him back to reality.

If he didn't focus on the party, life would overwhelm him.

Julie didn't seem all that disappointed when he told her he had to go home to change and get to work. She didn't ask him about the night's party.

She said goodbye and got in her car.

She didn't wave as she pulled out and drove past him.

He didn't wave, either.

But he wanted to.

He decided he had to call her.

They'd had a great time with Joy that afternoon. Yeah, they'd been met with grim news—but it was good news, too, for Edward. And for Joy, even if she didn't know it yet.

The little girl would be safe and secure and loved, no matter what happened. She wasn't going to be in foster care, regardless of how things turned out with her mother.

They should be celebrating.

He was about to call Julie, but his phone rang before he'd actually done it.

Mandy.

He was truly not happy to see her name pop up on his screen. Which wasn't her fault. She hadn't done anything wrong.

Anything different.

He was the who was acting differently, who seemed to be changing.

"Hey, Sexy, what's up?" His cheerful voice sounded like overkill to him. Hopefully she hadn't noticed.

"Now that's what I like to hear on the other end of the line when I call my main man," she said.

Her *main man*? That was a new one, and, perhaps oddly, it rankled. But, hey, they'd had lots of nicknames for each other over the years.

And it wasn't like she'd said *only man*. He wasn't her only man. They'd never been each other's *only*. And that had worked both ways. Mandy saw other men. He knew that for sure.

"So what's up?" he asked again, making a turn and then another. A couple of miles on a straight stretch of highway and he'd be home. Fifteen minutes to change into a tux and he'd be out the door.

"You, I hope. With me. Whenever you're done tonight, meet me at Yank's." She named a club they'd been to many times over the years. It was in Oxnard. She had a place there.

"I'd love to, Man, but I can't tonight. It's been one hell of a week. I've got a couple of bids to do and some follow-up reports."

"On a Friday night?"

He understood her disbelief. He'd never worked

on a Friday night after a gig. He was always too wound up. Ready to have a good time.

"I told you, this week's been crazy." He couldn't tell her about Joy. Or didn't want to. Joy and Edward…Mandy wasn't in that part of his life. As far as he could remember, she'd never asked him if he had living parents, let alone known anything about them.

It said something about his life that, until this moment, it hadn't even seemed strange to him.

"You sure it's not that beauty in black who's keeping you away from me?" A sultry, pouty tone entered her voice. One she used in bed.

It used to turn him on.

"Positive," he said. "Like I said, I have to work tonight."

"Because you've been playing with her when you should've been working?" Now there was doubt in her voice.

He didn't need this. He wished he could tell her that a woman had just died. At the hands of her own brother. For doing nothing more than loving him and his family.

Wanted to tell her a woman was missing, a young mother.

But he was afraid she wouldn't care. That she wouldn't see what it had to do with her. With them.

Truth was, it *didn't* have anything to do with them.

But it had a lot to do with him. If he told her,

he expected she'd ask why, and he didn't know what his answer should be. He couldn't predict the long-term ramifications, either.

In that moment, his time with Mandy, their relationship, seemed superficial to the point of waste.

He acknowledged that it wasn't fair to her. She was a nice woman. Easygoing. Fun-loving. And exactly like him. Like he used to be.

Like he would be again when things settled down?

He couldn't deny the possibility, but didn't think he'd ever be the man he'd been before he met Julie Fairbanks. He'd been living in ignorance—of so much.

One thing was for certain. He couldn't have Mandy maligning Julie, or his time with her, in any way. "I haven't been playing. At all," he finally said.

"I saw you today."

"You did? Where?" He hadn't seen her.

"You drove down to Oxnard. Stopped for ice cream."

She was right. He had. With Joy—and Julie. He hadn't even thought about the fact that he was familiar with the homemade ice cream shop because it was close to Mandy's favorite coffee place. And that she often stopped there on her way home from the hair salon where she worked. He hadn't given any thought to the fact that Friday was her early day, either. He'd known it, just hadn't thought about it.

"You were with her, Hunter. And some kid. A little girl. Hers, I'm guessing."

Shit. Now what?

"The little girl is my second cousin," he said, because it seemed the most innocuous answer that came to mind.

"You have relatives in town that you see?"

Nope. Hadn't been a good answer, after all. Nothing else he came up with was any better.

"My uncle's in town. Visiting."

"But you didn't think maybe I'd like to meet him? Or you didn't want him to meet me."

This was going all wrong. Fast.

"Come on, Sexy, this is me! And you! We don't make it complicated, right?" That's what they'd always said. What had always drawn them to each other. "I've never met a member of your family. Hell, I don't even know what family you have!"

"You ever stop to think that I didn't make it complicated because that's the way *you* wanted it, Hunter? All these years, I've been hanging around, willing to hang out, waiting for you to be ready…"

What the hell?

"You said you didn't want commitment. You didn't want a relationship. You just wanted some-one you could trust, to have fun with…" He hadn't dreamed that all up. She'd said it. Every word. Many times.

"I said that, yes. Because I knew that it was what you wanted. And you were worth the wait. But damn it, Hunter! After all these years of being your fallback girl, it's not right that when you finally decide to have a real girlfriend, it's not me."

"I don't have a girlfriend."

"You've never lied to me before."

"I'm not lying now."

"So...meet me at Yank's tonight. Convince me."

There was no way he could do that. Not now, knowing she was in way deeper than he was.

This was exactly what he *hadn't* intended to do to her.

"It's not going to work, Mandy." One thing he knew was that when a bandage had to come off, it had to be done quickly. "I'm clearly not what you're looking for."

If he ever did settle down—and that was a huge *if*—it wouldn't be with her.

"That's for me to decide."

Rip it off. Quick.

"I'm not in love with you."

"How do you know? We've never tried to be that couple. Where you're boyfriend and girl-friend."

"We've been hanging out for years. Don't you

think, if I was going to fall in love with you, I'd know?"

"You love her."

"I do not." It took him a second to realize he didn't have to ask who "her" was. Because there was only one "her" in his world.

"Wow. I turn my back for a second and that's it. I'm dumped out like the trash."

"That's not true." And it wasn't like her to react this way. Mandy really had been the most easygoing woman. He hadn't just imagined that. "What's going on, Man?"

"She's rich. I'm not. I get it. I see what you're doing. I don't even blame you. But…it's not right. You can't do this to me."

He could. He had to. "You've been lying to me, Mandy. About what you really wanted. We said we'd always be honest with each other, and you haven't been."

He wasn't even sure how he felt about that.

He wasn't devastated. He wasn't…much of anything. Except bothered. Which made him feel kind of sick.

"This is the end, isn't it? You've moved on, and there's nothing I can say or do to change that."

"I haven't moved on. But I think we need to call it quits," he told her. Julie or no, Mandy wasn't the person he'd taken her for all these years. He accepted half the blame for that. He hadn't looked at her hard enough to know who she really was.

He hadn't wanted to know.

"Yeah, well, thanks for the good times, Hunter."

"We had a lot of them."

"Yep."

"I wish things were different."

"Do you? Somehow I don't think so."

"I enjoyed spending time with you." He felt he owed her something, some kindness, some expression of gratitude. He just couldn't figure out what it should be. *You were great in bed*, wasn't it.

"Let's just stop, Hunter, before this gets any worse."

They'd hit rock bottom; it seemed they agreed on that much. Feeling like he'd failed her, and himself, he wished her well and hung up.

CHAPTER TWENTY-NINE

JULIE WAS SITTING at her desk in the office beside her studio just after ten on Friday night when her phone rang. She'd been going over a list of items needed, along with quantities, for the Thanksgiving dinner Sunshine Children's League was hosting at a children's home in LA. With the extra money made the night before, they'd not only be able to take care of the entire dinner at several homeless shelters, as well, but they could afford to provide little gifts for each of the Sunshine kids, too. She'd talked Colin and Chantel into joining her, and they were going to have dinner with the Sunshine kids that Thanksgiving.

Her phone almost rang a second time before she picked up.

"Hi." She'd wondered if he'd call. In her weaker moments that evening, she'd actually hoped that he would.

She'd wanted to speak with him—but wouldn't call him. It didn't feel right when she had so little to offer him in return.

"You're a late-nighter, too," he said.

"Yeah." Until this past week, those had always been lonely hours in her life.

"What did you do tonight?"

"Sat with Chantel while she had her first bout of morning sickness. Colin had a dinner with some clients."

Leaving her desk, she curled up on the silk floral couch, looking out toward the pool. Such an inane conversation shouldn't mean so much. Good thing she had her mind to keep her emotions on track.

"How was the hospital event?" she asked next. He'd mentioned that was where he'd be going as they walked out to their cars at the Stand.

"Really well. We had a fifties theme, with a Platters tribute band that's phenomenal. I've used them before. The dance floor was full. Pledges were plentiful, in addition to the plate charge. The hospital is going to get its new playroom. And I've got more prospective work."

"Do you have time for that?" The man seemed to work seven days a week.

"Kyle wants to do more on his own. If all goes well, we can hire another event manager and handle twice the business."

"But what about time off?"

"He's off two days a week. All three of them are." She'd met Trina and Bob, too.

"What about you? The ultimate party guy? When do you ever take a full day off?"

He wanted a friend, so she'd be the best one she could.

"Whenever I want."

"When was the last time?"

"I don't know."

"If you don't want to tell me, say so. Tell me to mind my own business. I can take it…" Her tone was teasing. She meant the words. Kind of. Considering everything else they couldn't share, she didn't want any pretense between them about the things they did.

"I honestly don't know. I don't remember."

"That's too long."

When he didn't respond for a moment, she asked, "What? You got all quiet."

"It just occurred to me that I didn't take time off because there was nothing I'd rather be doing than work."

She knew the feeling. Which was fine for her. Sounded sad for him, though. Especially since life all around him was filled with fun and with exciting things to do.

"It's good that you love what you do so much."

"Agreed."

"What's wrong with that? Loving your work, I mean?" His word hadn't said so. His tone had implied it.

"I was thinking that this week, there've been a few times I was doing something I'd rather be doing than work."

Oh. Her turn for silence. Just as well he couldn't see her smile. Or the way her lower lip was trembling.

Another aftereffect from her attack. She'd become a weeper.

"Anyway, the reason I called…"

He paused. She held her breath. If he asked her out, would she go? She wanted to. He already knew what she couldn't offer, what she couldn't do. He'd said that was okay.

When she heard a noise in the background, she sat up. "Where are you?"

"In my kitchen."

"I heard something."

"I just got home. Threw my keys on the counter."

Was it wrong that she wished she was there? Making him eggs in his kitchen?

"So…you said you called for a reason?"

"What do you think of this whole Edward and Joy thing? You think she'll be okay going with him? He's been through so much. Losing his wife. And then Cara. And now Cara again. He's alone."

Hunter was worried. She loved that. Not him. That.

The thought had her pulling back. Mentally. Telling her emotions to do the same.

"Lila's the greatest," Julie told him. "She'll take care of the transition process. And she'll know who to call if there's a problem. I'm going to talk to Joy about Edward tomorrow. I'll draw pictures of Edward and her doing things together. I've already sketched them out. During the hour or so Chantel was napping after dinner."

"I'm glad he's ended up with her."

"It's the best thing that could've come out of this whole situation," she said. "Joy had to get out of that abusive home, and with Edward having no idea what was going on, no way to contact Cara since she'd blocked his phone and social media accounts, Joy didn't have a chance. Now… the sky's the limit."

Assuming Cara was found—and came home to her father.

"What if Cara decides not to accept her father back into her life?" Hunter asked.

She didn't want to think about that.

"If Shawn's found he'll be in jail for his sister's murder," she went on. "Social services are involved. I think she'd have a hard time keeping Edward out of her life."

But it could happen. Because life came with no guarantees.

He was going to hang up soon. He'd have things to do. She didn't want to let him go. A precursor to what their relationship was going to look like in the future? Hunter coming into and out of her much smaller world. With her being grateful to have him there.

And mourning his loss a little bit every time he left.

"I need to talk to you." His words sounded ominous.

"I'm listening."

She heard something else in the background. Sounded like voices. "Are you a late-night TV watcher?" she asked, eager to prolong their conversation, to know the details of his life. Avoiding whatever the real reason was for his call.

When someone said "I need to talk to you" it generally wasn't good.

"I don't even have cable, I watch so little TV," he told her. "I've got music on."

"In your kitchen?" She liked that he'd have music in his kitchen.

"I'm in my den. I have my shoes, jacket and pants off. Still wearing my shirt. The tails are wrinkled. At the moment I'm walking from the entertainment system to my favorite chair—a recliner that I use when I'm working late—and I just opened a beer."

It was like he'd tossed her a ball, challenging her to return it. "What about socks?"

"I own some."

"On or off?"

"On."

She had another question. One a girlfriend could ask. Not that it mattered whether he was wearing boxers or briefs. His wrinkled shirt tails were covering them anyway.

"I need to get something clear between us." Wow, for a party guy he was gloom and doom that night.

She didn't want him to tell her that he didn't want to be her friend.

But she also knew she didn't have the right to stop him. And had to quit stalling him.

"I'm listening, Hunter. Whatever it is, just say it." No more fooling around. Getting up, she went to her little refrigerator and pulled out a single serving bottle of wine.

Uncapped it. Sipped.

"I need it clear between us, and particularly clear to you, that I'm not the guy who's always going to be there."

"I don't understand."

"You've heard the saying that 'when the going gets tough, the tough get going'?"

"Of course."

"Well, when the going gets tough, Hunter heads out."

"Okay." So he was telling her he was out? She was too…damaged for him? Too much angst. Too much drama.

She couldn't argue with that. She agreed. Wholeheartedly. So she paced her office.

"That's it?" He sounded...kind of put out.

"I was waiting for you to finish." She moved into her studio.

"I did."

Frowning, she took another sip of wine, and asked, "What do you mean, that's it? You haven't said anything yet. At least nothing you haven't said a boring number of times before. You think you can't be relied on to hang around through the hard stuff. Your actions show me that sometimes you can. So what else is there?"

"What do *you* mean, what else is there?"

"You aren't trying to tell me you're regretting your offer of friendship?" The wine let her say it. Or so she told herself.

"What?"

"You aren't trying to tell me that, now that Joy's future is secure, you're rethinking the whole idea of us staying in contact afterward?" She turned, headed back to the office.

"Hell, no!"

Oh. Well, then. She settled on to a corner of the couch. Pictured him in his shirttails. Those long legs of his bare, with the dark masculine hair that would be covering them.

"I don't get it," she said, softening her tone. It

was one she'd use if she was talking to Colin. Or
Chantel. Or Joy.

"My whole life, Julie, I'm the guy who goes
surfing. I've accepted that about myself, and I
just need you to know it. Don't count on me. I'll
disappoint you at some stage."

Was he trying to let her down gently, after all?
Didn't want to be her friend? It wasn't as though
she'd even asked anything of him. Had she?

And still, he obviously felt the weight of her
need.

She couldn't leave it there. "I don't understand
why you're saying this. Have I given you cause
to think I'm too needy? Trust me, Hunter. I can
fully take care of myself. Which is what I've been
trying to cram into my big brother's head. Yes, I
have issues. Yes, there are some things that challenge me. I know what those things are. I take care
to tend to them. I make sure I have safeguards in
place so I can deal with whatever comes into my
life. I don't need you, or anyone else, to make me
feel okay."

She might have said more, so she stuffed the
tip of the wine bottle in her mouth. Tipped it, too.

"Obviously I hit a hot button, which I'm going
to come back to at some point, but you missed
what I was saying."

Oh. She wiped at the dribble of wine on her

chin. It wasn't easy to drink with the entire tip of the bottle between your lips.

"My parents fought."

Hers hadn't. She'd had a blessed childhood. For which she was so thankful. "I'm sorry."

"Yeah, me, too. But the thing is, from when I was really little, every time they did, I'd turn my back. I'd leave. Mom would ask me to confirm something that had been said, and even if I could, even if I knew that Dad had actually said what she thought, or more often, that she'd told him something he claimed she hadn't, I stayed out of it. With him, it was usually some chore he was supposed to have done and hadn't, or someplace he was supposed to show up and didn't. Whatever it was, I'd just get the hell out. I wouldn't even bother with the answer."

"Parents are never supposed to use their kids to settle their fights."

"That's why I got into partying as a teenager. To block them out. And then I'd come back all het up and joking and distract them from the bitter silence that had fallen between them to a better mood."

"It's a normal response. Look at statistics. They'll tell you that. What matters is that you turned it all around. You're a huge success, spending your life helping people, and loving what you do."

"I got some kids in trouble back then. Led them to drugs. One of the guys I hung out with most in high school is in prison."

"You might've led him to some bad things, Hunter, but the choices were his."

His sigh wasn't encouraging. "What?" she asked.

"I'm not looking for a cheering squad here. I'm try to tell you something. To show you by example."

"Then show me. Because right now I'm obviously not seeing it."

"What I know is that anyone who relies on me, anyone who ever thinks I'll be there for them, ends up disappointed. So I don't want you to rely on me."

"Because you don't intend to be here." It was the only thing that made any sense. He had three employees, and their families, who relied on him. Had been relying on him for years. He had a list of clients, herself included, who relied on him. And he delivered, every single time. Over and above what he'd promised.

"No! Woman, you are giving me a headache."

She smiled at the change in his tone. It told her something, too. He was really floundering.

"I made a choice, Julie. A conscious choice. I chose not to bear the pressure of having people rely on me. I don't trust myself to be there."

"Hunter, if it makes you feel any better, I'm

thrilled that we're friends. It's like I've been walking on a different kind of air since our conversation. But I quit relying on anyone other than myself years ago. I'm happy for whatever time you're in my life. I'll miss you like heck if you leave. However, I'll also move on and be okay. That's one thing I know about myself."

"My dad almost went to prison because of me."

That was a new one. She sat up. "What? Why?"

"My senior year in high school, after I'd been accepted to college, my father told my mother he wanted a divorce. He'd found a practice to buy in Florida and he was going to move. My mother panicked. She couldn't let him leave her, leave the state. When he continued with his plans, she retaliated by filing charges of domestic violence against him. Said it'd been going on for years, but that she hadn't said anything because he'd never hurt me, and she knew she wouldn't be able to give me the chances in life, schooling and whatnot, that she wanted me to have without his financial support."

Julie swallowed. She'd heard the same story, versions of it, many times now. Women who'd stayed for financial reasons. Usually due to children. She'd seen the damage, broken bones that hadn't healed correctly, fresh bruises. Emotional stains that might never wash away.

"*Did* you know about it?"

"He didn't do it. If anything, he could've been accused of verbal abuse, in that he sometimes raised his voice to her. But even then, he didn't attack her. Didn't call her names or insinuate that she was stupid or anything. He told her she needed help."

"Did she?"

"They both did. Mom would've been fine, I believe, if she'd married a different man. Maybe not. She's high-maintenance. Needs a lot of re-assurance. And Dad put his career first. He was saving lives, so he kind of had to. She took his absence personally."

And Hunter hadn't? Maybe not knowingly. But the pieces fell into place for a moment. His lack of trust in himself. His thinking that he didn't have what it took to do anything but party. Could it be that little Hunter had determined at some point that he wasn't good enough, that he didn't mat-ter enough, to deserve a man as important as his father?

She was no psychiatrist. But it made sense to her.

"What happened to your father?" He'd almost gone to prison. Had he pled out?

"There was a meeting with Mom's attorney. To go over my testimony about all the fights. About how angry Dad would get. And then one with

Dad's attorney. He needed me to tell the court that I was certain Dad had never lifted a hand to her."

In her opinion, they should both have been hanged. Making him choose like that!

"What did you do?"

"The only thing I knew. The thing they'd both taught me to do. I told the truth."

So he *had* saved the day for someone. He'd saved his father from prison.

"I told them that my parents fought all the time. That Dad got really angry with her and raised his voice. And that I couldn't testify to any physical abuse because I never hung around long enough. I'd certainly never had to pull my father off my mother because I'd left rather than hang around to potentially protect her. I'd never asked, when I got back, if everything was okay. I breezed in. Cracked some jokes. Suggested a family outing. Ice cream. A game. And, for my sake, they always played nice."

Funny how at one time or another, life crapped on pretty much everyone. It was how you stood up, cleaned yourself off, moved on, that mattered. Hunter was far more of a success than he might ever know.

He was everything she'd ever dreamed a man could be.

"Wouldn't you have noticed bruises when you got back if he'd hurt her?"

338	FOR JOY'S SAKE

"She claimed it was where the bruises didn't show."

Not an uncommon occurrence.

"So what happened?"

"After I met with the attorneys—it wasn't legal deposition yet, just talking—I had a conversation with my mom. I had a feeling she was lashing out because she was scared. I mean, she wasn't being rational. Like, how would Dad being in jail help us? I mentioned that if Dad was off on his own in Florida, and successful, he'd able to help us financially. Help pay for my college. I mostly talked about how we could have fun, just the two of us. She agreed to drop the charges and Dad agreed to one hell of an alimony settlement. To make sure she'd be taken care of for the rest of her life."

Sounded to her like Hunter had saved the day. It was so telling that what he saw was that he'd almost been responsible for his father going to prison because he couldn't testify on his behalf.

"So you don't think he ever hurt her?"

"Not physically. I'm 100 percent certain of it. He grabbed her shoulders a couple of times to calm her down when she was getting hysterical. That was the extent of it. I made her tell me the truth."

"How did you do that?"

"Well, I asked her to tell me the truth and she did." His tone had lightened again.

She wanted to tell him that he hadn't let his

parents down. That it was the opposite, in fact. They'd let him down.

But she didn't think he'd believe her about his parents' responsibility in the whole mess. It was a realization he'd have to come to on his own.

"Chantel lied to Colin. She told him she was rich when she wasn't. She started a relationship with him based on a lie." He knew enough of the details. She didn't have to elaborate.

"I know."

"No one's perfect, Hunter. No one makes the best choices for everyone involved all the time. It's impossible when you're dealing with warring needs. You do your best. And that's all I'd ever expect of you. Not to take care of me. Not to fix me. Not even to always be there for me. Just do your best. That's the kind of friend I want."

"That's it?" He sounded as though he wasn't quite ready to believe her.

She thought hard. Looked deep inside herself. She needed to be completely honest with him. And he needed to be the same with her.

"There's one more thing," she said.

"What?"

"Honesty. Be honest with me. No matter what."

"Always." His voice was solemn.

"Me, too."

"Good night, friend. And thank you."

"For what?"

"I don't know. Sharing yourself with me."

Though she was certain she was getting the better end of that deal, Julie went to bed with those words in her mind, and a smile on her face.

CHAPTER THIRTY

HUNTER HAD A couple of hours on Sunday, between a morning golf outing and an evening tribute he'd been hired to coordinate in Santa Barbara at a private antebellum-style home. The evening event wasn't a fund-raiser but a sort of memorial paid for by the deceased's estate as designated in his will. He'd been a stand-up comic, and the one thing he'd wanted for his funeral was a grand party in his own home. His last party.

Hunter had managed to get a well-known LA comic to deliver the tribute free of charge. He'd offered to pay. The comic had refused the money.

The event wasn't due to start until six that evening, which left him from one until about three to do as he wished.

He wished to see Julie.

To have lunch with her, if possible.

He'd talked to her the night before. They'd decided together that until either of them came up with a reason he shouldn't call her every night, he would do so.

But they hadn't said anything about eating together on Sunday. Or seeing each other at all.

He called as he pulled out of the golf course parking lot. She was just getting ready to make herself a salad. Colin and Chantel were at the little apartment across town.

And he said, "You feel like slumming, too?"

"With you?"

"Of course."

"Where?" She wanted to. He'd heard it in her voice. But she was Julie. She was always going to be cautious. And that was turning out to be one of the things he loved about her.

Whoa! He didn't *love* her. Did he? A fast check assured him he didn't. He just loved things about her. It was an expression, that was all.

"I was thinking my place," he told her. No big brother in another wing. No one anyplace.

Maybe he wanted her to say no.

Or needed her to say yes.

"What are you fixing?" she asked.

"No clue."

"What do you have that I can fix?" Clearly his plan needed more thought. He was happy to stop at a fast-food drive-through.

She wouldn't be.

"I'm not sure," he told her. There was some stuff in the freezer.

"How about if I bring my salad and share it with you?"

He almost rammed into the vehicle in front of him. A two-ton pickup that would not have been kind to his Escalade.

"You're really going to come over?"

At the most, he'd hoped for an invitation to share lunch at her place.

"Do you really want me to?"

"Of course. I wouldn't have asked if I didn't want you to."

"Then, yeah, I'll come over. I want to see this den you sit in when you talk to me at night."

Shit. The den. He'd left last night's empty beer cans on the table. Because he'd fallen asleep in the chair. Spent the night there.

And had to be out of the house by five that morning.

Hunter sped the rest of the way home, counting himself lucky that he made it without a cop behind him.

SHE HAD AN escape plan. Her car. And she'd called Chantel and Colin to let them know where she was. They'd be texting. And if she didn't answer, Chantel and Colin would be hot on her trail.

Even though it was broad daylight.

And if she started to panic, she'd breathe. She knew how to handle that part.

With everything in hand, she was smiling for real as she approached Hunter's front door, carrying a disposable container filled with salad, half an hour after she'd spoken to him.

In jeans and a white blouse, with white tennis shoes, she felt...young. And with her hair down... free.

Thinking about whether she should knock or ring the bell when she got onto the porch, she kind of liked the flutters in her stomach.

Not quite a feeling of all-out joy, but pretty darn close.

As it turned out, she didn't have to make a choice. Hunter had the door open before she got to it.

The table was set, with paper plates, napkins and stainless steel forks that would've looked fine with her china. He'd poured a couple of glasses of tea, hers with lemon and a squeeze of lime. Just as she'd taken it during one of their early meetings for the gala.

She should've been nervous as she took her seat next to him at the big wooden table. She wasn't.

"I like this place," she said, gazing around. Big enough for a sizable family, his *little* place, as he'd called it, was anything but little. It was nicely painted, had art on the walls, and comfortable-looking, good-quality furniture.

Once again Hunter Rafferty had underestimated himself.

"You have a pool," she said, as she glanced up and saw the pool outside the window she was facing. That seemed so typical for him; rather than a place to swim laps, his pool was kidney-shaped with a hoop at one end, and would be shallow enough to play basketball.

"It's a tub," he told her when he saw her looking at it. But he grinned, too. "I'm quite fond of my home," he said. "Proud of it, actually. Bought and paid for it myself. It's just not what you're used to."

"Colin loves spending time at Chantel's apartment," she pointed out to him. "And that really is a little place."

Almost as though her sister-in-law had heard her speak, Julie's phone buzzed with a text. She took a moment to answer. Just a quick smile emoticon.

"I'm surprised they still keep that place," Hunter said, bringing bread over to the table to go with the salad and dressing she'd brought. "I would've thought the lease would be up by now. Didn't you say they've been married more than a year?"

"Yep. She actually bought the place. She says she needs it to keep herself conscious of who she is. She was afraid that in marrying Colin, she'd lose her own identity."

"And he's good with that."

"Of course. It's what people do when they care about each other. They deal with their issues…"

Her words trailed off as she looked up at him, afraid he'd think she was implying something about the two of them.

That she was implying they could do the same thing.

"Don't worry." He met her gaze. Stuck his tongue out at her. "I'm not getting any ideas."

She stuck her tongue out back at him. Remembering a gross joke she'd played to bug Colin as a kid, Julie said, "You're lucky I didn't have any food in my mouth or you'd be having *see*food."

"Ha, ha. Well, you'd be getting it right back, and I have to warn you, when it comes to playing with food, I'm the best there is."

Remembering his pancakes, she conceded the round to him with a smile.

HUNTER WAS HORNY as hell. Having Julie in his house might not have been the brightest idea he'd had that week. The more time he spent with her, the more time he wanted to spend with her. And the more he did that, the more he wanted to have sex with her.

He wasn't going to let it be a problem. But it did make him think—a lot—about the fact that

Julie couldn't feel even a hint of desire. That she had no idea how incredible an orgasm could be.

Or how satisfying and sweet slow lovemaking usually was.

"You wanted honesty." He blurted the words as they sat over the empty paper plates at his table. They had another hour together. He wanted to claim every second of it.

"Yes." For the first time since she'd arrived, he saw her frown.

And saw her texting again. "You did that the other night when we were together. Kept texting someone. Who is it?"

None of his business, that was who.

His clock was ticking.

And he was the one wasting the seconds, not her.

"It's Chantel," she told him.

"Does she know you're here?"

"Of course." And then it hit him.

"She's your safety valve. If you don't answer, she'll come running."

"Something like that. Or she could just call for a squad car that happens to be in the area to do a welfare check."

Maybe he should be offended. Or put out. Hell, he was the party guy. He grinned. "Impressive," he said.

He was relieved that she really did take care of herself. Down to the smallest detail.

He wasn't going to be able to hurt her or let her down. She had everything covered.

Except, perhaps, for one thing.

"I've been thinking about something," he told her. Tick tock. Tick tock.

"What's that?"

"Ways to show you how your body can experience pleasure without making you feel scared or threatened or panicked, or like you want to run and hide."

"This conversation pretty much just took me there. Into panic mode."

"No, it didn't. You aren't fidgeting with your hands."

"Well, that's because I know you're not serious."

"Oh, but I am. Say, for instance, some time you put on a swimsuit in broad daylight, at your house, with your brother and sister-in-law home, and let me touch your back." He'd had a dream about that one. It had been damned hot.

"Touch my back?"

"Yes. Just your back. Me. Touching it."

"Would Colin and Chantel be outside with us?"

"Not my first choice."

"How magical do you think this touch of yours

is?" She was grinning. Probably still half suspected he was kidding.

Fine, for the moment, since it kept her open to the conversation.

"The back can be quite an erogenous zone," he told her. "And yet, touching it is completely noninvasive, too. Plus, you wouldn't even have to see me. You could sit there and stare at your pool. Or you could close your eyes. Just feel the tips of my fingers on your back. Writing you a letter."

A woman he'd once dated had told him she and her girlfriend used to do that, write on each other's backs, when they had sleepovers. He couldn't remember the woman, but the story was one he'd never forgotten.

"Then there's the foot. Another noninvasive place and yet one of the most erogenous parts of the body."

"The foot."

He had a feeling the repetition was more because he was engaging her senses than because she doubted him. She was shaking a little.

But there was no fear in her gaze. No hint of distaste as she slid her tongue along her lips.

"You've heard of reflexology?" When she nodded, he went on. "They say the foot has pulse points that lead to almost every part of the body. You can be fully dressed, just like you are now.

Take off one sandal, and I could help you feel pleasure in places you've never felt pleasure before."

He was sure he could do it. Not sure, however, that he could do it for her.

But he was positive he wanted to try.

She wasn't giving him her foot. But she was sitting there. Meeting his eyes, with a slow smile forming on her face.

"And then there's—"

A hard knock sounded on his front door.

They looked at each other.

"You expecting someone?" she asked him.

"No."

Hunter was already making his way to the front room when the knock sounded again. It was loud. Commanding. Not like a neighbor coming to borrow a cup of sugar.

He looked through the front window first. If someone was up to no good...

Julie had her phone out, with text messaging open.

"It's a police car," he said, staring at her.

"I swear, Hunter, I sent her a smiley face."

"She must've asked them to send someone anyway."

She frowned, as she went toward the door. "No, as long as I text that things are fine, she wouldn't. Maybe, if for some reason my brother was concerned, he'd call 911 or try to get Chantel to order a patrol car. Though this is too much even for him. He just...he's always blamed himself for not watching out for me better."

She pulled open the door. "It's okay, I'm—"

She quieted abruptly as an officer pushed past her. "Hunter Rafferty?" the man asked with not the least hint of friendly cop in his tone.

"Yes?" Hunter stepped forward. He turned to her, then shrugged. They must be playing some kind of game with him.

A trick for the trickster.

"You need to come with me, sir. You're under arrest."

"What for?" he asked, half smiling. He glanced at Julie who looked horrified.

But she'd just told him how Chantel could have someone stop by for a welfare check. He hadn't read either her or Colin as pranksters at all, but the night before, Julie had talked about how, before the rape, she'd been a pistol. Taunting and teasing her brother mercilessly. Was this some kind of joke the three of them had come up with? An attempt to fit into his prankster world? It made no sense, but was all his shocked mind had come up with.

"Assault." The uniformed cop pulled out a set of handcuffs and slapped them on Hunter's wrists.

"I didn't hurt anyone," he was saying as the

man led him through the door, playing along. For Julie's sake.

Not his idea of a fun time. But at least she was trying to join his jokester world…

"Hunter!" Julie ran up to him, cold stark fear on her face. "I'm phoning Colin. He's a lawyer. Don't say anything, not a word, to anyone. Not until he gets there…"

"But I didn't do anything," Hunter said. He was still kind of grinning. But a knot of lead sank to the bottom of his gut.

"Don't say a word," she told him again.

And the cop led him away from her.

CHAPTER THIRTY-ONE

CHANTEL TOLD JULIE where they were taking Hunter. She stayed on the phone until Julie met her and Colin there. They were waiting outside in the parking lot.

Chantel spoke first. "He's being booked on charges of sexual assault."

Julie's gaze flew to her brother. "Colin?"

He nodded.

"Have you talked to him?"

"Not yet. But they know he's got a lawyer. Anything he says without me present will be inadmissible."

She nodded, feeling a little better, but not much.

And then it hit her.

Sexual assault.

Her gaze flew back to Colin's. It was as though he'd been waiting. "I need to know, Julie. Has he given you any reason to feel uncomfortable? Done anything that—"

"No!" Hunter was the least aggressive man she'd ever met. If you didn't count the number of times he'd asked her out before she'd finally agreed to attend the roast with him.

"And he's never made a move on you?"

He'd held her hand. And talked about touching her toes.

"I saw him that night at the pool, remember? When you were crying and he had you backed up to the fireplace."

Yes. Right. Colin was confusing her.

Sexual assault.

"Who made the claim?" she asked. "What do they say he did?"

"I don't know the answer to the first question yet. He's alleged to have forced sexual advances on a woman under false pretenses. Touched her inappropriately. Even had intercourse with her. Multiple times."

"False pretenses? What's that?"

"Not a formal charge," Chantel said, pushing a strand of hair away from Julie's face. Touching her. Gently. Reassuringly.

Chantel had been the one to first reach into Julie's hell and bring her out. Chantel, who'd known her own life of pain. Having had her best friend murdered in front of her, shooting the guy who'd done it but not in time to save her friend's life.

"There aren't any formal charges at this point," her sister-in-law continued. "Just a warrant for his arrest. To bring him in for questioning."

"Someone, a woman, says Hunter raped her?"

"She says he forced himself on her."

He raped someone? Multiple times?

Julie dashed to the far side of her car, but that was as far as she got before she puked up the salad she'd just shared with him.

For all his troubled youth, the mistakes he'd made, the chances he'd taken, the night he'd spent in juvie, Hunter had never been inside an adult jail cell. It felt worse than anything he could have imagined.

But he had no difficulty imagining how his father must have felt, a respected doctor, sitting on a bench with druggies and smelly alcoholics.

Confused. Angry as hell. And scared.

Hell, yes. Scared.

No one was telling him what was going on. He had to wait for his lawyer.

Colin Fairbanks.

He wasn't putting a lot of faith in the guy. Colin had probably left him there to rot. Whisking his sister as far from him—the bastard, Hunter—as he could. Hunter remembered the force with which Colin had come at him that night at the pool. He figured he was lucky if all the guy did was whisk Julie away.

Sexual assault. Sexual assault?

Who on earth… Why… His head hurt as he

tried to recall every woman he'd come in contact with over the past ten years of his life. Had he ever been too eager? Even a little? Too drunk to take care?

He'd swear not.

He was sure not.

But he'd partied a lot. Could there be a night he'd had too much to drink, a night he couldn't remember?

Not since high school.

He was sure of that.

Unless someone had slipped something in his drink...

The idea scared the shit out of him all over again.

Made him sick.

And even those thoughts weren't the worst ones.

Julie. She would've had it confirmed by now that there'd been a warrant out for his arrest because of a sexual assault charge.

Oh, God. He'd lost her. Right when he was so close to finally having someone worth sticking around for...

"Rafferty? Your lawyer's here to see you." The uniformed young woman who came to unlock the cell didn't look him in the eye. *I'm innocent*, he wanted to tell her, but he didn't waste his breath.

She probably heard the same every day. All day.

She wouldn't believe him.

No one would.

Least of all, Colin Fairbanks.

Funny, though, it wasn't Colin he was worried about. Or even himself. It was Colin's sister—and the thought of what Julie must be going through—that had him feeling like he had chains around his throat.

LEAVING JULIE'S CAR for Colin to drive, Chantel had taken Julie to The Lemonade Stand. She'd offered to take her wherever she needed to be.

That was where she'd wanted to go.

By the time she arrived, she was calm. Feeling empty. Dead inside. But calm. She could walk just fine—and went straight to Lila's office.

Where she sat, sometimes with Chantel, sometimes with both women, until Colin called to tell them that Hunter was out on bail.

"He didn't do it," she told the two women who'd been her backbone when she'd lost her own. Who'd given her legs to stand on when hers wouldn't work. "I know he didn't do it."

She did know. She knew Hunter.

"You ever hear him mention some woman named Mandy?" Chantel asked. She'd spoken with Colin the longest. "She's the one pressing the charges."

She nodded. Mandy. He'd had sex with her, by his own admission.

The woman had come looking for him that one time…

She hadn't seemed ready just to walk away, either.

Another memory. A few nights ago, on the phone, she'd heard a noise—he'd said he'd thrown his keys on the counter. Then there'd been voices—he'd said music.

Had he been in a bar? Someplace meeting Mandy?

Was he playing them both?

That was what men, did, right? Went for as many women as they could get? Talked about them. Took pride in getting them.

She shook her head.

Her father had been a one-woman man. There'd never been any doubt about that. Her mother had told her shortly before she died. She'd tried to convince Julie to make sure her father didn't feel guilty about dating again. She didn't want to think of him living the rest of his life alone.

Colin was definitely a one-woman man.

David Smyth. He'd dated a lot of pretty girls, but had chosen her. He'd married someone else. And then continued to take what he wanted from other women.

He'd been a charmer.

Hunter was a charmer.

Admittedly shy of commitment, he'd never been in a serious, one-woman relationship.

He didn't lie about who he was.

Couldn't even see his own value.

He'd talked about touching her feet—so she could keep her clothes on and feel pleasure.

He'd talked about physical pleasure with a woman who'd told him she'd been raped and never wanted to have sex. Yet there he was, trying to talk her into trying.

Because he wanted it that badly?

Or cared that much?

"He says Mandy called him the other night. That he told her he didn't want to hang out with her anymore. He said talking to her was like talking to someone he'd never met before. She was contradicting everything she'd ever told him about what she wanted and needed. Talking about how she'd been waiting around for him to be ready to have a girlfriend. And how it wasn't right that when he reached that point he didn't choose her."

Chantel was looking at her.

So was Lila.

"Colin says it's pretty clear, based on her statement, that she's doing this to get back at him," Chantel added.

"He's on his way here," Lila told them. "Edward's already here, with Joy."

"Edward," she said. "Good."

But Joy shouldn't see this. Any of it.

Not that Hunter shouldn't be around the little girl. He should. He was great for her.

He hadn't done anything wrong.

Right now, he needed Edward. Not Joy.

"He wants to see you," Chantel said to Julie.

"No."

"Julie." Lila sat beside her. Put a hand on her shoulder.

She shook her head. Felt a tear drop on the hands at war with each other in her lap.

"I can't," she said.

"I understand." Lila's words were firm, reassuring. "And you don't have to. Your fear is completely understandable."

"I'm not afraid of him."

"Then what?"

She looked up at Chantel first, then Lila. "It's like you said. Sometimes things happen to people, change them, and the change is irrevocable. That's me. I've got issues. I know about them. I'm on top of them. I'm in counseling to learn how to live with them. But the truth is, I'm going to have them for the rest of my life. And while I know in my heart that Hunter didn't do this, my mind…it keeps presenting doubts."

She could feel the storm coming. Knew she needed to bury her head and cry it out. "I thought

I had to listen to my head. That it was my heart that had let me down. But it wasn't. It was my head all along. I can't do this to Hunter, can't see him again. It wouldn't be fair to him. Or to me, either. I doubted him. I still doubt him. There's always going to be that 'what if.'"

"Don't you think that whether or not he lives with that is his choice? If he wants to take it on…"

"Do *you* think it is?" She turned to Lila. "You said yourself there are some people who've been so changed by life that they aren't meant for partner relationships."

Lila looked shocked. And shaken.

Julie took that as her answer.

CHAPTER THIRTY-TWO

HUNTER'S HEART FELT as if it had been ripped out. Mandy had turned on him. She was his accuser. Out of spite.

Because she'd waited around all those years for something he'd never even known she wanted—and then thought he'd given it to someone else.

He knew for certain he'd never abused her. Never, ever touched her without her consent. In fact, most times, she'd initiated their contact.

But she'd been right about one thing.

When he'd finally given his heart, it hadn't been to the woman who'd kept him company all those years. It had been to a woman he'd only known a few months.

One he'd never even kissed.

He could see how that would be hard to take.

He could also see—completely—why Julie refused to see him. Her worst nightmare was coming to life before her eyes.

He'd been hauled out of his home, in handcuffs, right in front of her. Charged with doing the one thing she feared most of all.

Sexual assault.

He couldn't fix this, couldn't joke his way out of it. She wouldn't even see him to give him a chance to try.

His whole life, through all the fights, the parties, the trouble, he'd always been able to find the bright side. And get others to see it, too. His mother. His father. His clients. Joy. Pretty well everyone he'd ever known. The one thing he could count on was knowing how to lighten the moment—or escape from it. Until the one time he couldn't.

"Joy was asking for you," Edward said as Hunter stood in the lobby of The Lemonade Stand, still wearing the golf clothes he hadn't changed out of yet. He'd have to prepare for the evening's comedic tribute.

He'd be later than he'd intended. He had time to get home. Get changed. He was going to make it to work. This was all so hard to believe. An hour for lunch, a couple of hours in jail, and off to work.

"I don't think I'd be good for her right now."

"I told her you were here. Can't you stick your head in for a second?" Edward was struggling to find solid ground with the little girl. Mostly because he didn't know how to be a parent to one.

Not because he didn't care. He'd just lost his confidence after Cara's defection.

Joy still hadn't said more than a few words to Edward. Hunter already knew that. Now Edward had told her Hunter was there. She'd smiled when he told her, and Edward asked if she wanted to see him. She'd nodded.

Hunter couldn't see Julie, but he couldn't not see Joy. So, with his feet heavy, he followed Edward through the Stand's main door and outside, across the grass, and to the bungalow where the girl was staying.

Joy's housemate smiled, then disappeared. He'd learned that she'd been abused by her adult son, a heroin addict. She was wonderful with Joy. And just as happy to leave the room when Edward or Hunter came around.

He got it.

Things happened to people, caused reactions they could neither help nor prevent.

People had triggers. Even olfactory ones. He'd learned that much in college. With his bachelor's degree in psychology.

And Julie—her trigger was any hint of sexual assault. That wasn't ever going to change.

Nor was the fact that he'd just been arrested for the very same thing.

Didn't matter if he'd done it or not.

She'd had doubt put in her mind. It would plague her.

He got it.

Joy sat on the couch, looking up at him, her head cocked to the side. She handed him a book.

One of the Amy books she was always carrying around with her. The one about a little girl who was afraid of her shadow.

He had nothing else for her, no tricks to pull out of his imaginary hat, so he sat down and read the book to her.

It was really pretty good. Exceptional for a children's book, if you asked him. Childlike and innocent. Full of funny pictures and color and words that, when he read them, sounded almost like song. But it talked about real things that a lot of children faced. The fear of what was lurking behind you. Or waiting ahead of you. The anguish of not understanding.

When he finished the book, Joy was studying him, her brown eyes serious. She didn't seem frantic, though. Or frightened. She just seemed... serious. Calmly serious.

She handed him another book.

It was almost as though he was on trial with her. As though she knew he'd been arrested and was trying to figure out if he was innocent or guilty.

But he knew that wasn't possible. She didn't know anything about his day. Or his life in general. So he took the book she handed him.

And read it aloud.

This one was about food. Healthy food and food that grown-ups made you eat. Food you liked. And about sneaking too much candy and getting sick. In the end, though, Amy was sick because of her guilty conscience for sneaking the candy, not for eating it.

He actually smiled as he gave the book back to Joy. He could see why she was so fond of Amy and liked that the little girl was so discerning.

He started to feel…hopeful again. For Edward. For Joy. For a world that brought Joys and Edwards together.

Joy handed him yet another book. He had to go. Get showered, especially now that he'd been in jail, and put on his tux. Then he had the drive to Santa Barbara.

He read the book quickly, getting through the first couple of pages without pausing to study the pictures. He didn't want to disappoint Joy, but he had to leave.

By the last few pages, he'd forgotten why he needed to head out. This Amy book was about doubts. About a little girl who got her feelings hurt. Who thought her mother didn't love her when she was naughty. And that her Sunday School teacher didn't think she was good enough because she fell asleep during the class. She believed other kids didn't like her because she had a big brother who was better than theirs. In the end, Amy finds out that all those fears were just her head playing tricks on her. She learns that everyone has an inner voice that tells them things about themselves—to keep them from getting too selfish. But that those things aren't always real.

Good God. Little Amy knew something Hunter had never figured out. That doubts could be good. But that they weren't the only thing. Or even the most real.

Doubt kept a man hardworking. Honest. Aware.

And a woman, too.

"This is a really good book," Hunter said, coughing as his voice cracked. He caught Edward's glance. The older man had been sitting in a chair across from them the whole time, and the look in his eye was direct. As though he was speaking to Hunter.

"Amy's a smart little girl," he said now.

Joy was watching him. She smiled at Edward and nodded.

Hunter had to go. He wanted to take the book with him, which was stupid as hell. He wasn't going to take it from Joy. From the Stand.

He didn't need a children's book.

He looked at the author's name, though. Fairy Child. What kind of name was that for an author?

But, then again, it was a children's book.

"Fairy Child. What's with the name?" he asked Edward. He *had* to go. But he didn't want to leave them. Or the book.

"It's a good name." Joy spoke clearly. With gusto. Her voice was confident, even with her lisp.

"It is, huh?" He turned to her, feeling a lightness he'd been lacking since he was shoved into the back seat of a police car. "How would you know?"

Joy was talking. With just him and Edward there. No way in hell was he leaving.

"Because."

Such a typical kid answer, he wanted to swing her up and hug her.

"Who comes up with a name like Fairy Child?" he said again. Teasing her. Not caring what they said as long as she continued to speak.

"Julie does," Joy said with such certainty he almost believed her.

"Julie does."

"Uh-huh."

"Julie isn't Fairy Child," Edward said. "She just reads the books to you."

"No." Joy shook her head. "You could be my grandpa when you wanted me to help Hunter read my Amy books, but you can't be my grandpa if you don't take that back." The rolled *r*'s didn't minimize the sting of those words.

Edward looked startled And…tremulous, too. "I take it back, then, because I am most definitely your grandpa."

"And Julie is Fairy Child," Joy said, stacking the books on her lap with precise movements. "It's a secret, and only us know and it's not a silly name."

Hunter started to feel hot. Overheated. Needed some air.

Julie with her art degree. Her studio.

The way she always talked about Amy whenever she spoke to Joy.

Could it be?

"Who told you Julie was Fairy Child?" he asked Joy. The girl might have a great imagination, she might invent things she wanted to be true, but she wouldn't outright lie to him.

"She did. 'Cause I'm friends with Amy, and Amy is her when she was little like me."

Oh, Lord.

Oh, good Lord.

Julie Fairbanks was a successful children's author?

On top of everything else?

"Go to her."

Edward's words hit him upside the head. Or his next thought did.

If Julie was Amy, then she knew that doubts were a good thing. That they kept a person from being too selfish. And weren't always real.

He wasn't at all sure what he was supposed to do with that.

But it gave him something to work with.

For the moment, that was enough.

JULIE WAS IN her studio about five minutes before she returned to herself, to an awareness of where she was.

The room…the easel… It hurt to look at them. She'd come to her safe place for comfort, and it mocked her. She was all about being honest, with herself and others. Being realistic. And she'd been lying to herself.

Hiding from herself.

She'd let her mind, her fears, her doubts, get the better of her.

Again.

Not just that day. Not just since Hunter's arrest, but since she'd first met him. She'd refused to let her heart have its say.

But what she knew, what her mother had taught her, what she remembered from Colin and her father when she'd come home with hurt feelings over one thing or another, had been that, yes, sometimes people do hurtful things. Mostly, though, hurt feelings were just our own minds being a little mean. It was for a good reason—to keep you humble. Aware. To keep you from getting too sure of yourself.

She knew this stuff.

She'd been raped. Not bludgeoned in the head and left mentally incapacitated.

She'd lost both her parents in a short period of

time. But she hadn't lost everything they'd been. Everything they'd taught her.

She'd just been thinking that afternoon about how her mother had asked her to make sure her father didn't feel guilty for loving again after her death. She hadn't thought of that conversation in years. Hadn't been able to bear it.

But because of Hunter, *for* Hunter, she'd remembered. She had to remind herself that not all men were like David Smyth. That would allow her to combat doubts about Hunter…

She remembered something else, too. Something she'd forgotten. Those first words had been on her father's behalf. Her mother had a different message for Julie. She'd begged her to listen to her heart.

She'd told her that her heart would never lead her wrong.

She'd thought she was listening to her heart when she'd gone to that party with David Smyth. But she hadn't been. What she'd done was stop listening to the voice of doubt in her mind. She'd become too cocky. Too careless. She'd listened to her head telling her how cool it was that the most popular boy in school wanted to be exclusive with her.

Shaking, she stood up. Got her purse. Her keys. She had no plan. She just knew she couldn't stay there.

Couldn't leave Hunter with her refusal to see him.

He'd think it was exactly what he deserved. And he didn't deserve it. Ever since the rape, Julie had been turning her back on reality and walking away. She hadn't gone forward with her accusations against David, not until Chantel intervened. She'd become a prisoner in her own hell. Still was.

Well, she wasn't going to be a prisoner anymore.

Hunter—and Joy—had shown her who she wanted to be. Who she *could* be. Hunter thought he was the one who didn't have staying power. He thought he'd let her down.

Instead, the opposite was true.

Passing her bedroom, she went inside, grabbed her swimsuit and headed downstairs.

Colin and Chantel were in their suite. She didn't want to take the time to go there. Instead she called them, told them she was going out and to expect her when they saw her. Before they could comment or question her, she left.

She got in her car and drove down streets she'd driven many times. To a street she'd only driven once. He wasn't going to be there.

She knew that.

He had a tribute in Santa Barbara that night.

She just hoped that when he got back, he'd be willing to see her.

HUNTER THOUGHT HE was imagining things at first when he reached his house around nine that night and saw a light shining from his backyard.

His second thought was to call the police. Memories of the afternoon put a rapid halt to that one. There were no cars out front. None in his driveway.

None in his garage when he drove inside.

If someone was waiting to hit him over the head and rob him blind, let 'em try. He was tired. And he wanted to be home.

His home. He'd earned it. And he'd damn well make sure that some thief who figured he could take anything that was his learned differently. He was done laughing.

He'd been arrested that afternoon.

He'd lost the one real relationship he'd ever had.

Life was no joke.

And neither was he.

He didn't own a gun. But he had a sledgehammer in the garage. Picking it up, he carried it in through the kitchen and out the back door.

He had a doubt or two as he walked boldly into the light shining directly in his eyes. But doubts were good, right? They'd made an honest man of him. A hardworking man.

One who wished he'd repositioned that damn light. He'd meant to. Planned to get out his ladder and adjust the fixture so it shone into the pool as he'd intended. He hadn't gotten around to it. It wasn't like he ever spent time out by his pool at night.

He wasn't Julie.

But...she was. Out there in the chill of the night. Lying on a chaise longue. In a bikini.

Hunter tripped—and fell into the pool. Tux and all.

Even the shock of the water didn't cool his skin. He came up swimming, though. He made directly for the edge of the pool closest to that chair. As though he'd meant to jump in all along.

In his tux.

Pulling himself out, he stood there, dripping and...hot. God, she was gorgeous. With a body that would drive any sane man nuts. And he didn't care about that. Not right now.

She was there.

In his home.

At his pool.

In a swimsuit.

Staring at him.

"You said if I wore a swimsuit, you could make me feel good," she said. Her voice shook. Her whole body was shaking.

She was going to catch pneumonia. It couldn't be more than seventy degrees out there. If that. With no sun to warm her skin.

She'd brought a towel with her. He wrapped

it around her—and realized that she was shivering from cold. And crying.

"I'M SO SORRY, Hunter. So sorry I wouldn't see you. Please, please, don't ever judge me by that. I won't do it again. Ever. I promise." The words were hard to understand at times. But he got the gist of them.

"I thought Mandy accusing me like that, me being in jail, was karma for what I'd done to my dad, not testifying for him," he said. There was so much to get out. So much he needed her to understand.

"No, Hunter…"

"I know." He picked her up. "I read your book…" Carried her inside the house. "About Amy and her doubts…" Straight to his bedroom.

And he realized what that would look like to her.

"The only blankets in the house are back here, and I don't think I have what it takes to just put you down. I plan to wrap you in a blanket and hold you against me. At least until I can get my heart out of my throat."

"You might want to change clothes. That tux is soaked."

Oh. Yes. Good idea.

He wrapped her in his bedspread and took

her to the den, where he placed her gently on the couch, propped up by pillows.

"I'm not sick, Hunter." She sniffed. Her tears came and went. But her strength was there every minute, shining from her eyes.

"But you should go get dry before you get sick," she said.

He was back in less than three minutes, wearing the sweats and T-shirt he'd had on the night before.

"You know I wrote the Amy books." She was sitting up. Waiting for him.

"Joy told me."

She smiled. And then frowned.

"Oh, Chantel called a while ago. They found Shawn. He was driving Dan's van in Nevada, in the middle of nowhere, but a cop had just seen the APB on the license plate and pulled him over. They think he was living in the vehicle, trying to stay under the radar out there. He's in custody. Swears he doesn't have any idea where Cara is. Even when they offered to see if they could help him out on the charges against him for Mary's death—second-degree murder since he didn't really mean to kill her—he still said he didn't know where she is. Swears he didn't do anything to her."

Hunter hadn't heard that. But he was pretty sure Edward had. And that he purposely hadn't told him. That was why Edward had been with Joy. He had some tough choices ahead of him. What did he tell Joy? How long did he wait before starting a new life with her?

Hunter had to call him.

"Lila said he's staying at the Stand tonight."

"It's probably bad news that Shawn isn't talking. It could mean he killed her. And doesn't want to face charges for her murder."

Julie nodded. "That's what Chantel said. But she also said he was pretty adamant about not hurting her. And they didn't find any evidence on him, or in Dan's van, to make them believe differently. No obvious blood, for instance. I'm sure they'll have someone going over it for any trace evidence. But they aren't holding out a lot of hope. If she is free, why hasn't she turned up someplace? From what Chantel said, they might never know what happened to her."

Hunter cared about that. A hell of a lot. But not as much as he cared about the woman sitting on his couch.

"Chantel also said that Colin has been in touch with Mandy's lawyer. I'm not sure what was said, but I think you can expect her to drop the charges."

At the moment, he didn't even care enough about that. Colin had indicated to him not to worry. He had anyway, right up until he'd arrived home.

Now all he cared about was Julie. There, in his home.

"I can make your back feel good," he said.

"I'm willing to give you a chance."

"I didn't *ever* touch Mandy without her consent."

"I believe that. But I doubted you." Tears sprang to her eyes again. "I doubted you…"

"Doubts are good. They keep you aware. Make you look at things, ask the important questions. They keep you safe. As long as you don't let them keep you hostage."

"I think I love you, Hunter. My mother told me to follow my heart, and here I am, in way over my head."

"I am, too. But I know I love you."

"I can't ask you to. I might never… I'm so scared."

He sat down beside her. Not touching her. Although the memory of holding her in his arms earlier was making him ache all over. "I'm scared, too. But what scares me most is living even a day of my life without you."

"Me, too."

"Marry me, Julie."

"How can I? I don't know if I can be a real wife."

"You're already more of a wife to me than I ever thought I'd find. Physically, we'll work it out.

I promise. One way or another, we'll work it out. I'm willing to do whatever it takes."

Tears rolled down her cheeks, but she was smiling, too.

"Hey." He wiped away her tears. "We'll do this together, Jules. You and me. We'll figure it out. All of it."

She nodded and stretched out her arms. "Hold me, Hunter. Please?"

The words brought the most incredible high he'd ever known. Hunter sat down beside her. Took her body, wrapped in her warm cocoon, gently against his, and had a feeling that he'd just slipped into the biggest party of his life.

One that was never going to end.

* * * * *

Look for the next
WHERE SECRETS ARE SAFE *book,*
coming in November 2017!

*And be sure to check out the other recent titles
in* WHERE SECRETS ARE SAFE

*THE FIREMAN'S SON
HER SECRET LIFE
THE PROMISE HE MADE HER*

*All available now from
Harlequin Superromance.*

Get 2 Free Books,
Plus 2 Free Gifts —
just for trying the Reader Service!

YES! Please send me 2 FREE Harlequin® Romance LARGER PRINT novels and my 2 FREE gifts (gifts are worth about $10 retail). After receiving them, if I don't wish to receive any more books, I can return the shipping statement marked "cancel." If I don't cancel, I will receive 4 brand-new novels every month and be billed just $5.34 per book in the U.S. or $5.74 per book in Canada. That's a savings of at least 15% off the cover price! It's quite a bargain! Shipping and handling is just 50¢ per book in the U.S. and 75¢ per book in Canada.* I understand that accepting the 2 free books and gifts places me under no obligation to buy anything. I can always return a shipment and cancel at any time. The free books and gifts are mine to keep no matter what I decide.

119/319 HDN GLWP

Name _____ (PLEASE PRINT) _____

Address _____ Apt. #_____

City _____ State/Prov. _____ Zip/Postal Code _____

Signature (if under 18, a parent or guardian must sign) _____

Mail to the **Reader Service:**

IN U.S.A.: P.O. Box 1341, Buffalo, NY 14240-8531
IN CANADA: P.O. Box 603, Fort Erie, Ontario L2A 5X3
Want to try two free books from another line?
Call 1-800-873-8635 or visit www.ReaderService.com.

* Terms and prices subject to change without notice. Prices do not include applicable taxes. Sales tax applicable in N.Y. Canadian residents will be charged applicable taxes. Offer not valid in Quebec. This offer is limited to one order per household. Books received may not be as shown. Not valid for current subscribers to Harlequin Romance Larger-Print books. All orders subject to approval. Credit or debit balances in a customer's account(s) may be offset by any other outstanding balance owed by or to the customer. Please allow 4 to 6 weeks for delivery. Offer available while quantities last.

Your Privacy—The Reader Service is committed to protecting your privacy. Our Privacy Policy is available online at www.ReaderService.com or upon request from the Reader Service.

We make a portion of our mailing list available to reputable third parties that offer products we believe may interest you. If you prefer that we not exchange your name with third parties, or if you wish to clarify or modify your communication preferences, please visit us at www.ReaderService.com/consumerschoice or write to us at Reader Service Preference Service, P.O. Box 9062, Buffalo, NY 14240-9062. Include your complete name and address.

HRLPI7R2

Get 2 Free Books,
Plus 2 Free Gifts—

just for trying the
Reader Service!

YES! Please send me 2 FREE Harlequin Presents® novels and my 2 FREE gifts (gifts are worth about $10 retail). After receiving them, if I don't wish to receive any more books, I can return the shipping statement marked "cancel." If I don't cancel, I will receive 6 brand-new novels every month and be billed just $4.55 each for the regular-print edition or $5.55 each for the larger-print edition in the U.S., or $5.49 each for the regular-print edition or $5.99 each for the larger-print edition in Canada. That's a saving of at least 11% off the cover price! It's quite a bargain! Shipping and handling is just 50¢ per book in the U.S. and 75¢ per book in Canada.* I understand that accepting the 2 free books and gifts places me under no obligation to buy anything. I can always return a shipment and cancel at any time. The free books and gifts are mine to keep no matter what I decide.

Please check one: ☐ Harlequin Presents® Regular-Print ☐ Harlequin Presents® Larger-Print
(106/306 HDN GLWL) (176/376 HDN GLWL)

Name _____ (PLEASE PRINT) _____

Address _____ Apt. # _____

City _____ State/Prov. _____ Zip/Postal Code _____

Signature (if under 18, a parent or guardian must sign) _____

Mail to the **Reader Service:**
IN U.S.A.: P.O. Box 1341, Buffalo, NY 14240-8531
IN CANADA: P.O. Box 603, Fort Erie, Ontario L2A 5X3

Want to try two free books from another series?
Call 1-800-873-8635 or visit www.ReaderService.com.

* Terms and prices subject to change without notice. Prices do not include applicable taxes. Sales tax applicable in N.Y. Canadian residents will be charged applicable taxes. Offer not valid in Quebec. This offer is limited to one order per household. Books received may not be as shown. Not valid for current subscribers to Harlequin Presents books. All orders subject to approval. Credit or debit balances in a customer's account(s) may be offset by any other outstanding balance owed by or to the customer. Please allow 4 to 6 weeks for delivery. Offer available while quantities last.

Your Privacy—The Reader Service is committed to protecting your privacy. Our Privacy Policy is available online at www.ReaderService.com or upon request from the Reader Service.

We make a portion of our mailing list available to reputable third parties that offer products we believe may interest you. If you prefer that we not exchange your name with third parties, or if you wish to clarify or modify your communication preferences, please visit us at www.ReaderService.com/consumerchoice or write to us at Reader Service Preference Service, P.O. Box 9062, Buffalo, NY 14240-9062. Include your complete name and address.

HP17R2

Get 2 Free Books,
Plus 2 Free Gifts—
just for trying the Reader Service!

HARLEQUIN
HEARTWARMING™

YES! Please send me 2 FREE Harlequin® Heartwarming™ Larger-Print novels and my 2 FREE mystery gifts (gifts worth about $10 retail). After receiving them, if I don't wish to receive any more books, I can return the shipping statement marked "cancel." If I don't cancel, I will receive 4 brand-new larger-print novels every month and be billed just $5.49 per book in the U.S. or $6.24 per book in Canada. That's a savings of at least 19% off the cover price. It's quite a bargain! Shipping and handling is just 50¢ per book in the U.S. and 75¢ per book in Canada.* I understand that accepting the 2 free books and gifts places me under no obligation to buy anything. I can always return a shipment and cancel at any time. The free books and gifts are mine to keep no matter what I decide.

161/361 IDN GLWT

Name	(PLEASE PRINT)

Address	Apt. #

City	State/Prov.	Zip/Postal Code

Signature (if under 18, a parent or guardian must sign)

Mail to the **Reader Service**:
IN U.S.A.: P.O. Box 1341, Buffalo, NY 14240-8531
IN CANADA: P.O. Box 603, Fort Erie, Ontario L2A 5X3

Want to try two free books from another line?
Call 1-800-873-8635 today or visit www.ReaderService.com.

* Terms and prices subject to change without notice. Prices do not include applicable taxes. Sales tax applicable in N.Y. Canadian residents will be charged applicable taxes. Offer not valid in Quebec. This offer is limited to one order per household. Books received may not be as shown. Not valid for current subscribers to Harlequin Heartwarming Larger-Print books. All orders subject to approval. Credit or debit balances in a customer's account(s) may be offset by any other outstanding balance owed by or to the customer. Please allow 4 to 6 weeks for delivery. Offer available while quantities last.

Your Privacy—The Reader Service is committed to protecting your privacy. Our Privacy Policy is available online at www.ReaderService.com or upon request from the Reader Service.

We make a portion of our mailing list available to reputable third parties that offer products we believe may interest you. If you prefer that we not exchange your name with third parties, or if you wish to clarify or modify your communication preferences, please visit us at www.ReaderService.com/consumerschoice or write to us at Reader Service Preference Service, P.O. Box 9062, Buffalo, NY 14240-9062. Include your complete name and address.

HW17R

Get 2 Free Books,

Plus 2 Free Gifts—

just for trying the Reader Service!

YES! Please send me 2 FREE Harlequin® Intrigue novels and my 2 FREE gifts (gifts are worth about $10 retail). After receiving them, if I don't wish to receive any more books, I can return the shipping statement marked "cancel." If I don't cancel, I will receive 6 brand-new novels every month and be billed just $4.99 each for the regular-print edition or $5.74 each for the larger-print edition in the U.S., or $5.74 each for the regular-print edition or $6.49 each for the larger-print edition in Canada. That's a savings of at least 12% off the cover price! It's quite a bargain! Shipping and handling is just 50¢ per book in the U.S. and 75¢ per book in Canada.* I understand that accepting the 2 free books and gifts places me under no obligation to buy anything. I can always return a shipment and cancel at any time. The free books and gifts are mine to keep no matter what I decide.

Please check one: ☐ Harlequin® Intrigue Regular-Print   ☐ Harlequin® Intrigue Larger-Print
                   (182/382 HDN GLWJ)   (199/399 HDN GLWJ)

Name   (PLEASE PRINT)

Address   Apt. #

City   State/Prov.   Zip/Postal Code

Signature (if under 18, a parent or guardian must sign)

Mail to the **Reader Service:**
IN U.S.A.: P.O. Box 1341, Buffalo, NY 14240-8531
IN CANADA: P.O. Box 603, Fort Erie, Ontario L2A 5X3

Want to try two free books from another line?
Call 1-800-873-8635 or visit www.ReaderService.com.

*Terms and prices subject to change without notice. Prices do not include applicable taxes. Sales tax applicable in N.Y. Canadian residents will be charged applicable taxes. Offer not valid in Quebec. This offer is limited to one order per household. Books received may not be as shown. Not valid for current subscribers to Harlequin Intrigue books. All orders subject to approval. Credit or debit balances in a customer's account(s) may be offset by any other outstanding balance owed by or to the customer. Please allow 4 to 6 weeks for delivery. Offer available while quantities last.

Your Privacy—The Reader Service is committed to protecting your privacy. Our Privacy Policy is available online at www.ReaderService.com or upon request from the Reader Service.

We make a portion of our mailing list available to reputable third parties that offer products we believe may interest you. If you prefer that we not exchange your name with third parties, or if you wish to clarify or modify your communication preferences, please visit us at www.ReaderService.com/consumerschoice or write to us at Reader Service Preference Service, P.O. Box 9062, Buffalo, NY 14240-9062. Include your complete name and address.